Vitamin Sea

JACQUELINE PARRISH

Vitamin Sea

JACQUELINE PARRISH

First paperback edition August 2025
Cover design by Bailey McGinn

ISBN: 978-1-7390491-5-7

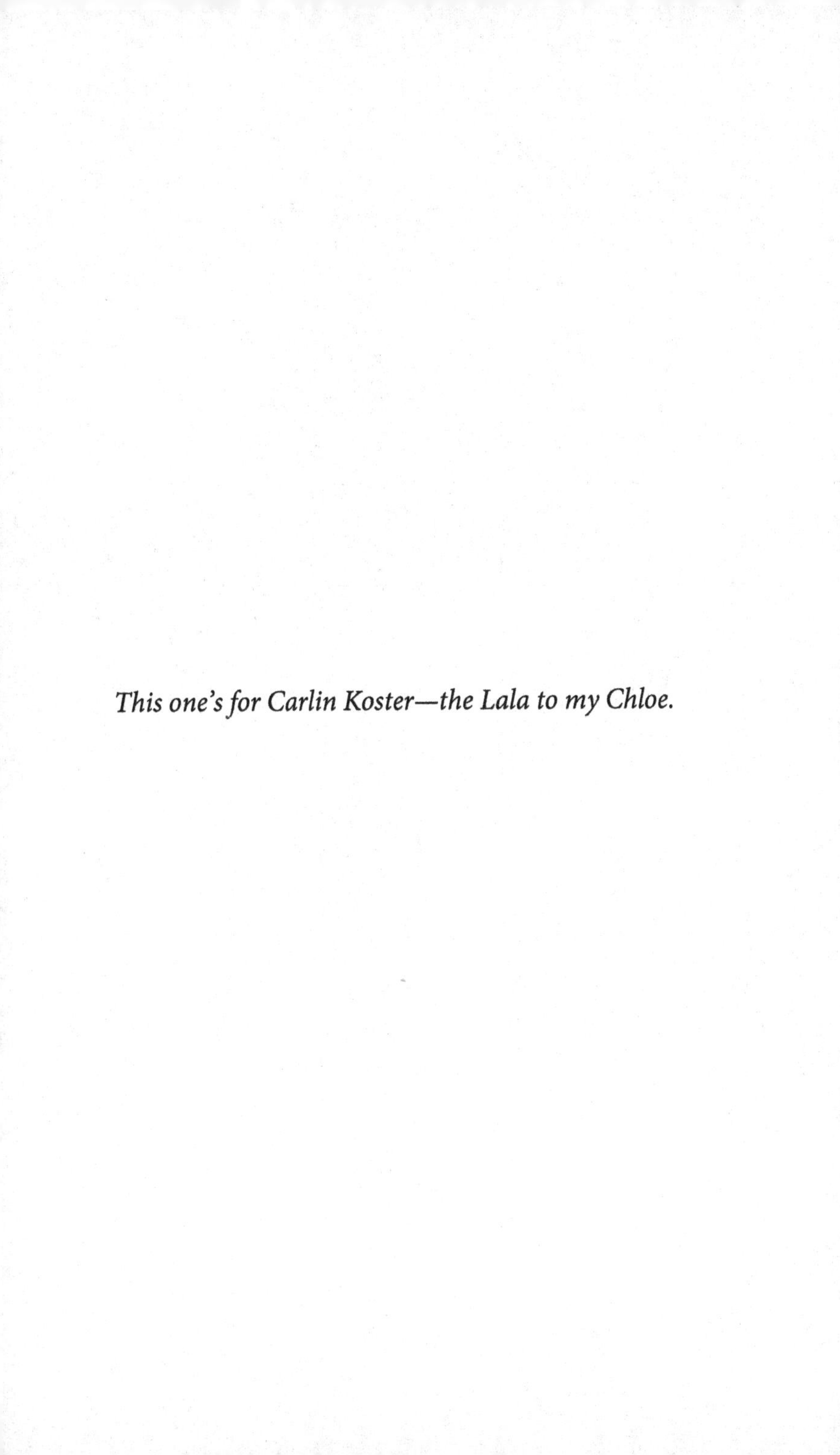

This one's for Carlin Koster—the Lala to my Chloe.

Prologue:
La Vie en Rose

"I am the luckiest woman in the world."

Chloe's stomach fluttered as Liam pulled her in for a kiss. It was crazy that he still did that to her, so many years later. Most couples she knew hit the roommate phase before the two-year mark.

Not she and Liam. Their relationship felt like a four-and-a-half-year-long honeymoon. And she knew without a shadow of a doubt that in a few short years she and Liam would be husband and wife. He hadn't popped the question yet, but it was coming. Marriage was something they were on the same page about, along with starting a family.

But her relationship wasn't the only reason Chloe considered herself to be lucky. In addition to her handsome banker boyfriend, she had a great group of girlfriends, a supportive family, good health, and the career of her dreams, which enabled her to travel around the world for free.

The stock ticker at the bottom of the T.V. flashed green as the clock changed to 9:30 a.m. She and Liam were both playing hooky that Friday, but that wouldn't stop him from keeping tabs on the market.

Not that Chloe minded. It was one of the many things she loved about Liam. He was hardworking and ambitious—out the door by 6 a.m. Monday to Friday, and back at home late most nights. Chloe, on the other hand, wandered into her office three hours later and, barring any magazine-related PR events or parties, was home at a much earlier hour.

That didn't mean that her work required less effort—it was just that Liam's job was more demanding in terms of time. As an investment banking associate at one of the Big Five, it was normal for him to sometimes work ninety-hour weeks. His schedule didn't exactly leave them tons of time to spend together, so it made her value the time they did spend together that much more. Which was one of the reasons why Chloe was so excited for today.

Skipping out on work had been Liam's idea. Of course, it wasn't a spur-of-the-moment decision. He had floated the proposal more than a month ago and blocked off his calendar to prevent any last-minute meetings.

For Chloe, it was a lot easier. As a travel editor, she often made her own schedule. She also had a lot of leeway with it, given the frequent after-work events her job required her to attend.

She wasn't complaining about that either.

The fashion, style, and beauty editors typically bagged the best invitations, but as a travel editor, she was invited to her fair share. The cult following of the print and online publication she worked for had garnered Chloe a long list of followers; her Instagram currently boasted a little over one million people, brands, places, and meme pages that were privy to her every work-related move. Not that she was one of those people who spent every waking minute on Instagram. Social media wasn't really her thing, but she understood the importance of it when it came to her job.

Brands and publicists invited her to exclusive events and comped her loads of products in exchange for social media promotions. When she was off the clock, however, she was more interested in enjoying her time with whomever or whatever it was she was doing—sans snaps.

She had been a bit surprised that Liam had been able to make the day off happen; she was used to going with the flow when it came to last-minute cancelations. His career was very important to him and Chloe was very supportive. Not to mention, she was busy with her own career and social life. She was often away for work on assignment—vacationing, for lack of a better term, in far-flung locales around the world.

Sunlight flooded their living room, dulled by a wall of sheer curtains that kept prying eyes from the neighbouring office building out of sight. With their other neighbour—a quaint park that gave them an unobstructed green view from their corner unit—they didn't have anything to worry about.

Liam was the one who owned the condo—Chloe had moved into it after their first year of dating. Hesitant to put her own place on the market, she had rented it out the past few years. Recently she had been thinking about selling it, but hadn't quite gotten around to setting the sale ball in motion. Which was seeming rather stupid, really. While their home was Liam's in title only, it was, for all intents and purposes, theirs.

When Chloe was working from home—a typical occurrence in the life of a writer; words, unlike the answers to a math equation, don't come on demand—she would take little breaks to observe the goings-on below from her desk. At the park across the street there was a never-ending parade of dogs, people milling about or sitting on benches and, in the summer, on the grass. It was so routine for some of them that Chloe practically knew their schedules.

From their eighth-floor view, she regularly saw Nugget,

an overweight golden retriever, waddle his way through the grass. She had met Nugget one afternoon after popping down to the park for a few minutes to catch some sun. The happy ball of fur had suddenly barreled over to her with a harried-looking woman in tow, sat down, and put his fuzzy paw on her lap.

"Sorry!" the woman attached to the other end of the leash had exclaimed. "He must think you have a treat!"

"Don't be sorry!" Chloe laughed. "I wish I did have one for him."

In the ensuing convo she had learned the chunky dog's name. Nugget had to make do with a head-and-back scratch that afternoon, but ever since that day, Chloe had taken to carrying Milk-Bones in her purse. And Nugget wasn't the only recipient of the bone-shaped snacks; there were many dogs in the park who could thank the golden retriever for the strange treat lady who carried Milk-Bones in her purse despite not actually having a dog of her own.

"So!" Liam's voice pulled her out of her reverie as he leaned back on the couch and gathered her into his arms. "What do you think we should do today?"

Chloe melted against him and snuggled her head into the crook in his neck.

"I can think of a few things . . .," she teased.

"Well, that's definitely on the list," he gave her bum an enthusiastic squeeze and Chloe squealed. "But what about the other eight hours?"

She pondered.

It was that transitional period of the season when summer is starting to turn into fall. Leaves go from green to autumn, and a crispness creeps into the night air; the days start to get shorter, and light jackets signal a promise of what's to come: apple picking, pumpkin spice, and spooky season.

"We could go to the ROM," she said inquiringly, referencing Toronto's Royal Ontario Museum. She loved getting lost in the exhibits; wanderlust—it was one of the reasons she was a travel editor. Exploring different cultures, histories, and art was one of her favourite past times—even if those cultures, histories, and art were trapped in the past.

"Or," she said switching gears, "we could go down to the waterfront, have brunch and spend the afternoon in the sun?"

While fall was fast approaching, the weather report that day had the temperatures in the high twenties.

"Brunch and some sun," Liam said firmly. "Let's bike down. That way we can get in some cycling along the lake."

Chloe smiled. Typical Liam—he would always find a way to get in a workout.

"Then we can bike to St. Lawrence Market and pick up some things for dinner," she suggested.

"Sounds great."

Liam started to rub her leg and shoulder.

"How about charcuterie for dinner?" she asked.

"Sounds great," Liam replied again.

Chloe had a feeling she could tell him they were having dog food for dinner and Liam would have the same response. His thoughts were clearly focused somewhere else.

Chloe shifted her body and fixed him with a devilish grin.

"What do you say we go back to bed for a bit?"

Liam didn't reply that time. At least not with words. An answering grin spread across his face, and he stood up before pulling Chloe off the couch and leading her into their bedroom.

*

She lay there in the mess of blankets and a feeling of happiness settled over her. There wasn't anything missing in her life. She had a career that fulfilled her, a handsome, hard-working boyfriend, a great group of girlfriends, supportive parents, a lovely home, a lovely life, and a wonderful future mapped out with Liam.

Next to her, Liam sighed, and Chloe snuggled deeper into his arms.

I am the luckiest woman in the world, she thought as her boyfriend planted a kiss on top of her head.

Present

Chapter 1:
La Fin

"*You are NOT the father!*"

"YES! I called it!" Chloe pumped her first triumphantly and put down the tub of vanilla frosting just long enough to take a swig from a bottle of red wine.

"Ahem."

She glanced at the redhead occupying the seat beside her. Lala raised her eyebrows and split a glance between the T.V., frosting, wine, and Chloe.

Through her half-a-bottle haze, Chloe interpreted her friend's raised eyebrows and pointed stare as a sign that she wanted in on the pity party.

"Sorry, Lala," Chloe took another swig from the bottle and then held it out to her in offering. "That was rude of me."

A look of disgust crossed Lala's face, and she shook her head.

"Look, Chloe," she took a deep breath. "I don't mean to

be a bitch and all but fucking pull yourself together." She sounded exasperated. "It's been three months. Are you really going to let him ruin your life?"

Chloe clutched the wine bottle a little tighter and averted her eyes. She looked back on unlocking the condo door and letting Lala in with regret. Nobody likes a killjoy. Not that Chloe had much joy left in her to kill. But still.

"Seriously, Chloe," Lala continued. "When you're not crying your eyes out and doing the bare minimum to scrape by at work, you spend most of your time shit-faced, stuffing your face, and watching trash T.V."

A grimace crossed Chloe's face, and she turned back to the T.V. Not that she was all that interested in *Maury* at that moment. It was just a way for her to avoid the conversation that she knew was coming.

Because, of course, Lala was right.

"Hey!"

She tore her eyes away from the T.V. and looked again at her friend, which immediately caused Chloe to cower. The steely-eyed glare Lala was fixing her gave new meaning to the term 'fiery redhead'. She sunk farther into the couch under her friend's withering stare as cheers from *Maury*'s studio audience reverberated in the background.

"But . . ." Chloe looked around helplessly. "He . . . I . . ." Her defiance faltered and her voice began to wobble.

A look of sympathy crossed Lala's face and Chloe crumpled on the couch in a mess of tears. The bottle of wine hung precariously in her hand, threatening to smash to the floor in an imitation of her broken heart.

Lala was suddenly there beside her—she took the bottle out of Chloe's hand and consoled her while she cried. After a few minutes, the sobs petered out into sniffles and the fountain of tears slowed to a trickle.

Lala patted her friend's hand affectionately.

"I know you're upset," she sounded calm and measured.

"I know you're heartbroken and I know you think you will feel like this for the rest of your life. But you won't. You're better than that. You are a great person, and most importantly—you are my best friend."

She paused.

"I know this is hard for you, but you need to get out and start living your life and stop letting that good-for-nothing bastard rule it. I love you. Your friends and family love you. The goddamned barista at the Starbucks on King loves you." She paused. "I saw him yesterday. He told me he was thinking of calling in a wellness check for you, but he doesn't know your number, address, or last name," she paused again. "But I digress. The point is, we love you and we are here for you, but this has gone on for long enough."

Chloe sniffled as Lala stood up, grabbed the frosting off the coffee table and headed over to the kitchen. The spoon clunked in the sink and the frosting landed in the garbage with a thunk.

She watched Lala head for the door.

"I'm coming to pick you up at noon tomorrow," she said. "You're going with me to yoga."

Chloe opened her mouth to protest, but Lala cut her off.

"No," her voice was sharp. "You are coming with me. No ifs ands or buts about it. I'll see you tomorrow," she said before strolling out the door and shutting down any opportunity for a retort.

Chloe sat there for a minute, staring at the door and cursing the indignity of it all. If she wanted to spend the rest of her life wallowing in self-pity, wine, and trash television, who was Lala to stop her?

Liam, the love of Chloe's life, was gone. He'd broken up with her, shattered her heart. Their relationship was finished. Finito. La fin. And she was supposed to just suck it up and soldier on?

It was the kind of strategy that might work for some

people, but it wouldn't work for her. Soldiers were stoic and disciplined. Chloe was . . . a mess. Compost was, if not how she actually looked, exactly how she felt—like decaying matter. The discarded bits that end up in the bin. And you can't turn compost into the statue of David.

If only I could recycle my feelings, she thought wistfully and let out a sigh.

She had been in this sorry state for three months. Three months and five days, to be exact. Not that Chloe was keeping track or anything.

Her friends and family had rallied around her initially, but as the days had dragged on and the world kept on turning, one by one their sympathy began to wane. Lala had been the longest-lasting outpost of support and was just the latest in a long line of people in Chloe's life who had had enough of her moping.

The results of *Maury*'s lie detector test sounded off in the background, but she was no longer paying attention. The poorly concealed elephant in the room, which seemed to be a permanent houseguest, reared its ugly head and forced Chloe to confront the problem. A grimace washed over her at the prospect of attempting to process her feelings.

The worst part of her and Liam's breakup hadn't been the sadness—although that was pretty bad. It was the conflux of emotions. There was misery, heartache, despair, and depression. But there was also yearning, anxiety, desperation, and regret. One minute she was crying her eyes out in bed, the next minute she was staring listlessly at the ceiling. Once or twice, she had even caught herself staring at Liam's number, the 'call' icon tempting her like a half-off sale at Saks. Maybe she could pretend she had accidentally called him. Pocket dialed him. He would text her to see why she called, she daydreamed, and somehow they would end up back together.

Fortunately, she was led not into temptation. But only

because she knew Liam would see right through the high-school ruse. And if there was any hope of the two of them getting back together, coming across as desperate would be a one-way ticket to Single-ville, population: her.

A fresh surge of sobs bubbled up inside of her as her mind flashed back to the night Liam had taken a meat tenderizer to her heart. She took a deep breath to quell the emotion and Maury's voice suddenly cut through her thoughts: *"Sometimes the hardest truths are the ones we need to hear the most."*

She looked at the T.V.

The daytime talk-show host was giving a pep talk to a woman who, according to the short description on the screen, had just found out her husband was sleeping with her sister.

Chloe sat back for a moment.

Obviously, she wasn't in the same situation, but there was a large grain of truth in Maury's pearl of wisdom.

The hardest truths are the ones we need to hear the most.

Maury was right.

Lala was right.

Was she really going to let Liam ruin her life?

She didn't want to. He was a good-for-nothing bastard. But that didn't stop some part of her from hoping that he would change his mind. Even though she knew that wasn't going to happen. Which was yet another unpleasant emotion she had to contend with.

A wave of resolve suddenly washed over her and Chloe sat up a little straighter. She narrowed her eyes and scrunched up her nose.

Screw Liam.

She wasn't going to let him rule her life. She was going to get over him. She was going to walk the walk, talk the talk, and put him in her past.

Her features softened as her determination faltered, and her back slouched as thoughts of doubt started to creep in.

She sat back on the couch.

She would work on getting over Liam, yes.

Starting tomorrow.

As for today?

She headed for her fridge and rummaged around for the chocolate cake she had hidden in the crisper.

*

Bees. Everywhere. Angrily swarming her body. Panic engulfed Chloe as the buzzing got louder and a bee headed right for her face.

"No!"

Chloe awoke with a start, her heart pounding like Tommy Lee on a drum set.

She looked around wildly, her heart still racing. It was a relief for her to find that the buzzing sound was not a swarm of bees but, in fact, her phone. She had fallen into a wine-and-cake coma the previous evening and passed out in bed a little after 9 p.m. Which was where she had stayed until ten minutes to noon according to the clock on her phone that hovered just above Lala's name on the screen.

Chloe winced and pressed the green button.

"I swear to Christ, Chloe, you'd better be ready to go," Lala's voice came from the speaker.

She sounded deadly.

"If I have to hog-tie you and drag you from your building, you're coming to hot yoga," she threatened.

A moan of displeasure escaped Chloe's mouth: "I don't want to," she whined. "But I'm coming. Give me ten minutes."

One hot-yoga class later and Chloe had sweat out her cake-and-liquor sins from the previous evening. Her tank top was drenched, her thighs stuck to the yoga mat, and her arms had nearly given out during downward dog. But she did it.

It had been disappointing but not entirely surprising to

find that her workout clothes had somehow shrunk two sizes. She wanted to put it down to her poor skills as a laundress instead of the sad 'fuck my life' diet she'd resigned herself to for the past few months, but denial was a state she had been living in for far too long.

She was almost in disbelief that she had let herself go that badly since the breakup. Although, in all fairness, she figured that it's hard to gauge your size when you live in sweatpants and pajamas.

Yoga had never been one of her favourite forms of fitness, and she had agreed to go only because she knew Lala would have made good on her threat. So, it was somewhat of a surprise to find that the class had done something for her. Whether it was the sweat, the stretching, the remnants from last night's poor choices, or just being out in public, Chloe felt a bit better afterwards.

A weight hadn't necessarily lifted. But something in her had definitely shifted. For that, she was grateful.

"I told you!" Lala beamed after Chloe confided in her. They had stopped in at Starbucks after class. Not the one on King Street—Chloe wasn't ready to face that barista yet.

"I knew if you got out of your condo and did something productive you would feel better."

*

In the following weeks, she made several strides with the encouragement and accompaniment of her friend.

Gone were the sweatpants, unwashed hair, and tear-streaked complexion. Not that she didn't still cry herself to sleep some nights. She just made it a rule to put on a few swipes of mascara when she first woke up and kept herself occupied morning, noon, and night.

Podcasts kept her company when she woke up; work—entirely from home—kept her busy during the day; and in the evenings, she filled her social schedule with outings and exercise.

Plastering on a smile and feigning happiness was hard at first, but as time wore on, she found she was no longer faking. She found genuine joy in small talk, in seeing a happy dog trot by her in the street. Contentment came from a latte at her favourite shop and a bubble bath with a good book.

Her gym—the place she hadn't seen the inside of for one entire quarter—welcomed her back with open arms and she had taken to the treadmill to work out her frustration. Any time she felt a spiral coming on, she laced up her shoes and went running.

"I threw up at the gym," Chloe, mortified, confessed to her friend. She had pushed herself extra hard on the treadmill that session, but it wasn't in an effort to beat her personal best. It was because she thought she had spotted Liam in line at the Mos Mos coffee shop that morning. The jolt that went through her when she set eyes on the man, who was not, in fact, Liam, alerted her to the fact that she was definitely not over her ex.

A whole host of negative emotions had bubbled up inside, and she channeled those feelings into her workout. Apparently, she had overdone it. Although, when she thought about it, she figured it could potentially serve as a very useful form of negative reinforcement. If every time she thought of Liam she pushed herself to the limit at the gym, at some point she would associate him with throwing up. If she was really lucky, at some point, the mere mention of his name might induce her to gag.

"Hell, yes, you did!" Lala clapped at her friend's confession.

Chloe was appalled.

"You're applauding this?"

"No," Lala shook her head. "I'm applauding the effort you're putting in. You're working out, combing your hair, *washing* your hair, and being social. A few weeks ago, your place looked like it was inhabited by hoarders and the only thing you were motivated by was wine. Now, you're leaving your condo all on your own. I don't even have to threaten you anymore," she added brightly.

Chloe could see her point. She really had come a long way. She reflected on the several months she had spent wallowing. It added up to more than one quarter of a year.

It was crazy what a bad breakup could do to a person.

*

"You look so much better, honey." Chloe's mom opened the fridge and put away a carton of milk.

It had been six weeks since Lala had staged her intervention and Chloe was sipping coffee in her parents' kitchen, watching her mom put away a bag of groceries. Her dad was away fishing.

"Thanks." Chloe was sincere. "I've been working out and eating better. I'm starting to fit back into my old clothes." She traced her finger around the rim of her mug.

"Oh, well, I didn't mean that," her mom said, pulling an avocado out of a cloth bag. "I mean your spirit. You have a human spark in you now. You look alive."

Shades of Frankenstein aside, Chloe didn't know how to respond to that and scrunched her mouth to the side. She supposed she *had* been in some bizarre kind of walking-dead limbo the last few months. She had been alive. Technically, at least.

"Speaking of—now that you're back in the land of the living, have you thought about going on a date?" her mom continued. "It's been nearly five months. And you know what they say—the best way to get over someone is to get under someone else! Or someones!"

Chloe choked on her coffee and began to splutter.

"Oh my god, Mom!"

Was her mother really suggesting a wild run of no-strings-attached promiscuity? It appeared that yes—yes she was.

Her mom put the last of the groceries away, arranging green apples into the porcelain bowl on the island before plopping down in the seat beside her daughter.

"I mean, really, Chloe. I don't know how you've even managed to keep your job these past five months," she said bluntly.

Truthfully, Chloe didn't know how she'd managed to keep her job either. Being given the nod to work from home was a godsend. Getting by on the bare minimum, delegating tasks to her assistants, and begging off work events due to 'sickness'; it was a miracle that her boss at *Strut* hadn't canned her. What kind of travel editor wouldn't even travel outside of her home?

"I know, Mom," she said. "But I'm making an effort now. I love my job, and I definitely don't want to lose it. I've just been so depressed that I didn't care about anything. Not work, not life, not friends, not family—" she paused.

"Not hygiene," her mom prompted helpfully.

Chloe looked at her, eyebrows drawn and shaking her head. "Thank you, very helpful."

"Well, darling, I call it like I see it," she shrugged.

Chloe sighed.

Chapter 2:
Strut

Dasha Kulakova was a blonde-haired boss bitch with a penchant for cutting-edge fashion and an aversion to moving her face. The jury was still out as to whether it was a deep-seated hatred of wrinkles or an over-abundance of Botox that left Dasha's face expression-free, but either way, the end result was the same—a powerful woman who was made all the more intimidating because you could never quite tell what she was thinking.

As the formidable president and editor in chief of *Strut*—a one-stop-shop print and online magazine that catered to the 'ladies who lunch' clientele—Dasha had been at the helm of the publication for the past fifteen years. Chloe had worked her way up from intern to lifestyle editor before obtaining the coveted position of in-house travel editor.

When she had first started at *Strut*, Dasha had scared the living daylights out of her. But in the several years since, she had grown close with her boss. She didn't quite consider her to be a friend, but she did consider her to be a mentor. And, in that vein, when it came to Chloe's breakup, Dasha had been the only person at the office who she had told. For the rest of her colleagues, Chloe's relationship status remained a secret.

Not that the disclosure to Dasha happened immediately. After finding herself single, Chloe had emailed her boss asking for a couple of days off. Dasha, who trusted her staff implicitly, had been very understanding. In Chloe's email she hadn't gone into detail about what had occurred, but in a subsequent Zoom meeting her boss had set up to check in on her, Chloe had tearfully revealed it all.

It hadn't been her finest moment and the contrast between her and Dasha's demeanors was like night and day. After she had stopped sobbing, she thought it was entirely possible that her boss would relieve her of her duties. Dasha's sympathy, therefore, had come as a surprise.

"You can work from home," she had said, her features unmoving. "Take as long as you need and keep me updated."

With that, HR signed off on Chloe's modified working arrangement and she hadn't set foot in the office since.

Which was why Chloe was so nervous this morning. That weekend she had sent Dasha an email letting her know she would be back in the office at the start of the work week. It would be the first time she would be seeing her colleagues in person in almost six months.

Morning came early for her that Monday; her alarm clock had been set for 7 a.m., but Chloe had found herself awake two ungodly hours before then. Despite that, she felt refreshed, recharged, and ready to get back to her office.

Letting out a big sigh she rolled over in bed, snuggled up under the covers, and stared off into the darkness.

It was deafening.

She wasn't entirely over Liam. She didn't know if she would *ever* manage to get over him or if he would be a permanent black cloud she carried around for the rest of her life. Maybe she would turn into one of those jaded people who carried around the pieces of their last relationship and protected themselves from further harm with bitterness and avoidance.

Maybe.

But she hoped not.

Hot water cascaded down her body and the sweet smell of pomegranate filled the air as she scrubbed herself clean. She took her time toweling off and, minutes later, had a steaming mug of coffee cupped in her hands. A plush housecoat was wrapped around her body as she leaned her head against the living room window and took in the stillness of the city. Jenga blocks towered into the sky and stood silent, belying the tens of thousands of people—office workers, support staff, maintenance crew, restauranteurs, and retailers—that bustled in the buildings during the day.

It was something she used to savour some mornings with Liam: waking up while the rest of the city was sleeping and slowly sipping her coffee while watching the sunrise.

Now she was doing it alone. One mug, one person. That was her new normal.

Chloe shook off the thought.

The dishwasher door creaked as she put the mug inside and clicked the door closed. This was another one of her rituals. During what she referred to as her 'period of mourning', her living conditions would have offended a packrat. Her place was clean now, but to avoid falling back into the hoarding trap, she followed a very carefully crafted routine. Granted, she hadn't cleaned up the multi-month mess that had accumulated on her own. Lala's encouragement had pushed her to get out of her home and out of her head, yes. But what it didn't do was give her the motivation to clean her condo, which more closely resembled a garbage dump than a home. Fortunately, her friends had come over one day, armed with an assortment of cleaning products, and taken charge. After that, Chloe had been careful not to make a mess. She realized it was harder to fall back into a pit of despair when your surroundings were pristine.

Not impossible, mind you. There had been a time or two where things started to accumulate, but she discovered that immediately forcing herself to pick it up and put it away was one part of the 'back to feeling like Chloe' equation. She was hoping that going back into the office would be one of the final pieces.

In the bathroom mirror she caught a glimpse of her reflection; her blonde tresses just skimmed the top of her shoulders. She'd gone to her hairstylist, Ricardo, that weekend, and had him take care of her three-inch roots. Ricardo, who hadn't seen her in six months, had gasped in horror when he saw her. A look of revulsion crossed his face as he fingered the three inches of brown hair that protruded from the top of her head. Chloe could understand why—he was a stylist who took his career very seriously. Her natural colour scarily contrasted with the rest of her bottled blonde locks. It gave her a look that Ricardo, deadpan, had referred to as 'the reverse skunk'.

Ricardo, bless his heart, had worked his magic and, three hours later, she had walked out of his studio missing several months of split ends, and sporting a fully blonde, bouncy blow-out. Her hair still kept its shape this morning and bobbed along as she trudged through the snowy sidewalks to *Strut*'s fifteenth-floor offices. They were situated in a tall building on Bay Street and Richmond Ave that housed a bank and a handful of other institutions.

As she walked past Hy's, the restaurant where she had first met Liam, Chloe fought back a wave of nausea. An upscale steakhouse situated on the ground level of the skyscraper, Hy's catered to lawyers, bankers, and businessmen who conducted round-the-clock meetings along with round-the-clock drinks. It was a last-minute decision to grab drinks there that had led to her meeting Liam Hollingsworth. A decision they had laughed about afterwards, often joking about how lucky they both were that she hadn't gone to the other side of the block and hit up The Chase instead.

Liam and some of his banking colleagues were seated at the table next to Chloe that evening, and the happy hour drinks were flowing. Three of Chloe's close friends had joined her, and it hadn't taken long for Lala, her bold-as-brass best friend, to strike up a conversation with the tableful of suits sitting beside them.

Liam had first caught Chloe's eye as she followed the hostess to her table. His dirty-blond hair was flecked with premature gray, and his slanted blue eyes twinkled when he caught Chloe looking his way. She had him pegged as early thirties, which was in stark contrast to the four other men sitting with him who all looked to be at least half-a-century old.

Her curiosity was piqued, but she minded her own business after she sat down and busied herself by studying the restaurant's drink menu. Despite Hy's being situated in the same building Chloe worked in, she had never found herself patronizing the place. Her job at *Strut* didn't pay her enough to be dining out at expensive steakhouses. Not to mention, while she shared the elevator with bankers, lawyers, and businessmen on the daily, she felt out of place when it came to mingling with them. She didn't dress up in fancy suits or discuss business deals while drinking old-fashioneds. She wore casual clothing and gossiped about men while sipping seltzers.

Not that her dating life at that point had been anything to write home about. The last three men she had been out with had been total duds. One was still pining for his ex, another mentioned that he was into polyamory (she didn't judge, it just wasn't what she wanted, and she was less than pleased that he had neglected to mention that tidbit on his dating profile). The third had spent the entirety of their date, which lasted sixty-seven minutes, boasting about himself. It had been more than two years at that point since she had broken up with her ex-boyfriend and, not to be too pessimistic, she had resigned herself to singledom for the rest of her life. A begrudging acceptance had settled into her heart and that night the last thing she had been looking for was a man.

As she scanned through the menu—beer, wines, cocktails, and mocktails—she had felt the blond man's eyes on her again. She glanced at him through her lashes, and he had responded with a sexy smirk.

Chloe had blushed furiously. She managed a small smile back and then had buried her head back in the menu, studying it as intently as if she was preparing to write the bar. A waitress soon came over and took her order—an espresso martini—which she sipped while she waited for her friends.

Lala, her closest friend in the entire world, was a sales executive for a tech company and worked just a few blocks away. She was a forceful personality and excelled at her job. In fact, Chloe wouldn't be surprised if Lala someday ended up running the whole corporation. Alejandra and Opal, the other two friends she was waiting for, were a dental hygienist, and an associate lawyer, respectively. Alejandra had a perfect set of pearly whites, which served as great advertisement for her services, and Opal was a reasoned and seasoned corporate lawyer who was working her way up the Bay Street ladder.

The four of them had been friends since their undergraduate university days, and their friendship had only grown as they found themselves living and working in the city. Of course, with busy lives and schedules, they saw each other less often than they did during their four years at university, but they still found time for a tri-weekly meetup.

Chloe's work assignments—read: multi-day all-expenses-paid vacations that she, incredibly, was salaried to write about—often allowed for a plus-one. It was something that Lala joined when she was able to, but Chloe had also brought along her parents, a close cousin, and once, when she had been able to swing it, Alejandra. She worked long hours at two dental clinics just to make ends meet, and Chloe knew her friend would never have been able to afford a trip like that on her own.

Not that Chloe was swimming in cash either. Her pay wasn't anywhere near top tier, but she really couldn't complain. Her job allowed her to see the world without spending a dime. And not in a hostel-hopping, back-pack traveling kind of way that most people did in their twenties. No, no—she stayed at luxury hotels and resorts and got to experience the cities, towns, beaches, and bushes the way the ultra-wealthy did.

In Nunavut she had gone on a polar bear trek where she slept under the stars, saw the northern lights, and participated in traditional Inuit ceremonies. In Johannesburg, she stayed at the newly renovated Four Seasons, spent a day at their spa, ate exquisite cuisine, and saw lions, giraffes, and zebras on a safari. In the South of France, she slept in a castle, went on wine and cheese tours, and stuffed her face with as much French bread as she could stomach.

After she had gotten together with Liam, he had joined her on a few of her assignments. Their first trip together, after they had been dating for over a year, was to London, where they were reopening the newly renovated The Langham, London. They had spent four luxurious nights at the hotel, which had included a black-tie reopening soiree, butler service, the spa, heavenly pastries, fine dining, and all the sights, sounds, and experiences that London had to offer.

Well, all the sights, sounds, and experiences that they could reasonably squeeze into three days.

They started officially cohabitating shortly afterwards,

with Chloe moving into Liam's place—her 500-square-foot condo was hardly big enough to house two people. Liam, on the other hand, had a two-bedroom condo right in the downtown core. Not that moving in together had meant much anyway given they basically already lived together. Which was for reasons both personal and practical. Personal because they loved each other and practical because the location of Chloe's condo meant that it took her, on average, forty-five minutes to get to work. When she stayed at Liam's place, that extra forty-five minutes in the morning were spent either getting some extra shuteye or savouring her coffee.

She had been shocked at how quickly the two of them had gotten together, she and Liam. Prior to meeting him, she had mostly found dating to be a revolving door of commitment-phobes, men wanting to 'keep their options open', bitter people laden with baggage, and desperate clingers.

Which was why it had come as such a surprise that Liam was even single. He checked none of the aforementioned boxes and there was nary a red flag in sight. As Liam told it, much like Chloe he had broken up with his long-term girlfriend the year before and, since then, had only been on a handful of dates. Long hours spent at the office as he worked on closing deals and climbing his way up the cutthroat banking ladder meant that he didn't have much time to meet anyone, let alone go on any dates.

It was just as well then, perhaps, that the two of them hit it off that fateful night at Hy's. Over three espresso martinis (Chloe's) and several vodka sodas for Liam, they discovered that they worked in the same building but on different floors. They also discovered a shared love of travel; Liam had been intrigued by her career.

"You get paid to go on vacations?" he had sounded incredulous.

"Yes," Chloe took a sip of her martini and put it down before elaborating. "Not handsomely, but it pays the bills.

And I get to travel and have experiences most people only dream of."

A live, three-piece band started strumming the intro to a popular rock song and the volume in the restaurant increased.

"And they're not vacations," Chloe said with mock indignation. "They're assignments."

Liam laughed.

"Sheesh, I wish my work involved luxuriating on yachts in the Mediterranean," he shook his head with a smile, recalling the story Chloe had just told him about her latest assignment on the Amalfi Coast

She was used to getting that response when she told people what she did for work. And she did consider herself lucky. Very lucky. But she didn't put her position down to only luck. There was a lot of hard work that had gone into it. She had gone to school for journalism and was editor in chief for two on-campus magazines while attending the University of Toronto. After graduation she had interned for two magazines—*Strut* and *Elle Canada*. The internships, unpaid of course—money was scarce in the writing industry—had been supplemented by a waitressing gig at a restaurant near her home. In between her three-job juggling act, she found time to write freelance pieces for various magazines, which paid peanuts, but gave her more work for her portfolio.

She had been dismayed, but not altogether surprised, to find that after the internships ended, neither magazine had any job openings. Neither did any of the other print or online publications she researched. Newspapers, lifestyle magazines, beauty magazines, parenting magazines, technology magazines—none of them had job openings. At least not any job openings for an entry-level copy editor's position.

Because of this, three months after her internships had ended, she was waitressing full-time while picking up whatever freelance work she could find on the side. Then, Mylene, Chloe's manager at *Strut*, had called to let her know that they were hiring.

Along with all the other applicants, she submitted her resumé, cover letter, and portfolio, and had been called in for an interview. To Chloe, it felt like her first foray into the adult world. Sure, she had gone to school, lived alone, and done freelancing and internship work, but interviewing for her dream career at a magazine she loved felt like she was hitting a milestone.

She was unsure of herself after the interview, but had received a phone call the following day from Mylene.

"Congrats, Chloe!" she said enthusiastically. "I'm so happy you'll be joining us. You were such a great intern, and I just know that you're going to do great things at *Strut*."

Chloe, *Strut*'s newly minted copy editor, had sported a perma-smile for days afterwards and had taken it as a feather in her cap when Mylene told her that Dasha had been the one to float Chloe as a potential candidate for the position.

It came as a shock to her that Dasha even knew she existed. When she had interned at *Strut*, her job had consisted mostly of answering phones, scheduling appointments, picking up merchandise, packaging items and mailing them back to suppliers, designers, and PR agencies. She knew that Dasha had approved two pieces she had written for the online version of the magazine. But she also knew that *all* pieces were approved by Dasha, so she hadn't thought anything of it. Apparently, though, Chloe's work had left an impression on the no-nonsense blonde. It led to her forming a close connection with Dasha that had only strengthened as Chloe rose through the ranks and settled into different editorial positions.

Strut was a widely circulated magazine with a large readership throughout North America, Europe, and Australia. It was primarily a fashion magazine but also had a beauty and travel section—which was the one that Chloe was now in charge of—and always featured hard-hitting articles that delved into everything from human rights abuses—one piece had investigated a luxe fashion house's line of sweaters that were sold for more than $6,000 but whose Indigenous farmers who supplied the wool were compensated pennies—to overconsumption and fast fashion. Each issue also, of course, included a travel feature written by none other than Chloe Ryder herself.

The magazine was a beacon in a sea of drowning magazine and media companies. Mostly, Chloe believed, because Dasha pushed her employees to be the best. And while some people might not like a boss who demanded nothing short of perfection, the staff at *Strut* responded positively to the pushing. Their bi-monthly all-staff brainstorming sessions were Olympic-level competitions to see who could come up with the next great idea for a captivating feature or a show-stopping editorial. All the employees, even the entry-level editors, were considered top players in their industry. And it was because of Dasha's pushing that they all had jobs. With the advent of the internet, print and online magazines had fallen away and there were now only a handful of publications—all of which were fighting for longevity. Magazines had to be at the top of their game, which meant that their staff had to be at the top of their game too.

In mainstream and alternative media, *Strut* had been described as 'bold', 'forward', and a 'force to be reckoned with' and Chloe was proud to be working there. When she had started studying journalism, there wasn't any subject she had felt particularly drawn to. But that changed after she started interning at *Strut* and got to see up close what Aurelie, the travel editor at the time, got to do. Aurelie, a second-generation Canadian whose family hailed from France, had blown into the office one winter morning with a golden tan, a raffia handbag, and looking like she had had the best sleep of her life.

"Ritz Carlton Bahamas travel feature," she had tossed off in response to Chloe's jaw-dropped expression.

Before that, Chloe had had vague notions of what a travel editor did. Which was much like what any other editor or writer might do—research and then write. What Chloe hadn't appreciated or understood was that, like the fashion editor who goes to Paris, London, and Milan to write about fashion, *Strut*'s travel editor went to the locations, hotels, and locales to write about travel. She had liked Aurelie, but from that moment on, Chloe had had one goal in mind—to get Aurelie's job.

Chloe had slowly risen up the ranks of the magazine until the celebrated day came, six years on, when Aurelie tendered her resignation. Her husband had been offered a job in New York City, and it was too good an opportunity for them to pass up.

Dasha, knowing what a loss Aurelie would be to *Strut*, had offered to let her work remotely, but Aurelie had turned the opportunity down. Her husband would be working long and odd hours with his new career and she wanted to ensure she was there to support him and their family, the same way that her husband had supported her. After all—without him she wouldn't have been able to take all those trips she had gone on and written about. With two children at home who couldn't very well be dragged along with her, she had often required him to be a stay-at-home dad on weekends and on weekdays.

When Chloe had heard that her colleague was leaving, she had almost leapt out of her seat with joy. She was sad that Aurelie would be leaving, yes. But she was also out-of-her-mind excited. She was confident that she would do a bang-up job in the travel editor's position if she was given the opportunity. Not that she was so arrogant as to think she was the top candidate for the job.

Nevertheless, when the position was posted, Chloe had immediately submitted her portfolio and, after an informal interview with Dasha, Chloe had been offered the position before leaving her boss's office.

It was all Chloe could do not to leap across the table and tackle Dasha in an enthusiastic hug. She had dreamed of this moment. Literally. Some of her dreams had her jetting around the world in bizarre situations as a travel editor—visiting a remote region of the Amazon to stay in a grass hut with Indigenous tribes; scuba diving with the president of France—and now her dream was coming true.

The other staffers had all been supportive. To the best of Chloe's knowledge, no one else had put in for the travel editor's position. The women and men at *Strut* were mostly happy with their roles. It was largely a fashion-based magazine so it kind of made sense that no one wanted the travel section. But there were hundreds of external applications—who didn't want a job that involved all-expense-paid luxury vacations?

Chloe was given Aurelie's old office and moved her things in that afternoon.

She had gone out and celebrated after phoning and texting her friends and family the good news. Champagne, shots, and margaritas had flowed like a river, and the next morning, Chloe thanked her lucky stars that she didn't have to work that holiday Friday—she felt like death warmed over.

She had quickly settled into her role and went to Greece on her first assignment. Her mom had come along as her plus-one and her dad had bought a plane ticket to join them.

Chloe couldn't think of a better way to celebrate reaching her career goal. It was a short trip—three days, four nights, which was the length of most of her travel assignments. But it was a trip she knew she would remember forever.

They had spent three glorious days experiencing Santorini like the one percent. They ate fantastic food, took in the picturesque sights, soaked up the sun, and toured the ancient ruins. It was the perfect celebration to mark the start of her dream job, and she felt unbelievably grateful to be able to experience it with her parents.

Several years later, she still considered it to be one of the best trips she had ever taken. Which was really saying something considering what she had experienced in the years since.

It had taken her a while to get used to flying business and first class and being catered to hand and foot. It was something she was more comfortable with now, but it wasn't ever something she took for granted. She knew that whenever her travel editor gig was up, she would be like Cinderella when the clock struck midnight—back to flying economy, saving up for vacations, staying at affordable hotels, and being budget conscious when it came to restaurants.

Fortunately, there seemed to be a semi-permanent pause on Chloe's clock. Its hands had been frozen in time—stuck at a very reasonable 7 p.m. Which meant there was plenty of time for her to keep enjoying the perks of her position.

And that was the story of her career.

And of Liam.

The rest, as they say, was history.

Just like her five-year-long relationship.

*

"Chloe!" Dasha exclaimed as she passed Chloe in the office. Her boss sounded happy, but her facial expression stayed the same.

It was earlier than most staffers arrived, and besides her and Dasha, the office appeared to be empty.

"I'm glad to see you back in the office. You look great." Dasha paused before getting back to business. "We need a hot travel feature for our October issue. Stop by my office once you've settled yourself in."

Chloe nodded. "Thank you," she said sincerely. "I'm glad to be back. I'll drop my things off and come by in five."

Despite Dasha having approved Chloe's multi-month work-from-home arrangement and allowing her to offshore a few months' worth of travel features, there was a knot in the pit of Chloe's stomach. She hadn't been a model employee the past few months. What she had been was a champion loafer. Snacking, sobbing, and sleeping wasn't a recipe for success, and she was grateful that Dasha had been compassionate towards her.

But, she thought, maybe it had more to do with labor and employment laws in the province.

She dropped her coat and bag off in her office—she had a small space close to the kitchen—and had been hit with a wave of nostalgia when she unlocked her office door.

She hadn't been in it since her life had been turned upside down.

With effort, she pushed the thought to the back of her mind and headed for Dasha's door.

Her boss ran a tight ship, but it was one of the reasons why the magazine was so revered. It was also one of the reasons why Dasha was so well paid and popular. Chloe knew from gossip around the office that magazines and corporations were always trying to poach the fierce editor, but *Strut* was Dasha's baby.

Literally.

The editor in chief and her long-term partner, Mikhail, who also ran a company and worked long hours, had never had children. For Chloe, she hadn't minded the fact that Liam spent most of his time at work, and she had often wondered if that was how Dasha's relationship worked too.

Liam had met the editor in chief a handful of times at events that she had brought him to like the company's annual Christmas party. Which usually consisted of dinner in a private dining room filled with staff dressed in high fashion and their toned-down but dressed-up partners.

She had seen a barely perceptible hint of disapproval on Dasha's face the first time she had met Chloe's boyfriend. Which was really saying something, given that most of the time Dasha's face didn't move. The slightest of creases between her boss's brows had alerted Chloe to the fact that Dasha didn't seem pleased with Liam.

She didn't understand why.

"Take a seat," Dasha gestured to one of the chairs across from her desk.

Chloe did as she was told.

"We've gotten by with the pieces you front-loaded for our last few issues and two freelance features," Dasha sounded measured.

The pit in her stomach tightened and she suddenly felt sick. She knew the articles Dasha was referencing and the freelancers. Chloe had recommended them herself. Was this a preamble to being fired?

"The freelance articles were good," her boss continued, "but they weren't Chloe Ryder good. For our October issue, I want something exciting. You're one of my best writers and I'm happy to have you back."

Chloe's body relaxed.

She wasn't being fired—thank her lucky stars.

It was a good reminder to her that, from here on out, she needed to bring her A-game.

"I understand," Chloe nodded. "There's a hotel in Nairobi that reached out last month. They have giraffes," she suggested.

Dasha's expression remained impenetrable.

"I also received invitations from Mardan Palace in Turkey and Aman Kyoto in Japan," she suggested.

Dasha continued staring and then finally spoke.

"I received an invitation to a resort in Costa Rica," she

said. "They opened a few months ago and I think it would make for a good feature."

Chloe was game. She had been to Costa Rica before and found it to be a beautiful country with rich culture and warm people.

"I'm more than happy to check it out," Chloe said enthusiastically.

Dasha nodded in approval.

"What's the resort?" Chloe inquired.

"It's called Costa Morpho. I'll forward you the invitation."

And with that, her meeting with Dasha was over. Chloe headed back to her office, unpacked her things, and opened her laptop.

She had heard the email notification sound from her cell phone and the promised invitation from Costa Morpho that Dasha had forwarded appeared on her computer screen. The email offered her and a guest a week-long stay at their resort and requested a response along with available dates.

She hit the reply button and began to type. A few minutes later, after consulting her calendar, she hit send before looking at the invitation email again.

Costa Morpho—it was a bit of an odd-sounding name, but no stranger really than Sandals, Moon Palace, or Breathless.

She wondered what the resort's schtick was. With the existence of Google, she could find out within seconds, but in her role, Chloe made it a rule not to look up the resorts and hotels she was staying at in advance. That way, she was seeing and experiencing the site with fresh eyes and no preconceived notions. She felt it made for a more authentic experience.

She was looking forward to going on assignment and seeing what Costa Morpho had to offer. And it wasn't just because she had spent several months veritably locked inside her condo. She genuinely loved her job, and when it came to new resorts, they were always looking to try and get one up on their competition. Often, that meant the companies worked to up the ante when it came to their offerings. One hotel she had stayed at had offered goldfish companions for their guests' rooms. On request, a butler would bring up a fishbowl with an aquatic friend that sat on the dresser for the duration of the guest's stay. It was odd, but what made it even odder was that the hotel was situated in the Caribbean, literal steps away from the ocean where fish were a dime a dozen.

Chloe guessed the fish companions were for those guests who wanted round-the-clock reminders that they were in an oceanic paradise. Still, given the size of the bowl that the poor fish was housed in, she saw it as cruel. She had made mention of it in the travel feature she had written about the resort and the unhappy postings on X and barrage of emails they had received caused them to put their 'goldfish for guests' program on hold.

A hotel in Texas had a quirky amenity that Chloe had found fun—a podcast recording studio in their lobby. While she wasn't interested in being a podcaster herself, she had taken advantage of the studio and filmed some clips for her Instagram. After all, as a travel editor, it was her job to test out all aspects of the hotel and its offerings to be able to inform potential guests about the good, the bad, the odd, and the ugly.

On assignment in Switzerland one spring, she had found herself staying at a hotel with an amenity labeled Meet the Sheep. It was, exactly as the name stated—an opportunity for guests to meet and pet some sheep. She had been delighted to be able to mingle with and pet the fluffy creatures, although she had been a little put out when she came to the realization that one of the hotel's restaurants offered a couple of entrées consisting of their wooly next-door neighbours.

At the Fairmont Hotel MacDonald in Canada, she had fallen in love with a chubby yellow lab by the name of

Smudge. The dog was part of the Fairmont chain's Canine Ambassador program, which donated a portion of their pet fees to a non-profit that gave guide dogs to the vision impaired. Smudge had her own spacious doghouse and would greet guests when they walked into the lobby. Chloe wasn't surprised to see that she wasn't the only one who enjoyed the sweet and friendly labrador. She had watched one morning as a serious-looking man in an expensive suit had gotten down on the floor to give the dog a belly rub in the middle of the hotel. A smile had spread across her face as he talked to Smudge in a sugary-sweet voice while the dog wagged her tail ferociously and lifted her paw in hopes of more belly rubs.

Chloe had also experienced a robot butler, a cake buffet, and—perhaps the strangest amenity of all—a Snoopy tuck-in service.

Which was exactly what it sounded like.

A person, dressed up as Snoopy in a set of striped pajamas, showed up to her room to tuck her in for the evening. She supposed it was all part of the experience, given it was a hotel that catered to kids, but as an adult, she found it quite unnerving.

Snoopy, like his cartoon counterpart, didn't speak. He had instead wordlessly indicated that Chloe needed to get into bed. She had lain there awkwardly as Snoopy had then gone around the room and turned out all the lights except for the lamp beside her bed and then thrown a fuzzy blanket over top of the duvet.

After the life-sized Snoopy had left, she had immediately jumped out of bed, locked her hotel room door, and looked out of the peephole to make sure the costumed human wasn't lurking outside of her door. While she could definitely see the appeal of having Snoopy come to your room as a kid, for Chloe, it was the stuff that nightmares were made of.

That particular assignment had been part of a feature that

focused on the 'best' places to stay for families, singles, couples, and sightseeing. And despite being creeped out, she didn't report on it negatively. She knew how popular it would be with families, but in the article she had alluded to it being a strange experience for an adult. She loved dogs. She just didn't love the two-legged, costumed, human kind. There were conventions for that kind of thing; it had occurred to her that the Snoopy tuck-in experience might actually attract people who frequented them. She had snorted with laugher as she pictured it in her mind—an unsuspecting Snoopy coming to tuck in a guest only to be reverse Uno'd at the door by a furry.

She wasn't sure what Costa Morpho would have to offer in the way of innovative or odd amenities, but she was hoping that a change of scenery would buoy her spirits and help to heal her heart. And even if the resort didn't have a host of spectacular amenities, she was just glad for the opportunity to get away. She was hoping she would be able to bring Lala with her and wasn't sure if her best friend could swing it.

She sent an inquiring text Lala's way.

How's your schedule looking next month? She wrote. *Fancy a trip to Costa Rica?*

Minutes later her phone pinged, and an enthusiastic reply popped up on screen.

Yessss!!! Girls trip!!! Give me the dates and I'll make it happen!!!!!

Chloe smiled at the message.

She really loved her best friend. And after the intervention Lala had staged, thankful didn't even begin to describe how Chloe felt towards her.

"Chloe!"

Her head snapped up and she saw Zhang, her colleague who worked in the beauty department, standing in her doorway.

"Hi!" Chloe smiled back.

"Welcome back to the office! We've missed you."

"Thanks, I've missed you all too."

Chloe's morning was filled with a lot of that—people stopping by to say hello and tell her how happy they were to see her back. A few of them had taken a seat across from her desk and settled in for a lengthier chat.

"People have been commenting on your Instagram," Jude, the very dramatic head of accessories, said seriously. "Some of them think you've died."

A laugh escaped Chloe's mouth and, seeing the serious expression still on Jude's face, she quickly turned it into a cough.

Her Instagram, the only social media that she used, was kept strictly for work-related endeavors. When she went to events, which, before her breakup, was at least once per week, she took photos and videos and posted pictures and stories. When she went away on assignment, she did the same, but waited to post most of them until the magazine article came out to entice people to read about it. She also reposted content from *Strut* and from her colleagues.

What she didn't post was anything personal. Liam, her friends, her family—none of them had ever graced her Instagram account. *And a good thing too,* she thought. She couldn't imagine how awkward it would be for her to have to go through her Instagram and delete all the happy couple photos of her and her ex. Having been on the receiving end of text messages telling her that various people's accounts had suddenly been wiped of all traces of their significant other, Chloe was glad to know that no one would be pulling apart her relationship and wondering what had happened.

Still, it was unsurprising that people had been speculating about her circumstances, given she had deleted the photo-sharing app on her phone a few days after the breakup. For someone who posted at least once per week, a sudden months-long disappearance was concerning. Most people with large followings who posted with regularity tended to give their followers a heads-up if they were taking a social media break.

Chloe had done no such thing, and she was now a bit apprehensive about reinstalling the app on her phone. It was something she would have to do, given her upcoming work assignment, and that wasn't the only thing she was worried about.

In the past six months she hadn't done any writing. Her features had been written in the months before, and all her work, aside from editing, had been outsourced. She was itching to get back to the keyboard—to pick up a pen and start outlining an article. But there was no small part of her that felt a little scared that her writing might not be as sharp as it used to be.

Chapter 3:
Highs & Lows

I'*m in!!!!*

Chloe was elated.

Costa Morpho had booked her in for a week-long stay at the end of the month. With the room, meals, and airfare comped, all she had needed was confirmation that her best friend could make it.

Which Lala's text had just provided.

She had been back at the office for over one week and it had made her realize how much she missed being there. From the impromptu cubicle conversations and the team brainstorming sessions to the endless racks of clothing and accessories littering the space and her fashionably dressed colleagues.

Curiously, no one made any inquiries into her six-month-long absence and, happily, no one had inquired about Liam. She was sure that the notoriously private and professional Dasha wouldn't have said anything about Chloe's absence. But she also knew that downtown gossip spread like wildfire.

It was a safe bet that someone—a friend of her colleagues or one of her colleagues themselves—would have run into Liam or one of his friends. All it would have taken was an innocent inquiry about Chloe's well-being and . . . bam—her relationship status would have been known all over the office.

When she thought about it, it was better this way. Six months later, Liam's name still made her stomach turn and her heart rate increase. This way, everyone avoided the topic.

She had gotten up the courage to reinstall Instagram on her phone over the weekend and was overwhelmed by the number of messages she had received from followers inquiring about her well-being.

It was both touching and a tad alarming. There were so many that, instead of replying to each person individually, she posted a story thanking her followers for their concern and letting them know that she had taken some time off for her well-being.

She had also RSVP'd for a beauty launch, which she would be attending that Thursday night. It was something she was apprehensive about. While her coworkers had enough tact to avoid any questions about her relationship, she knew that there would be those at the event who were either not so kind or who hadn't been apprised of the situation.

She wasn't so self-absorbed as to think that her relationship was newsworthy enough to end up in the gossip pages, and industry acquaintances were unlikely to be informed. Chloe just hoped there wouldn't be any questions.

*

Bisha Hotel was situated a bit west of the financial district on a crowded street. An imposing building, it was done up in blacks, grays, and blues with soft lighting that gave the interior of the hotel a dark, dramatic feel. The launch party was for a new line of Korean skincare products and was taking place on the rooftop restaurant which, in contrast to the rest of the hotel, was light and airy in taupe and beige tones.

Chloe wasn't the only staffer from *Strut* attending and she walked over with Jude and Luna, the senior beauty editor.

A sign in the hotel lobby indicated that Kost, the rooftop restaurant, was closed that evening for a private event. At a desk off to the side, a girl from the PR company sat with a clipboard and checked their names off the list before they made their way upstairs.

The usual assortment of industry people—influencers, editors, local celebrities, and those in the media—packed the restaurant. Lights were turned down low and a DJ was spinning. Specialty cocktails had been made for the event, which also featured an open bar, and patrons got live demonstrations of all the products.

Familiar faces greeted Chloe, many of whom remarked about how long it had been since they had seen her. She brushed it off by telling them she had taken a step back to deal with some things and, mercifully, no one had asked past that.

She laughed and chatted, posed for photos, took photos, and filmed some of the carryings-on. After two cocktails, she bid adieu to her colleagues, three more of whom had shown up in the time she had been there. A quick thank-you to the PR team and one over-stuffed gift bag later and Chloe was in an Uber on her way home.

Her stomach was full of Asian-fusion canapés, and she felt a warm glow from both the cocktails and the comfort of feeling like she was almost back to normal. After the months she had spent in isolation, it was a surprise to see how easily she was able to slide back into her old life.

Before bed that night she scrolled through her camera roll to see all the videos and pictures she had taken at the event.

Her thumb accidentally hit the scroll bar, which leapt backwards in time, and suddenly she found herself staring at photos of her and Liam.

Chloe's heart started racing and she got a sick feeling in the pit of her stomach.

She stared at the pictures. They had been taken the night they had celebrated their fourth anniversary. They both looked so happy, so carefree, so in love.

She was overcome with a wave of nausea.

She had worked on processing her emotions, she had committed to cleaning up her condo, and she was back in the swing of things at work. But one thing she hadn't been able to bring herself to do during the past six months was to go through her phone and delete the photos of her and Liam.

Part of it was to avoid the pain she knew that pictures of them together would bring. And part of it was because, while she knew in her head that she and Liam were done and dusted, somewhere in her heart she was still holding out hope for a reconciliation.

What a fool she would feel like, she had reasoned with herself, if they got back together and she had deleted five years of their life. It was better, she told herself, to just avoid looking at them altogether.

With a few deep breaths she scrolled back to the top of her camera roll, exited out of the app, and put down her phone.

The lightness she had felt minutes before dissipated and she buried her head in her hands.

One day it wouldn't feel like this, she hoped. And that day couldn't come soon enough.

Past

Chapter 4:
A Sinking Feeling

T here's nothing I'd rather be doing this evening," a playful smile crossed Liam's face. "Except for you." He pushed himself up off the comfy nest they had created on the couch and pinned her wrists to the cushion.

"No!" Chloe giggled and made a futile attempt to wiggle out of his grasp.

Selling Sunset—the only reality show she had managed to rope Liam into watching—blasted in the background.

"Yes!" Liam's grin widened.

Chloe laughed and gave up trying to wriggle free.

"At least push the table out!" she said with a squeak.

He momentarily released one of her wrists and grabbed for the remote, pressing the mute button before dropping it onto the coffee table and pushing it away.

Chloe hadn't tried to move from her position underneath him while she had the chance to. She was enjoying this far too much. Besides—she didn't want to get away from her boyfriend.

"Now," Liam said, turning his attention back to her and putting his hand around her other wrist once again. "Where was I?"

Chloe gasped as he leaned down and planted several kisses along her neckline.

A jolt went through her as she was pulled out of her reverie and found herself alone, on the couch, with takeout for one on a Friday night. It was hard to imagine that things between her and Liam could be so different just a few months later.

Things between them had always been so easy. It had caught even her by surprise with how quickly the two of them had fallen into step together. There were no awkward stages; none of the back-and-forth game-playing or let's-just-casually-date-and-see-where-it-goes type of thing that seemed to be de rigueur these days. Neither of them had been looking for a partner when they met, but they had both also recognized a good thing when they saw it.

Of course, Chloe had had some initial reservations. Bankers weren't typically known for honesty or, for that matter, monogamy. So, while she had gone into the first few months of dating Liam as hopeful, she had also not allowed herself to fall into any fantasies. She had been down that road before and knew that nothing good could come from it. She wasn't pessimistic per se, just cautiously optimistic. Due to her previous forays into dating, she had been entirely prepared for Liam to turn out to be one of those men who came in hot and heavy initially but then turned into a ghost when he finally had her hooked.

It was a happy surprise, therefore, for her to discover that Liam was not of that sort. He was everything she had ever wanted in a man without knowing it. He was supportive, smart, and cared about his family; he helped with the cooking, was generous and thoughtful—often sending her flowers or bringing her a new bauble—and he loved Chloe unconditionally.

Even with all her faults. Of which, she was convinced, there were many.

She could be a bit neurotic, which had caused grief in previous relationships, but Liam didn't seem to mind—and, miraculously, it hadn't become an issue between them after the six-month mark. She supposed that, aside from working on the issue herself, Liam's consistency had helped in spades.

And while Liam wasn't perfect, he was perfect for Chloe. He snored—like a freight train—but it hadn't turned into her wanting to smother him in the middle of the night.

It was funny how things like that happened. In the first six months of dating, your partner's quirks and quarks are endearing. After that, the little things that would previously bring a smile to your face could easily induce rage.

While Liam's snoring, which used to make her smile, still woke her up in the middle of the night, she didn't find it annoying like she knew had happened to some of her friends. They were many, *many* years past the typical honeymoon period at this point, but they still retained some of that initial spark. They hadn't turned into roommates or people who lived together because of financial or familial commitments. They truly loved one another.

She accepted the long hours he spent at the office and had known when they first got together that it was part of the deal. It had never bothered her before because she knew that it was what came with dating Liam. Over the past few months, however, she had noticed that he had been spending less and less time at home. Not only that, but during the time they did spend together, Liam seemed distracted.

Something about it was niggling her.

That had never happened before, and she weighed the pros and cons of saying something before discussing it with her best friends.

All of them agreed that it was something she should talk

to him about, and she did so, cautiously, when he came home late one Tuesday night.

It was just after 10 p.m., and the leftovers from the dinner she had made were sitting stone-cold in the fridge.

Liam had listened and immediately reassured her. He was working on a new project, he said. A deal that they were trying to close. He apologized for the negative impact it was having on their relationship, but he promised that when it was done, they would take a vacation together.

With that, Chloe had been placated.

After all, she knew what Liam did for a living. And he was ambitious—always vying for a promotion and higher pay. There had also been periods in the past where he worked until around 10 p.m. practically *every* night for a month straight. So, she took his reassurance at face value and kept herself from feeling sad by checking out different places they could vacation together when his deal was done.

Which was something that really did keep her occupied. As someone whose job involved staying at some of the top-rated hotels and resorts around the world, she had a lot of options to choose from.

It was November and, if Liam was right and the deal took another couple of months to get done, that would put them right into the middle of winter.

She contemplated going to a place they had previously vacationed at but nixed it in favour of a new adventure. A few evenings of Googling had given her some ideas and she casually mentioned them to him one Saturday morning.

Normally he was an early riser, but that day he had slept in until nearly noon. The late nights at the office, Chloe reflected, were clearly taking their toll.

"How are things going at work?" she inquired when he finally emerged from their bedroom. She hadn't even seen him the previous night, having gone to bed before she heard him crawl into bed around 1 a.m.

He grunted in reply to her question and headed for the kitchen before joining her on the couch with a cup of coffee. Chloe had finished hers four hours ago. Along with breakfast.

"The deal is . . . progressing," he had said vaguely before bringing the mug to his mouth.

Chloe had pursed her lips to one side.

"Progressing," she said flatly.

"Babe," he gave her a look. "You know I can't discuss it with you."

She knew that, but she also knew that compliance and NDAs had never stopped him from telling her about what he was working on before. He changed the names of the people and companies so that Chloe wasn't fully in the know, but she had enjoyed hearing about the inner machinations of the business world. Even after living, sleeping, and dating one of those cogs for several years, she still found the industry very foreign.

She considered calling him on it but held her tongue. The last thing she wanted that morning was for things to turn into a fight.

She changed the subject.

"I've been looking at some options for after your deal gets done."

"Options?" He looked confused.

Chloe furrowed her brow. Now wasn't the time to get upset, but did he really not remember the conversation they had had a few weeks ago?

"Yes," she said, working hard to keep the exasperation she felt out of her voice. "You said when your deal was done that we would go on a vacation."

A flicker that Chloe couldn't quite place went across Liam's face, and he leaned back on the couch.

"Oh, right," he nodded, sounding less than enthused. "What have you found?"

She mentioned three places—one in Europe, one in Asia, and one in South America—and showed him some photos from each of the hotels and cities. He had nodded along, but he didn't look very interested.

"Whatever you want, Chlo," he had said, picking up his phone after she showed him the third option.

She was stung by his apparent lack of interest and was sure that it showed on her face. Not that Liam would notice with his face buried in his phone. She had hoped that a vacation would help them reconnect and was disappointed that she seemed to be the only one excited for it.

Liam's long hours at the office didn't usually bother her, but for the past few months, it had almost felt like she lived alone. Which *was* unusual. On previous projects, he would ask her to grab a quick drink before he went out for business dinners. Or he would ask her to meet him for lunch or pop over to her office for a quick coffee.

During this deal, there hadn't been any invites for a quick lunch, drink, dinner, or coffee. The ones that they did have were all initiated by Chloe. Even on weekends he had seemed reserved and distracted.

It made her uneasy, but she reminded herself it wasn't like she hadn't seen him this way before. It just hadn't been for months-long stretches.

She didn't know what that uncomfortable feeling tugging inside of her was, but she brushed it off determinedly. Once they had their post-deal vacation, she knew that things between them would be back to normal.

Present

Chapter 5:
Without a Stitch

Chloe's off-the-shoulder white-linen dress fluttered around her body in the warm breeze. She pulled her suitcase with one arm and used the other to frantically grab at her dress, trying to hold down the fabric. Outside the airport in Liberia scores of tourists were lined up along the sidewalk, all bustling for a shuttle or a taxi. It was a riot of different colours, different sizes, and different languages.

She pulled her sunglasses onto the top of her head and scanned the crowd for any sign of Lala—she had gone ahead when Chloe had been pulled aside for a random bag check.

She squinted and tried to search through the people. It felt like a real-life version of one of those *Where's Waldo?* books.

"Chloe!"

She jerked her head in the direction of her friend's voice and tried to pinpoint her location. It took a few moments before she spotted Lala—her friend's arms waving wildly in an effort to grab Chloe's attention. She was standing next to a car with her suitcase and motioned Chloe over. Costa

Morpho had sent the transportation for her and Lala, and it looked like Lala had happened to find it first. Resorts often offered buses to shuttle their guests to and from the airport, but when you were writing a story about a property that would be read by millions of people, the companies always wanted to cater to the writer's every need.

The driver was hoisting Lala's oversized suitcase into the back of the trunk as Chloe squeezed her way out of the crowd.

"Gracias!" Chloe smiled as the driver grabbed her bags.

Lala was already seated inside the air-conditioned vehicle, reapplying her lipstick in the mirror.

"Six hours on a plane," Lala moaned, throwing her head back on the seat as the taxi navigated away from the airport. "I can't wait to get to the resort. I need a shower and champagne, stat."

Chloe laughed as palm trees flew by her window.

"Champagne, snacks, massages, entertainment—all taken care of," Chloe said lightly. "I still can't believe Dasha sent me on a week-long assignment in the tropics after the past six months."

Chloe wasn't kidding. She *was* still incredulous.

It was akin to slacking off at school and being crowned class valedictorian. She had half expected to be sent on a fifty-mile sherpa-trekking experience through Siberia.

Latin music blasted throughout the vehicle and sunlight beamed through the window as they sped down the highway. Chloe had kept to her rule of not Googling the resort ahead of time, so where they were staying would be just as much of a surprise to her as it was to Lala. She hadn't told her the name of the resort to keep her from spoiling the surprise; all either of them knew was they were going to Costa Rica for a week.

A warm breeze flowed through the open windows as the car bumped its way along the road. Chloe's blonde hair whipped around her face, obscuring her vision as palm trees, vehicles, and buildings flew by.

The winding, one-hour drive took them on a scenic tour through the hills. Mindful that her trip was technically work, Chloe took out her phone and recorded some of the drive.

Eventually, the vehicle began to slow as the resort came into view. Perched on the edge of the coastline on a peninsula, Costa Morpho promised, from what Chloe could see, incredible views. Towering palm trees and lush greenery surrounded the resort's entrance, which was flanked by two imposing stone structures that stood on either side. They pulled into a large circular courtyard that served as a drop-off area for guests, which was large enough for several buses. In the middle of it was an oversized fountain made up of a kaleidoscope of butterflies that floated above a sign spelling out the resort's name. Palm trees dotted the perimeter of the courtyard above exotic, jewel-toned flowers that sat amidst a sprawl of greenery.

It looked like something out of a magazine and Chloe let out a contented sigh. This was her happy place. She loved her job, and she was so happy to be on an assignment with her best friend.

While their driver took out their luggage, Chloe documented the courtyard, taking close-up pictures of the greenery, fountain, and building. She hit 'record' as a bellboy dressed in black shorts and a white linen button-up bearing the name of the resort came to collect their luggage.

Luis, his nametag indicated, led them into the massive, open-air lobby whereupon Chloe's jaw dropped, and her eyebrows shot up to her hairline.

There, in the middle of the lobby, was a completely naked man.

Shocked, she stopped in her tracks and stared as the sandy-haired man sauntered past her.

"Ooof!" Lala's voice came from behind her as she

smacked into a suddenly static Chloe.

"Why did you stop!" she said, sounding annoyed.

Chloe couldn't speak. She was rooted to the tile floor in shock. Lala poked her head around her friend and slapped a hand to her mouth, muffling a fit of laughter.

The bellboy, Chloe noticed, inexplicably did not seem the least bit perturbed, and was several steps ahead of her and Lala.

"Is security not going to do something?" Chloe's face furrowed as she looked around in search of someone who looked like they had some authority.

Surely a guest walking around in the nude had to be against the rules of the resort?

The more her eyes searched for help, the more confused she became. The nonchalance with which several staff members seemed to be treating the naked patron was puzzling. There had been instances of guests getting seriously hammered at hotels she had stayed at before, but usually staffers were quick to attend to the scene and cart them off. The casualness with which the staff seemed to be treating the man, who was now helping himself to complimentary coffee, was astounding. Their behaviour almost gave Chloe the impression that nudity amongst guests was okay. But that was too bizarre for her to even comprehend.

Lala, too, was watching the scene unfold, and she appeared to be arriving at a conclusion much faster than Chloe.

"Um, Chloe?" she whispered. "Did your boss tell you what exactly your assignment is?"

"No!" Chloe said desperately, averting her eyes from the man's bare backside as he left the lobby with his cup.

Her head snapped to the left as she saw two women, looking to be in their fifties, enter into view. Both were in their birthday suits and carrying towels. They walked past a fully clothed Costa Morpho employee who smiled and greeted them as they placed their towels on two of the plush teal chairs in the lobby and took a seat.

"Well," Lala deadpanned beside her friend. "It looks like Dasha's forgiven you. It also looks like she has one sick sense of humor."

Another naked woman walked into the lobby and shot the two of them a friendly smile. Chloe, still in shock, couldn't muster anything back and she watched the nude woman's bronzed body waltz out of sight. She had a purse slung over her right shoulder, which seemed absurd. Surely a simple pair of shorts or a sundress with pockets would make more sense than lugging around a purse? *Where else would she keep her credit cards?* A voice went through Chloe's head.

She shuddered at the thought and then was hit with another.

Costa Morpho. The name of the resort.

'Costa', she knew, was Spanish for 'coast'. But 'Morpho'? She hadn't the faintest idea. The word had initially given her flashbacks to the time she had ended up in the Emergency Department for a migraine so terrible that only morphine would touch it. She didn't like to read too much into things, but her first thought was that the name was an allusion. As in *our resort is so tranquil, you'll feel like you're on drugs.* Goodness knew she had come across hotels, resorts, restaurants, and experiences more strangely named than that. Now she was wondering if it had something to do with 'metamorphosis'. As in *stay for a week and transform from within in nothing but your skin.*

The busboy was standing expectantly with their luggage next to the check-in counter and Lala urged Chloe forward

"Go on!" She nudged her friend. "Don't be rude!"

Chloe, her video still recording, clicked her phone off, stuffed it in her pocket, and headed to the check-in counter.

"Ola!" a dark-skinned woman with short black hair and a toothy smile greeted her.

"Ola." Chloe gathered her wits and responded with as much enthusiasm as she could muster.

"Welcome to Costa Morpho," the woman continued. "My name is Carmen and I'm here to help you. Checking in?"

"Yes," Chloe nodded.

She gave Carmen her information and received two key cards, a map, an itinerary, and a printout that contained an overview of the resort and FAQs.

"Cocktails are served in the lobby at 6 p.m. every evening, and this outlines all of the activities that are available for your stay." Carmen slid a colourful-looking pamphlet across the desk.

Chloe glanced down and saw that it included a list of rules.

No gawking, she read the first rule on the list. Who knew that nudist resorts—she now had zero doubts as to the type of establishment she and Lala would be staying at for the next week—had specific rules about staring? She supposed it made sense—you wouldn't want other patrons to feel uncomfortable.

But still.

Had she known that this was where Dasha was sending her, she would have spent the last couple of weeks brushing up on her poker face. Or asked Dasha for a referral and gone to her doctor for a full-face application of Botox.

"Gracias and please enjoy your stay!" Carmen beamed as Chloe and Lala turned to follow the bellboy to their rooms.

Outside the lobby, they were led to a golf cart, which their suitcases were loaded onto before she and Lala climbed in.

They zipped past naked bodies as they bumped along the path towards their room, colloquially known as the Reserve Suite, which was more of a cottage than a simple room.

It was stellar—a beach view, two bedrooms—one on each side of the cottage—with outdoor showers, free-standing tubs, a living room, wet bar, and a dining table. Sandy shades and aquamarine accents, which seemed to be the resort's signature colours, lent the space a beachy feel. A large plush sectional faced a television, and a breeze ruffled the white cotton curtains through the sliding patio doors.

"Wow," Lala said from behind her. "This is gorgeous."

Chloe wheeled her suitcase into the master bedroom on the right side of the room and collapsed happily on the pillowy bed.

"I'm going to put my clothes away," Lala said from her bedroom on the other side of the cottage.

"I'm going to take a quick shower," Chloe called back.

Ten minutes later she was lying on top of her duvet, wrapped up in a fluffy housecoat. She picked up the Costa Morpho printout Carmen had given her and started to read. 'Awe-inspiring views', the first sentence promised as the myriad of nude guests she'd been subjected to in the last hour flitted through her head. *Awe-inspiring indeed*, she thought. Maybe not exactly how she would describe it. Ugh-inspiring would maybe more accurate.

Not that she had a problem with nudists. She supported people's choice to live their life clothing-free. She just didn't want to see it. She wasn't a prude or a 'keep your clothes on at all times' type of gal, but she thought the whole notion of a clothing-free resort was rather odd.

Further reading informed her that, contrary to her initial thought, 'morpho' didn't refer to morphine—something she wished she had a week-long supply of right now. Nor did it refer, directly at least, to 'metamorphosis'. It was actually a type of butterfly that was native to Costa Rica.

Fitting, she mused, because she sort of felt, with this trip, like she was finally stepping out of a cocoon.

Which didn't mean she would be joining in with the nudists.

No, no. The cocoon she was thinking of wasn't made of fabric, it was more figurative. It was the one she had wrapped herself up in from the minute Liam had broken her heart.

The last few months she had been doing a hell of a lot better, and she was doing a hell of a lot better at managing her emotions. But the sadness was still there, lingering in the back of her head.

She was hoping that this assignment, her first trip since the breakup, would prove to be the final piece of the 'getting over Liam' puzzle. That week, her aim was to transform from a mushy pile of sadness into Chloe 2.0—fierce and fabulous and void of sadness with her wings fluffed for takeoff.

There was a knock at her door and Lala poked her head in. Chloe patted the space beside her on the bed and her friend climbed over her and took a seat.

"So," Lala said, "a nudist resort." She paused. "We're really spending a week at a nudist resort?" She chuckled.

"I didn't know!" Chloe exclaimed with a giggle. "And besides," she said with an air of superiority, "according to this printout, it's a naturist resort. Very upscale. Much classier than a nudist resort."

"Po-tay-toe, po-tah-toe," Lala said wryly.

"I still can't believe this is where Dasha sent me," Chloe said in disbelief. She wasn't kidding. She was still feeling floored.

"Ah, it will be fine." Lala shrugged. "Live a little!"

"Four drinks and staying out past midnight is my version of 'live a little'," Chloe mused before cringing. "Boobs, butts, and nuts is not my idea of a good time."

"Don't knock it 'til you've tried it!" Lala smirked. "Besides—with what passes for a bikini nowadays, it shouldn't be that far off of being at a regular beach."

Chloe sank back onto the feather pillows and pondered that for a second.

Lala had a point.

"And at least you'll have an interesting article to write," Lala said pointedly. "And something to talk to a therapist about in the future."

Chloe laughed while Lala climbed off the bed.

"Let's get organized and head to the pool. I need a tan and a margarita," Lala declared. "Not necessarily in that order."

Chloe busied herself putting away her suitcase and half an hour later there was a knock on her bedroom door.

"Are you ready?" her friend's voice came through the light-coloured wood. "The pina coladas are calling my name!"

"I thought you needed margaritas?" Chloe questioned.

There was a momentary pause.

"Margaritas too!" Lala exclaimed. "I don't discriminate when it comes to vacation drinks."

Chloe laughed.

"Okay, just let me get dressed." She opened one of the dresser drawers and grabbed a tropical-patterned swimsuit.

"We are at a nudist resort, Chlo!" Lala said in mock exasperation. "Clothing is not only optional, it's discouraged."

Lala had her there. But just because she was at a naturist resort didn't mean she was going to participate. Besides, her tropical bikini was one of those itsy-bitsy teeny-weeny suits that qualified as more of a suggestion than actual swimwear. Surely that had to count for something? Swimsuits really were little more than scrap-cloth coverings. In fact, she had seen some bikinis in her time that seemed more overtly sexual than a nude body. Everyone was completely naked underneath their swimsuits but there was something off-putting to her about bare-naked bodies in the pool. There was something about a bit of fabric that provided a flimsy but firm barrier. A no-go red light.

Not that she thought there would be any untoward behaviour at Costa Morpho. One had to only look at the luxury of their surroundings and refer to the resort's list of rules. The most important of which was numero uno: no gawking.

"Give me two minutes!" Chloe called to her friend as she pulled on her triangle bikini, and threw her phone, sunscreen, and purse into her beach bag. She pulled on a white linen cover-up that just brushed the tops of her thighs, slid into white foam flip-flops, and stepped into their living room.

"About time!" her friend ribbed her.

Chapter 6:
Sad Girl, Happy Hour

"Oh, holy Jesus."

Chloe was lying on the sun lounger and, turning to grab her phone from her bag, found herself face-to-crotch with the heavy-set man to her right. Her eyes bugged out of her head, and she quickly turned away, trying to erase the image from her mind.

"Take this!" Lala's voice came from beside her and she felt a shot glass being pushed into her hand.

"What is this?" she looked at her friend.

"Shhh," Lala shushed her. "Don't ask, just drink."

She took the proffered shot and threw it back, feeling a warmth grow in the pit of her stomach. Her phone forgotten in the shock of the assault on her eyes, she lay back down on the sun lounger and closed her eyes.

It was better that way.

Without the benefit of sight, she didn't have to worry about any unsolicited full frontals. It had brought up the memory of one of her first experiences on Tinder, which had involved a seemingly normal-looking man who had proceeded to send her an unwelcome dick pic mere moments after they had matched.

The heat made her limbs heavy as her mind wandered and daydreams crept in.

*

"Phwa!!!"

A spray of cold water shocked her out of a deep slumber. It was a sleep that she hadn't consciously fallen into, and when she came to, she wasn't quite sure where she was. It took a second for her to orient herself and, as her eyes came into focus, she realized that she was not in Toronto.

A warm breeze sealed it.

Ah, yes. Now she remembered. She was on a work assignment. At a nudist resort. *Naturist resort*, she corrected herself as she sat up and half-heartedly stifled a yawn.

A glance at the empty lounger next to her indicated that Lala was missing. She wasn't sure how long she had been asleep for, but the sun appeared to have moved quite a distance across the sky. Salsa music pumped through the air and Chloe wondered how exactly she had managed to sleep through all the noise.

The pool, which had been almost empty when she and Lala first arrived, now resembled a red-light district due to the number of naked patrons occupying it. That, Chloe surmised, was the obvious source of the sleep-ruining splash. Two very busty women were presently engaged in a mostly male game of pool volleyball—their breasts flapped like rocks in a sock every time they jumped to hit the ball.

That can't *be comfortable*, Chloe winced before her mind went back to rule number one at Costa Morpho—*no gawking*.

She tore her eyes away from the scene and leaned back on the lounger. With naked people everywhere, it was odd to be the odd one out. Sort of like how one would feel if they were the only naked person surrounded by a resort full of people who were fully clothed. Chloe was doing something perfectly normal—she was wearing a bathing suit and lounging by a pool while on vacation at a luxury resort. But in this particular environment, wearing clothes meant that she was the weird one. Status quo, she reflected, is a funny thing.

So was what was considered 'normal'. It really did depend upon a person's frame of reference. And really, she thought, it was no different than traveling to another country and being unfamiliar with their customs.

The staff, Chloe had noticed, were nonplussed. She assumed they probably just got used to the nudity over time. The resort had only been open for a few months, but maybe that was all the time they needed to grow accustomed to it.

Did they talk about the guests, she wondered?

Likely.

She didn't see how it would be different from other resorts or customer-service jobs. Several years ago, when she had a part-time waitressing job while interning at *Strut*, the staff often talked about the customers. If someone was particularly rude or, in contrast, incredibly pleasant; if a customer was difficult or strange. Sometimes the men were lecherous, and she had to let the manager know so other servers were on the alert if that customer came in again. They also had customers who placed weird orders, people on awkward dates, and people who thought the restaurant was a good place to tell their partner they no longer wanted to be together. That was always the worst. Trying to be a good server while one half of the table was in distress was the definition of awkward. Doing your best not to interrupt while staying attentive and personable in that sort of atmosphere was harder to balance than two trays of drinks.

She wondered what the staff at Costa Morpho were saying about her and Lala. After all—what kind of people signed up to go to a naturist resort only to stay covered up the entire time?

It was nonsensical. Like going on a booze cruise when you're sober.

There had been a second, maybe even less than a second, when Chloe had considered stripping down. 'When in Rome', after all. But she reasoned, they weren't in Rome, and really she just wasn't personally comfortable with the concept.

The wind picked up and a warm breeze ruffled her hair when a sudden thought went through her head.

A heaviness descended on her.

She was supposed to be on vacation with her long-term boyfriend right now. With Liam.

It had come seemingly out of nowhere and was quickly followed by an overwhelming feeling of despair. It wasn't that she was unhappy to be spending a week in the tropics with her bestie, she reflected. But there was something about it that was bittersweet.

Six months ago, she had certainty. Certainty of a husband, certainty of a family, certainty—as juvenile as it might sound—of a happily ever after. That certainty had been brusquely torn away, and a hollowness had settled in instead. Which was an apt description of how she was feeling in that moment—hollow.

She took a deep breath in and tried to reframe her thoughts. The breakup was bad, yes. But, she thought, it could have been worse. If Liam had cheated on her and ended up with a baby, that *definitely* would have been worse.

A wave of nausea swept over her as it suddenly hit her that, not today, maybe not tomorrow, but someday, he would end up with a baby and a partner. She had known with every fiber of her being that the two of them were going to get married, have a family, and grow old together. It was a fact. Something she had known just as she had known that the sun would rise in the East every morning and set every evening in the West.

Being hit with that realization while on a vacation she was supposed to be taking with her ex was shattering.

Chloe's stomach suddenly turned and she thought she was going to vomit.

"You're awake!" Lala's jubilant-sounding voice cut through her thoughts and Chloe looked over to see her friend.

Alarm crossed Lala's face as she took in Chloe's expression.

"Hey." Lala's voice took on a more serious tone. "What's going on?"

Chloe grimaced.

"Liam," she said with misery. "It just hit me. At some point he's going to have a family with someone else."

"Whoa," Lala said emphatically. "That's a lot." She paused. "Listen—I don't know how to help you out with that one right now, but let's get you some tequila," she turned to a passing waitress in a black skirt. "Two margaritas, por favor." She glanced again at Chloe and then turned back to the waitress. "Better make them doubles."

The sun lounge next to Chloe creaked as Lala flopped down onto it.

"I'm sorry." Chloe was apologetic. "I'm not trying to be a downer. My mind just started to wander. I think keeping myself so busy the past few months has kept me from thinking about it. But being here . . .," she trailed off.

Lala nodded.

"I get it. Don't beat yourself up over it. We're here to relax, rewind, and refresh. And," she added as an afterthought, "for you to write. On that note, we're going to start off with some relaxation."

Chloe spied the waitress on her way back with a tray that held two margaritas.

"Margarita relaxation?" Chloe inquired.

"Something something—'tequila makes her clothes fall off.'" Her friend quoted a popular country song about the harsh-tasting liquor. "If your clothes are falling off you, I don't know how you can get much more relaxed than that."

Chloe pondered then conceded.

"You do have a point."

The waitress set the margaritas on the table between their loungers while Lala rummaged around in her purse for a tip.

"Gracias," the woman smiled as she took the American money and the two of them thanked her back.

"Cheers!" Lala lifted up her glass and clinked it against Chloe's.

She picked up her own glass and was just about to take a sip when Lala put her hand on Chloe's arm to stop her.

"Wait!" Lala said dramatically.

Chloe was confused.

"What—?" Chloe started but Lala cut her off.

"First off," her friend said fiercely, shooting her a fiery-eyed stare. "Fuck Liam."

Chloe's eyes widened as Lala continued.

"This trip is to get away from him, forget the shit he's put you through, and celebrate the radiant, kind, caring, smart, sassy, and all-around fabulous person you are." She raised her margarita again and tapped it against Chloe's glass.

"Cheers to you!" she clinked her glass against her friend's again. "Here's to you, to vitamin sea," she gestured towards the ocean, "and, if you're lucky—some vitamin D."

A smile spread across Chloe's face, and she took a big drink of the margarita. Which immediately caused her to sputter.

"Christ!" she coughed hoarsely as the liquor burned her throat. "This is a *double*?"

"That," her friend said pointedly, "is the magic of the all-inclusive free pour," Lala deadpanned before taking a big drink of her own.

"I took a walk around the resort while you were sleeping." Lala put down her glass. "It's so beautiful here. They've done a great job on the landscaping. Thanks again for taking me."

"Of course. I'm so happy you could come," Chloe said sincerely. "Without you I'd probably still be knee-deep in squalor and despair."

Her best friend laughed.

The margarita and Lala's presence served as a good distraction and completely took Chloe's mind off the dark path that it had wandered down. They spent the rest of the afternoon by the pool before heading back to their cottage to get ready for dinner. The itinerary that Carmen, the front-desk clerk, had provided Chloe had tentative reservations scheduled at Costa Morpho's Italian restaurant that evening. Lala, it turned out, had come across it, as well as two other restaurants and the buffet, while she had been out exploring.

Italian was a curious choice to Chloe. It seemed like an odd type of cuisine for a Latin country to be showcasing for a travel editor's first night's stay, but she supposed the resort catered to guests who didn't want to venture too far outside their culinary comfort zone. Which wasn't necessarily true for all of *Strut*'s readership. Some subscribers craved adventure and unique experiences; others were happy to travel to exotic locations but only to high-end hotels with familiar amenities and food.

Despite finding the first night's choice of restaurant a bit strange, she was looking forward to seeing the décor and what the chefs had to offer. Aside from getting to stay in places most people only dream of and experiencing different countries and culture, Chloe's second favourite thing about her job was the food. Some high-end hotels had Michelin-starred or destination restaurants known throughout the world for their fare. As someone who considered herself to be a bit of a foodie, she loved being able to explore new restaurants. It was an experience that was only improved upon by being able to share it with someone she loved. Which she was fortunate to be doing on this trip.

Cucina Cibo, the Italian restaurant, was a pleasant surprise. It was done up in dark tones with warm lighting, and soft jazz music provided a soundtrack to their dinner which was punctuated by the bustling sounds of a busy restaurant. To Chloe's amazement and horror, they discovered that patrons actually ate at the restaurant in the altogether. Which was in stark contrast to the dressy outfits Chloe and Lala were wearing. Funnily enough, while their fellow guests were clothing-free, most of the women were wearing makeup and some of them had accessorized their skin. Chloe had barely stifled a laugh when she saw a curly-haired redhead wearing nothing but a necklace with a large blue gemstone and a smile— shades of Rose DeWitt Bukater in *Titanic*.

Each guest, as the resort's rules stipulated, brought a towel, which they draped over their seat and sat on. Napkins, mercifully, covered diners' nether regions although Chloe wasn't sure if that was for reasons of modesty or just to prevent crumbs and accidental burns in sensitive places. Still, it was weird and almost felt like she was eating dinner at an all-sexes topless bar. Even if it felt like a very upscale one sans flashing lights and pervy patrons.

Seating was available for around fifty people and a five-foot-long charcuterie buffet served as an appetizer or full-meal platter for the snacking-inclined. Fine cheeses, meats, breads, and spreads were laid out as nicely as any fine-dining establishment Chloe had encountered. She and Lala had grabbed a couple of items from the charcuterie spread and then ordered mains. Branzino for Lala and a mushroom tagliatelle for Chloe, which they had with a glass of Super Tuscan wine. For dessert, the chefs, aware that they had a travel editor in their midst, put together a delectable and delicate tiramisu with a Latin twist.

Overall, it was a great meal and, with the exception of being a little put off by the naked people serving themselves up from the charcuterie buffet, it was a pleasant experience.

They left after giving their regards to the chef and headed towards the resort's lobby. Just outside of it, in the back, was a tiki bar strung with lights and comfy padded furniture. Salsa music played softly in the background—the volume not loud enough to drown out the sound of the ocean waves—and brilliant pinks and oranges streaked across the darkened sky as the sun began to set.

Chloe leaned back into the squishy patterned chair and breathed in—the salty scent of the ocean enveloped her and the humid air lay sticky on her skin. This was relaxing. This was what she had been looking forward to. Her minor blip earlier about Liam had been a one-off. She figured it was all a part of the grieving process and instances like that would taper off with time.

In an identical chair across from her, Lala looked equally at peace—a happy expression on her face as she observed her surroundings. It was quiet—most of the resort's patrons appeared to be having dinner—although they had passed a number of people sitting in the lobby.

Lala stifled a yawn. It had been an early morning for the pair, and Toronto was two hours ahead of Costa Rica.

"It's not even six and I'm wiped," Lala said sleepily.

"Technically it's almost eight our time and we've been up since two a.m.," Chloe reasoned.

"You're just feeling refreshed because of your two-hour nap," Lala teased back.

Despite the validity of Lala's statement, Chloe found herself feeling rather sleepy.

They were both a bit toasty from the wine they had at dinner and decided to head back to their cottage and call it an early night.

Luxuriating in the perfectly made-up bed, which had been

fluffed and fixed during turndown service, Chloe was fast asleep the moment her head hit the pillow.

Past

Chapter 7:
How Do You Solve a Problem Like Sophia?

Small beads of wax dripped down the side of a white pillar candle; its flame flickered intermittently. Tea lights dotted various surfaces in the condo—the kitchen counter, the media stand, the coffee table, but they had burned out long ago. The pillar candle perched on the dining room table was the only thing still burning—a bright flame flickering in the dim light. The remainder of the room was lit ever so slightly by the living room light's dimmer switch.

On the dining room table there were also two wine glasses, a decanter, two dinner plates, two cloth napkins, two forks, and two knives. In front of one place setting, Chloe sat slumped at the table. The chair in front of the other setting sat empty. An expensive bottle of wine was down to its last five ounces and the crystal decanter sat there, untouched. *Soft Jazz*, Chloe's carefully curated playlist for relaxing evenings that involved charcuterie and wine, contradicted the slow rage that was burning inside her.

Soft Jazz had just started its second run-through. She knew this because Louis Armstrong and Ella Fitzgerald's *Stars Fell on Alabama* was on its second play. She had a feeling that her favourite playlist for relaxation was soon going to turn into her most hated one. Unless, of course, Liam had some damn good reason for being two-and-a-half hours late for dinner.

So far at least.

The way her evening was going it might turn out to be a much longer wait. She knew he was working hard on his latest deal, which he hoped would clinch him a big promotion. But he also knew how important dinner this evening was.

At least she thought he did.

Today was their five-year anniversary and Chloe had pulled out all the stops. She had never been a Barefoot Contessa in the kitchen, but she had secretly been taking cooking lessons at St. Lawrence Market for the past few weeks. It was all in an effort to perfect the meal she had wanted to make this evening. Steak au poivre, fingerling potatoes with rosemary and thyme, vegetables just the way Liam liked, and for dessert a special kind of French cheesecake called 'basque'.

Last week she had mentioned to him that she was looking forward to their anniversary this evening and hinted she had something special planned. He had been up and out the door this morning before she had woken up, like most mornings. And while she hadn't expected him to do anything elaborate, especially with his workload lately, his lack of acknowledgement of the special date had stung. Forget flowers—which had been an annual staple—today there hadn't been a card, a call, or even a text.

Their anniversaries weren't typically cause for over-the-top celebrations and were usually marked by a bouquet, cards, and going out for dinner. This year, however, for many reasons, Chloe had been fixated on their anniversary date. One, it was a milestone—five years together was nothing to sneeze at. And two, she was hoping they could spend the evening celebrating and, if things went well, sparking some romance back into their relationship. Hell—at this point she would even settle for a kiss.

Liam's physical and emotional absence over the past several months had been eating at her. He was rarely home, spending evenings and weekends at work, and when he was, he seemed distant and distracted. Even more worrying was that they hadn't been intimate in several months. Liam kept brushing it off as stress-related disinterest. She wanted to take him at his word, but there were lingering doubts. Albeit ones she tried very hard to push to the back of her mind.

He had worked on big deals before, she reasoned. And stress seemed to be a built-in part of his job. But in the entirety of their relationship, they had never had a dry spell that had lasted more than a month.

The unease gnawed at her and was made worse because she kept the state of their relationship to herself. Where her friends and family were concerned, Chloe and Liam's relationship was great. Status quo. And any thoughts that popped into her head of what might actually be going on with Liam were pushed to the deep recesses of her brain. Which wasn't doing her any favours—her mounting concerns and inability to voice them had sent her stress level skyrocketing. She did her best not to dwell on any thoughts that crept into her head, but there was something lurking in the back of her mind that was setting off alarm bells.

Still, she chose to ignore it. If nothing was going on and Liam really was just working hard to secure a promotion, she would feel terrible if she voiced her feelings to her friends and family. If word somehow got back to him, it would put a nasty wrench in any celebrations. She would look like an ungrateful and gossipy spouse—unable to just be supportive of her partner when he was working so hard to secure their future. That wouldn't be a good way to start off their sixth year together. And so, she kept her feelings and her doubts to herself.

With one curious exception. Her boss—Dasha.

While the stoic blonde rarely revealed any hint of emotion, she had an uncanny ability to detect bullshit. She was like the human equivalent of a lie detector test, at least when it came to her employees; Chloe couldn't speak to her abilities outside of *Strut*'s staff. Although given Dasha's quick climb to the top of the magazine's ladder and her success at expanding its readership in an era where print magazines were in steep decline, it stood to reason that her abilities likely extended to business dealings as well.

She had called Chloe into her office—literally called her on her cell despite being no more than twelve steps away from Chloe's office—one Thursday morning. Liam had been pulling away for three months at that point and Chloe's stress level was at an all-time high. She did her best to keep it under wraps, but cracks were beginning to show in her facade.

During their Tuesday-morning staff meeting, Chloe had snapped at her coworker Merrill. She had also stumbled over her travel pitches. After the meeting, she had taken Merrill aside and apologized. She blamed her lapse in manners on a lack of sleep and work-related stress. As for the travel pitch fiasco, she had returned to her desk and hoped that Dasha would write it off as a non-event. By the end of the day, she thought she was out of the woods, but the second Dasha's name popped up on her phone the next morning, Chloe knew what was coming.

Or so she thought.

One of the many things she appreciated about her boss was her ability to surprise. Chloe thought it was actually one of Dasha's business tactics. In sports and business, the element of surprise is an advantage. If an opponent isn't sure of their adversary's next move, it leaves the adversary with the opportunity to gain the upper hand.

Chloe had taken a deep breath, clicked out of Outlook, and headed to Dasha's office. She gave a hesitant knock when she reached the door and a muffled "come in" came through the frosted glass.

Steeling herself for what she thought was coming and mentally preparing an apology, Chloe pushed open the heavy glass and walked inside. Her heels clicked against the wooden floor of Dasha's sparsely decorated office. Like its nine-to-five inhabitant, it was all business. Several *Strut* cover photos dotted her walls, and a shelf held various awards the magazine had won: Best Cover, Best Fashion Feature—accolades doled out by the fashion and beauty industry every year and typically voted on by industry insiders. Chloe had some similar-looking trophies in her office, too, having been the recipient of some awards for her travel features.

Aside from that, there weren't any personalized items that would identify the occupant of the office. No family photos, no fancy degrees. A robot could have been helming their publication for all the lack of personality the room displayed. Which was pure Dasha. No personals, no knick-knacks, and nothing unnecessary.

Dasha had given Chloe a slight smile and indicated, with a single nod of her head, for Chloe to take a seat in one of the chairs across from her. Which she did. They were simple, stylish, and pricey leather chairs from a well-known designer.

Over the top of her laptop, Dasha fixed Chloe with her ice-blue stare.

Unnerved, she squirmed a bit in her seat.

"Er, you wanted to see me?"

Dasha stared at Chloe for a few seconds before she closed her laptop and sat back in her chair.

"You've been snappy in meetings, unfocused when

pitching your features, you've lost weight, and you have dark circles under your eyes that even Dior concealer can't hide."

Chloe was silent. She had no idea what was coming. She knew that Dasha was observant, but holy shit. Or, a thought went through her head, it was also possible that she, Chloe, wasn't as good at masking her inner turmoil as she thought.

"You're still doing a good job in terms of what you're producing but I can tell you're distracted." Dasha kept her eyes trained on Chloe. "Stressed."

Chloe winced.

"You haven't mentioned Liam in a couple of months, and you haven't pitched an international feature in that same amount of time," she continued.

Chloe's eyes widened at her boss's keen sense of observation. And by "keen sense" she meant FBI-profiler level of perceptiveness.

"What's going on, Chloe?" Dasha fixed her with a hard stare.

Chloe took a deep breath, not knowing how to begin, when suddenly she blurted it out.

"It's Liam," she said, sounding distressed.

After that, the floodgates had opened, and all her words came quickly. Before Chloe knew it, she unleashed a torrent of thoughts onto her unblinking boss. The state of her relationship, her fears, Liam's excuses, her suspicions, and her work to keep everything looking picture-perfect to everyone on the outside.

Chloe didn't cry, although she had teared up. Finally, unburdened by the jumble of thoughts, she realized that by voicing them, she had been fooling herself the last several months. The expression on Dasha's face didn't change as Chloe kept spewing—she took it in like a Stanford-trained psychologist and let Chloe get it all out without any outward signs of judgement.

At one point, Chloe realized she wasn't even sure what

she was saying anymore and the stream of words became less of a torrent and more of a trickle. Finally, a few minutes later, she found she had nothing left to say. A quick glance at her watch revealed that she had been in Dasha's office for twenty minutes.

Cripes. Twenty minutes and only a vague notion of what she had said in her emotional blackout.

Across from her, Dasha's poker face gave no indication as to just how graphic or unhinged Chloe had gotten. Dasha continued to stare at her and then finally spoke.

"Well," she raised, just barely raised, one eyebrow, "it sounds like you are under a lot of stress. Relationship issues can wreak havoc on a person's self-esteem."

Chloe nodded as Dasha's last line hit her. It was very insightful and for the first time she realized that her relationship wasn't the only thing that had taken a nosedive. So had her confidence. It wasn't something she had noticed about herself, but now that someone had voiced it, she thought back to some of her recent behaviour. Instead of meeting the world wide-eyed and smiling, she now avoided eye contact and wore an expression that could best be described as dour. The helplessness she felt on the inside with regards to her relationship was shining through to the outside.

"From someone who has gone through something similar, I'm not going to tell you what to do," Dasha said evenly, "but I will tell you that a woman's intuition is rarely incorrect."

Chloe sat there and pondered what her boss was saying.

"I'm not saying Liam is doing anything," Dasha continued. "But it sounds like you have suspicions. Well-warranted ones," she continued in a measured tone, "that you're keeping bottled up. Keeping it bottled up won't help your relationship with Liam, or your relationship with your friends and family, or your work."

Dasha sat back in her chair and rested her arms on the armrests.

Chloe didn't know quite what to say, but she was grateful for the advice and to have been given the space to vent.

Which she had done. Like a volcano. She knew it was probably inappropriate for her to bring her personal life to work, but damn if it hadn't felt good. But after, oddly, she had felt a bit deflated.

Chloe shook herself out of her reverie and looked at the candle, which had melted down another few centimeters. The wine in her glass was down to the last dregs and she placed the pricey and now empty bottle on the kitchen counter.

Tears sprung to the corner of her eyes and she blinked several times to hold them back. She wasn't sure if it was the wine that was making her weepy, but she knew it hadn't helped. It was now nearly 9 p.m. and there was no sign of Liam. She turned off the *Soft Jazz* playlist, blew out the pillar candle and, as ill-advised as she knew it was, grabbed another bottle of wine. A loud 'glug' punctured the air as she poured out a mega pint before grabbing a glass of water and heading for the couch.

So much for a romantic anniversary dinner.

Clicking the T.V. onto Netflix she clutched her wine as she scrolled through her watchlist until she hit on *Bridget Jones*—one of her favourite comfort classics. She didn't identify with the thirty-something British singleton looking for love, but there was something very feel-good about the film.

She draped a fuzzy black blanket over herself as she curled up on the couch. In the hopes of injecting a bit of romance into her and Liam's celebration dinner that evening, she had put on a short, sexy dress. The bouncy blowout she had had done at the salon was meant to give her a bombshell look. Now, as she lay on the couch defeated, she felt annoyed by her bouncy hair. The come-hither makeup she had practically troweled onto her face was slick from the wine, which had made her feel hot and flushed.

Which was just wonderful.

It was in the spirit of hope that she had made dinner, set the scene, and dolled herself up. She imagined that by the time Liam got home, she would look a lot more like 'nope'.

Bridget Jones began speculating about her future as a single woman, ending in being eaten by wild dogs, at which point Chloe checked her phone for any missed messages from Liam.

She knew he hadn't texted, but a small part of her hoped she had somehow missed the sound of his custom notification. Notwithstanding the fact that two hours ago she had turned her notifications on to the loudest volume possible.

Her black phone screen came to life, and she was hit with disappointment that her boyfriend had not sent her a message.

With a sigh she set her phone on the couch and took a big drink of wine. The glass clinked as she set it on the table and snuggled herself under the fuzzy blanket.

*

The sound of the lock turning in the front door jolted her awake.

Chloe's eyes flew open and she lay there, mentally trying to gather her bearings. It took her a second. Her head was hazy.

A glance at the television showed rolling credits for *Bridget Jones*. There was a wet feeling on the side of her mouth, which, she surmised, meant that she had been drooling.

Fantastic.

The romantic evening she had planned and prepped for had turned into a total disaster.

As Liam ambled through the door, Chloe wiped the side of her mouth and blinked a few times before letting out a sigh. Liam didn't say anything as he busied himself with his shoes and briefcase.

She did a quick calculation—*Bridget Jones* was finished, which meant she had slept for almost an hour and a half. That meant Liam was just walking in the door around 11:30 p.m.

"Hey." Liam sounded surprised to see her lying on the couch.

"Hey," she replied back, trying to keep the emotion out of her voice. She was thoroughly sloshed by this point, but she didn't think that letting her emotions get the better of her would help the situation.

"Why are you all dressed up?" Liam sounded genuinely perplexed. He walked over with his briefcase before glancing at the table and seeing the special settings she had done.

"Did I miss something?" He sounded just as confused as he looked.

Chloe stayed silent and pulled the blanket tighter. She didn't trust herself to talk.

Liam dropped his briefcase on the kitchen counter and came over to sit on the couch next to Chloe.

"Chlo?" he said.

She sat up and the blanket fell off her shoulders. Her glass of wine somehow found its way back into her hands and she took a sip.

Nice, Chloe, she thought. The last thing she needed was more wine.

Liam looked at her expectantly. She knew what a mess she must look like—smudged makeup, drool stain on the side of her mouth, blowout smooshed on one side, and red-wine-stained lips.

"You forgot our anniversary," Chloe said, her voice wobbling. She didn't want to cry, but her feelings seemed to be a lot stronger than her resolve.

"Our what?" Liam said.

"Our five-year anniversary," she said, sounding a little stronger.

"Oh, fuck." He closed his eyes. "I completely forgot."

"I learned how to cook steak au poivre and bought a bottle of Tignanello." Her voice was a little stronger. "I thought I would surprise you. I thought you would remember. I reminded you last week." Her voice started to wobble again.

Liam pursed his lips together.

"I'm really sorry, Chlo." He looked at her glass of wine and then stood up to get himself one. "I'll make it up to you this weekend. I was stuck at the office."

Insecurity washed over her and she waited until he had made his way back from the kitchen before she blurted out: "Was Sophia there?"

There was a pause in which Liam's body tensed and he answered back angrily.

"Jesus Christ. Yes. Sophia was there. She's my coworker. We're working on the deal together. *Obviously* she was there."

Chloe said nothing. The revelation that Sophia had been working late with him, even though she knew she would be— she *was* Liam's coworker for goodness sake—stung. Like a taser to the face. Or, in this case, like a taser to the heart.

Liam sat back on the couch with his wine; his attitude was markedly changed from just one minute ago. Through her wine haze, Chloe wondered how it had all gone so wrong. She had spent time learning how to make this dinner, had cooked it, set up their condo with candlelight and music, dolled herself up, and had waited patiently for her boyfriend of five years to show up and be surprised.

Instead, her boyfriend had spent the evening at work in the company of a tall, blonde coworker named Sophia, and Chloe was now the subject of his annoyance. Even with a blood alcohol content of 'toasty' she knew that this wasn't the way it was supposed to be.

Present

Chapter 8:
A Soggy Situation

"Oh, this is too much," Lala moaned.

They watched as a naked guest strolled up to the sausage station at the breakfast buffet and Chloe giggled.

"Weren't you the one telling me not to knock it until I've tried it?" she said in a low voice to her friend. "Do you want to modify that statement?"

"I've tried it and I'm knocking it," Lala declared, giving the sausage man a serious side-eye while a topless woman carrying a plate of fruit walked by. "At least when it comes to the buffet."

They quickly grabbed an assortment of pastries, sausage, eggs, and toast and headed for the outdoor sitting area. Lala, still feeling a bit affronted by the full frontals, ditched her coffee and went straight for a mimosa.

"And keep them coming!" she exclaimed as the waitress walked away. "The sights in there," she lowered her voice and gestured towards the buffet with her chin, "are more of a kick in the face than a triple-shot espresso."

Chloe nearly choked on a piece of cantaloupe.

She had slathered on sunscreen before heading for breakfast, and a good thing too. She would look like a tomato without it. The sun was shining and, despite it being an early hour, it was already sweltering. Lala, on the other hand, was sunblock-free and somehow managed to always maintain a beautiful golden tan—a veritable miracle for a natural redhead.

The itinerary the resort had provided hadn't booked them in for anything that day. It was typical of longer assignments and was meant to give her some time to relax and see the resort or hotel sights for herself. As a VIP guest—a luxury she was afforded through her job title and not something Chloe considered herself to be—the resort wanted to ensure that she had adequate time to relax before they hit her with a whirlwind schedule.

And whirlwind schedule it was.

Costa Morpho had booked her and Lala in for spa services, breakfasts, lunches, and dinners, an ocean excursion, an aerobics session, a tour of a nearby beach town, a talent competition, and a beer-and-rum experience, just to name a few.

So, for the two of them, today it was all about relaxing. The calm before the proverbial storm.

They finished up breakfast and found themselves seated in the same bar just outside the lobby that they had ended their night with the previous evening. It was equally as picturesque during the day as it had been last night, but in an entirely different way. Instead of the pitch dark being punctuated by soft light, stars, and low-volume salsa, the raffia of the tiki bar sat in front of a bright blue, cloudless sky with Latin music loudly pumping from the sound system. Abrasive buzzing sounds broke through the music as the landscapers mowed the grass and trimmed the trees.

During the day, the foliage could be fully appreciated. It was like walking into a garden paradise and rivaled some of the top hotels Chloe had stayed at during her travels.

She hadn't known what to expect with Costa Morpho, aside from the obvious fact of knowing which country it was in. After the shock of finding out it was a naturist resort, it had come as another surprise to see just how luxurious and detail-oriented Costa Morpho was. She had thought, rather judgmentally, that a nudist resort probably wouldn't be very high end—catering to the granola-crunching crowd who cared less about five-star luxury than they did saving the Earth.

It just went to show the unconscious bias she had when it came to that kind of vacationing. She had never given nudist resorts a second thought before. Mostly because never in her wildest dreams did she think it would be something she would end up covering. Which were all beliefs that she was quickly being disabused of. And while she was starting to get used to it all, it was still strange to feel like the odd ones out. She and Lala stuck out like sore thumbs in their clothes, but it hadn't stopped staff and other guests from being friendly. Discomfort with the sausage man at the buffet aside, they had chatted with two of the tables next to them during breakfast.

One table was occupied by a married couple in their mid-fifties who were visiting from North Carolina. The other table was occupied by two friends—women in their late sixties—who told them all about the best naturist resorts they'd been to.

At the tiki bar there were three other patrons aside from her and Lala. Two were sitting beside them on towel-covered chairs at the bar, and one was sitting on the same couch they had sat on the night before.

Lala, having drank two mimosas with breakfast, ordered herself up a Bahama Mama before eyeing up the laminated cocktail menu with interest.

"Oh, this one sounds fun!" She pointed at a drink ominously named Shark Bite.

Chloe looked apprehensively at the ingredients—it had four different types of liquor.

"That one looks like it should come with a waiver and a medic," she said dryly. "But we're on the vacation, so what the hell."

Her friend eyed her with interest.

"Does that mean you'll have one too?"

Chloe laughed and shook her head. It tracked that Lala was looking for a kindred friend who would indulge in spirits.

Lala crinkled her face.

"Suit yourself, Chlo. My vacation bucket list is to work my way through this menu," she said matter-of-factly.

Chloe considered.

"So, you're planning on returning to Toronto with liver damage and a tan?"

"Excuse you," Lala said with mock indignation. "This is cultural research." She directed her attention to the bartender. "Juan? I would like a Shark Bite," she said politely. "And a pina colada for my friend."

Chloe smiled. She wasn't a fruity cocktail type of woman like Lala, but her one weakness when she was on a beach vacation or assignment was a pina colada. One of the sugary drinks was enough to tide her over until the next tropical trip.

Minutes later two drinks were placed in front of them. A buttery-yellow blended drink for Chloe, and a bright blue concoction for Lala that was accompanied by an umbrella pick and a potent smell. Juan turned to some other guests and moments later the grating sound of the blender drowned out the bar's music.

Lala took a sip, and her head rolled back in ecstasy.

"I'm going to marry Juan," she said decisively.

"That good, hey?" Chloe inquired. "I don't mean to rain

on your parade, La, but I think I saw a ring."

An exaggerated pout sprouted on her friend's face.

"Well, the week is young and if the other bartenders can make a drink half as good as this, I'm proposing."

Chloe lifted her glass in the air and toasted.

"Here's to terrible choices and great stories."

"I'll drink to that!" Lala clinked her glass against Chloe's and they both took a drink.

Three hours later, Lala had worked her way through one half of the menu. Granted, there were only four drinks on each side as well as a variety of beers and canned beverages, but four drinks was a lot. They had loaded up on protein and carbohydrates at breakfast, but it had become increasingly evident that it hadn't been enough for her friend. The remnants of a bright green concoction sat in front of Lala as she wobbled unsteadily on her chair.

"I need to have a nap," she slurred.

"Good call." Chloe nodded her head. She had kept her wits about her and stuck to virgin drinks, aside from the single pina colada. "I'm going to take a walk on the beach after this." She gestured to her lemony mocktail, which was one-quarter full.

One-quarter full.

See?

She was already acting more optimistic. The work assignment was serving her well. Even if it did require her to be in the presence of nudity anytime she left her room.

Lala slid out of her seat and stood up. Chloe noticed she had a slight sway to her. Which was no wonder, given the number of shots she had seen Juan dump into Lala's drinks.

"Do you want me to walk you to the room?" Chloe was concerned—she wanted to support her friend, and Lala clearly looked in need of it, but she also didn't want to impose.

Lala giggled

"I think I'll be okay," she said, grabbing her purse and trying to pull herself together. It was a feat that she didn't entirely accomplish due to her sunglasses being slightly askew and one portion of her hair that she had run her hands through sticking up at an odd angle.

"But thanks." She leaned over and put her arms around Chloe in a big bear hug. "If you find my dignity out there on your walk, bring it back."

Chloe giggled and hugged her back.

"Okay, well at least send me a text when you get to the room," she implored. "So I know you made it safely."

"Will do, Chlo. And if you find anything with abs, bring that back too," Lala said. And with a flourish—a slightly unsteady one at that, Chloe was alone. Just her and Juan and the naked couple sitting next to her.

She was surprised to find she was getting used to the sights of the resort. Which wasn't just limited to the architecture and scenery. Really, it was just like being in the sauna at the gym. The brain's ability to adapt to different situations was wild. Habituation was it called? She had taken a psychology class where she had learned all about that sort of thing, but the details were hazy.

She turned back to her mocktail and sucked the blended ice up through the straw when her phone lit up with a text from Lala.

Made it!

She had also included a photo of her wrapped up in a bathrobe, lounging on the bed and wearing her sunglasses. Chloe also spotted a big bottle of water on the nightstand beside her.

Good choice, La, she thought to herself.

She sent a text reply letting Lala know she would message her when she was on the way back from her walk, to which she received an emoji thumbs-up. With a sigh she pushed the empty glass away from her and slid two American dollar bills towards the bartender and got up to leave.

"Gracias!" she said loudly to Juan who was busy mixing up drinks.

He turned and gave her a wave.

"Gracias, señorita!"

Chloe smiled, slipped her phone in the pocket of her shorts, and headed for the beach. To get there she had to pass the main pool. Which also meant a hoard of sunbathers. She averted her eyes as she walked through a salsa dancing party that one of the activities coordinators was currently hosting.

It really was a sight to be seen and averting her eyes from that was more of a struggle. She marveled at how much the human body wiggled and jiggled while dancing. Naked yoga, she knew, was on that afternoon and she hoped she wouldn't be around to see that one.

Shiny sand-coloured tiles trimmed the perimeter of the pool and they were covered in an expanse of sun loungers. Almost all of them were occupied, with people either oiled up and soaking up the sun, under umbrellas reading books, sleeping, or talking with other guests and spouses.

One thing she had noticed about the resort was that most people seemed to either be alone or a part of a couple. Aside from the two women they had met that morning, there didn't seem to be many people who were vacationing there with their friends. Which made sense when she thought about it.

Unless you were used to no-pants parties with your friends, there would be no reason to go to Costa Morpho together. That is, of course, unless your boss, with a sick sense of humor, sent you there on assignment and you, unaware, chose to bring a friend. She loved Lala, Opal, and Alejandra dearly, but a naked vacation together was not something she wanted.

Palm trees lined the outer edges of the pool and four tiled steps led down to the sandy beach—also nude, of course.

Lounge chairs dotted the sand, some of which were occupied with towels, people, or both, and wait staff wandered around bringing drinks and snacks for the guests and clearing away empty plates and glasses.

She walked down the wide steps and onto the sand, which spilled over the top of her flip-flops and onto her feet. She slid off her shoes and took them in one hand before setting off along the shoreline.

The calming roar of ocean waves crashing against the sand mingled with the squawking of birds and the laughter of people playing in the water. She had intentionally not brought her AirPods with her that morning. She was looking to soak up the experience and immerse herself in the here and now.

It was something she had learned from the mindfulness classes Lala had started dragging her to shortly after the inaugural hot-yoga session.

Well—she had dragged Chloe to the first couple of classes. After that, Chloe had gone willingly with nary a threat or a nag. Leaving her headphones behind was her putting into practice the tools she had taken from the classes—focusing on the present and centering herself to avoid getting overwhelmed by thoughts of her past or her future. Along with keeping a busy schedule and a clean home, if she stayed in a mindful headspace, she was able to stop herself from spiraling out of control and heading back into the land of sadness.

Sand squished between her toes and cold water rushed up and covered her feet, providing a welcome respite from the heat. Boats of different sizes dotted the shoreline—small, motorized fishing boats, catamarans with large sails, yachts, diving boats, and jet skis. Waves crashed over the bow of a yacht that was cutting through the water, hurrying on its way to a different part of the ocean.

A strong wind picked up and her blonde locks blew around her head. She could almost taste the ocean air and was confident she was now rocking an authentic beach 'do' that people pay a pretty penny for in a salon.

While the Costa Morpho property was located on a peninsula, the resort itself was situated on the edge of a long, sandy cove. Eventually Chloe came to a rocky area that required her to climb carefully amongst the water-drenched boulders to get around the cliffs to, presumably, a beach on the other side. It didn't look too far and the boulders didn't look too difficult to traverse.

Her flip-flops in hand, she climbed her way up onto a tall rock and eased her way down onto a neighbouring one with a flat surface. The boulders were wet with ocean water, and she made her way from one rock to the next until she had made it several meters from the shore. As she climbed along the jagged rocks, a barrage of waves hit her in rapid succession.

She climbed unsteadily on top of one sharp-edged rock as water crashed around her and she and looked around to try and figure out which one to go to next. The boulders, which had looked so friendly when she had first started out, were starting to look more lethal. They wouldn't be so bad to climb across if it wasn't for all the water; it made the rocks slippery and made her unsteady on her feet.

A hint of doubt crept into Chloe's head as a spray of ocean struck her in the face. Maybe heading this way hadn't been such a good idea.

She glanced behind her to see if she should head back towards the resort when a rogue wave knocked her off balance and smashed her onto the rocks. She floundered for a second, her body throbbing, before another wave hit her and pulled her off the rock and towards the ocean.

She thrashed around blindly. Salt water obscured her vision and stung what she presumed were cuts sustained from the fall. Her knee and ankle were throbbing and so was her right shoulder. Tomorrow, she knew she would have some nice big bruises to show for her little beach adventure.

If, that was, she managed to get out of this situation alive. Water sloshed around her as she tried to grasp onto a boulder, and she flailed around helplessly as another wave crashed overtop of her head.

A thought flitted through her brain as she fought to keep her head above the water.

This is bad.

It was followed by a succession of absurdities. What a tragedy it would be, her mind whispered, to go all the way to Costa Rica to get over her ex—okay, mostly for work—and, in a cruel twist of fate, meet a watery, oceanic demise.

She wasn't trying to be melodramatic, but her limited vision combined with her injuries and not knowing how to navigate her way out of and away from the water had her scared. She could tell she was bleeding in several places from the sting of the salt water, but how badly she was injured was a mystery. It also wasn't exactly low tide right then, and people died from drowning all the time. As she had climbed her way amongst the rocky outpost it hadn't occurred to her that the waves might knock her off balance and drag her into the water.

Another wave crashed over her and slammed her into the rocks below. As the water receded, she tried to claw her way up onto one of them and reached up to wipe her eyes with the bottom of her shirt.

It was about as useful as rubbing salt in a wound, given her clothing was just as soaked with ocean water as she was.

"Fuck!" she said aggressively, trying to squint through the stinging in her eyes as another wave crashed into her.

It smashed her against another rock and her heart began to quicken as another wall of water hit her seconds later.

Her hands slid across the rock, slick with ocean slime and salt water, as she desperately tried to find something to hold onto to.

She was smarter than this, she cursed herself. She knew better than this. How could she have been so stupid?

She thought of Lala waking up to find her friend missing and the entire resort sending out a search party. And what they would find? Her flip-flops or her body, *if* they managed to find any evidence of her at all.

A shiver went through her.

"HELP!" she yelled, hoping against hell that someone around would hear her. Once she had walked past the resort, she had found it to be pretty secluded. She hadn't seen anyone else around, but she didn't have many options at this point.

With her eyes squinted shut because of the salt, she tried to climb her way closer to the rocks she had been dragged from. It wasn't easy going and her body throbbed as she slipped, tripped, and stumbled while waves broke around her.

"HELP!" she yelled again, taking refuge on a rock she thought she had a good grip on. Her heart was in her throat and she yelled another cry for help that was suddenly cut off by a huge wave that smashed into her and pulled her back into the ocean.

No! she thought to herself, panicking. *No!* This could not be happening. This could not be how she died.

She cried as she tried to tread water and keep her head above the water, which felt like an impossibility with all the waves.

Would it be worse to die from the blunt-force trauma of being repeatedly smashed into rocks or from being dragged out to sea and drowning?

Terror gripped her as she sobbed and a wave crashed over her head and dragged her under the ocean. Her arms flailed about as she tried to navigate her way to the surface, but she was so disoriented she couldn't tell which way was up. She thrashed wildly as the current dragged her this way and that and her final thought before she gave up the fight was of her mom and dad. How heartbroken they would be when they were told that their only daughter drowned.

And then, just like in the movies, a montage of her life flashed before her eyes. Her school birthdays, vacations with her parents, high school graduation, her internship, meeting Liam, sleepovers with her girlfriends, Liam breaking up with her, and finally, her elation at being in Costa Rica with her best friend.

The irony.

Suddenly she felt something grab onto her arm and pull her downwards. Or was that upwards? Underwater, she couldn't tell.

Oh no, she thought, *even worse than drowning or blunt-force head trauma—I'm going to get eaten by a shark.*

The thought paralyzed her with fear and suddenly everything went black.

*

Chloe's eyes were closed but it seemed she was no longer in the water. In fact, it felt like she was on solid land. Hard, ocean-free, solid land.

But that was impossible.

Unless she *had* actually died, and heaven was a place with solid ground. That really would fly in the face of all the cartoon cloud depictions she had seen.

Still, it had to be heaven—the absence of burning hot fires told her that, despite jokes she and her friends had sometimes made, she definitely wasn't roasting in the pits of hell.

Her entire body ached, and her eyes still stung; her skin felt sticky, and her lips were parched. Suddenly, she felt a hand on her arm and, what felt like, hair, brush her neck.

"Hey!" a low male voice said urgently.

Chloe moaned softly, and the male voice urged her again.

"Hey! Wake up!"

She felt a hand on the side of her face.

"Are you okay?" the voice asked urgently again.

Chloe groaned and felt the rim of a plastic water bottle being gently pressed against her lips.

She lifted her head a bit and the bottle tilted so a trickle of liquid dribbled into her mouth.

"My friend has gone to get a medic." The voice sounded concerned. "Stay with me."

A medic. Hmm, she thought through a fuzzy haze. *I must not be dead.*

Which should have come as a relief and probably would have if she didn't feel so awful. How had her morning of enjoying the sea, sand, and sun, and centering herself in the here and now turned into bruises, bangs, cuts, a near-death experience, and an apparent savior?

She didn't know, but she thanked her lucky stars that someone had intervened.

"I . . . can't . . . eyes," she gasped hoarsely. "Salt."

"Oh!" said the man. "Of course, yes!"

Seconds later she jolted as cold-water splashed over her eyes and rinsed out some of the salt. There was a plastic clicking sound as, Chloe surmised, the man unscrewed the cap off another bottle of water before pouring it over the top of her eyes. She squeezed them shut and then felt a rough fabric gently rub against them.

A towel, she mentally placed the fabric. She wasn't sure if in the near drowning she had lost a few neurons or if the shock of it was just taking her brain a bit to process.

Finally, the burning ebbed and she slowly opened her eyes.

"Hey!" the man said, his voice sounding much happier at seeing progress with his patient.

Her body was not cooperating—she tried to move her limbs and fingers, but it didn't seem like they wanted to cooperate with her brain. She wasn't sure if it was due to shock or if being smashed into the rocks had done some permanent—read: spinal—damage.

She tried to lift her right arm and it trembled.

The man noticed and placed a reassuring hand on her arm.

"Try not to move too much," he said coaxingly. "We want to make sure the medic gets you checked out."

Chloe obliged and gave up the body-mind struggle and tried to get a better look at her surroundings without moving her head. Her tongue darted out and licked her lower lip—it was dry and cracked from to the salt water.

The man took it as a cue to offer her more water, which he trickled into her mouth, and she drank gratefully.

"Thank you," she said, her voice still hoarse. She cleared her throat and then asked him what had happened.

"I was out here with my friend, we were taking a walk on the beach, and we saw you get caught up on the rocks. You slipped and the waves smashed you into the rocks. We got to you as fast as we could. We were yelling at you, but you probably couldn't hear us because of the water. It looked like you were trying to feel your way closer to the shore, but then a big wave swept you off a rock and dragged you under."

Chloe's brain tried to process this.

She remembered climbing on the rocks in an attempt to see what was on the other side of the beach. And she had a vague memory of being in the water. But she didn't remember being tossed around and pulled into the ocean.

Her body, on the other hand, definitely remembered; the stinging and throbbing of her bumps, bruises, and cuts made it very apparent that what he was telling her was true. Her brain was probably just traumatized.

"I didn't think we were going to get to you in time," the man said, somewhere between relief and concern. It occurred to her that he might still have adrenaline coursing through his system.

Not that she could blame him. She didn't remember what had happened to her, but it was terrifying to hear about. It must have been more terrifying to watch it happen.

"Thank you," she mumbled. The gratitude she sincerely felt didn't translate into her tone because of the sorry state she was in, but she had a feeling the man would understand.

He patted her arm reassuringly.

"I'm just glad we reached you in time."

Chloe had been squinting due to the bright light of the sun, but it was suddenly blocked out and she opened her eyes a little wider.

And holy hell was she glad she had.

The man positioned his head so he was blocking out the sun; he was looking at her with marked concern.

Her eyes focused on his handsome face. Skin tanned to a golden perfection? Check. Cheekbones that looked like they belonged on a Roman God? Check. Deep, soulful eyes that were framed by haughty dark-brown brows and a head full of beach-tousled softly curled brown locks? Check.

On second thought, maybe she *had* died and gone to heaven.

A small smile involuntarily spread across her lips and her saviour's expression turned from one of concern to one of astonishment and then a mirrored grin.

"I'm glad you're going to be okay," he said sincerely.

"Thank you," she repeated, starting to regain her composure. "What's your name?"

"Jack." He smiled.

"I'm . . ." she took a deep breath, "Chloe," she breathed out.

"Chloe," he repeated.

Jack's head turned to the side and relief washed across his features. She saw him wave.

Seconds later she heard voices and noticed three more people had joined them. Two appeared vaguely medical, and one was clearly Jack's friend.

"Miss." A man kneeled next to her and looked into her eyes. His dark skin was lightly wrinkled, and he had salt-and-pepper hair. "I'm Doctor Vargas." He pulled out a small pocket flashlight and shined it into her eyes, one eye at a time.

As he went about his doctoring business, Chloe was cognizant of a woman doing other medical things to her. The woman lifted Chloe's left hand and placed a blood oxygen monitor onto one of her fingers.

"Do you know where you are?" Doctor Vargas asked her seriously after he instructed her to follow the movement of his finger with her eyes.

"Costa Rica," Chloe said a little hoarsely.

"Can you tell me what your name is?" he prompted her.

"Chloe." Her voice was a little stronger now. "Chloe Ryder."

"Chloe," the doctor repeated. "Okay, I'm going to do a quick test of your reflexes."

Her brain function had almost entirely returned to normal, and Chloe braced herself for whatever Dr. Vargas's reflex test would consist of. Seconds later she felt a short, sharp whack to her knee and winced as her limb jerked in reply.

She was aware of Dr. Vargas and the woman, probably a nurse, speaking to each other in Spanish. Then she watched as the woman lifted up her left arm, wrapped a blue rubber band around it, and squeezed it tight. A sudden coolness swiped across her skin, followed by a sharp prick and seconds later Chloe felt the bizarre cold rush of saline course through her arm and into her system.

The adrenaline in her body started to wear off then as her brain finally realized she was no longer in danger. Which was good on one hand, but also bad because she began to feel the full extent of her injuries.

They were superficial of course—Dr. Vargas hadn't put on any tourniquets to stop any bleeding—but she had a vague notion that one or two of the cuts might require stitches.

While Dr. Vargas and the nurse tended to her injuries and made sure she didn't have anything internal going on, Chloe could hear Jack and his friend murmuring in the background.

Minutes later two more people appeared with a stretcher board, which they helped Chloe, who was moving gingerly, onto before buckling her in. Her body hurt with every step the medics took through the sand as she bumped along while strapped to the stretcher.

In addition to feeling pain, she was also starting to feel a creeping sense of embarrassment.

She was grateful that Jack had saved her from imminent death and thankful for the medical attention and appearing to only have sustained superficial injuries. But there was something mortifying about being strapped to a stretcher and carted down a beach by medics.

Her head was turned away from the sun and she squinted at the people lounging on the beach as they stared at her in curiosity. She felt like a circus freak—a sideshow for people to stare at and wonder what had befallen the bedraggled woman.

Suddenly, Chloe remembered her phone. What had happened to it? She had tucked it into the front pocket of her denim shorts when she set out on her walk. What were the odds that it hadn't managed to get dragged out to sea during her near drowning? Her flip-flops were long-since forgotten—they had likely been ripped out of her hands the minute the wave had dragged her into the ocean.

A wave of pessimism suddenly rolled over her. There was no way it had stayed in the loose pockets of her shorts. And even if someone did find her phone, there was no way it wouldn't be completely waterlogged. It was small in comparison to what she had apparently gone through, but she would be lying if she said it didn't make her a bit upset. After all—while she was gainfully employed and financially sound, things were going to get tight after she moved out of

Liam's place, and she was once again living on a single income—something she hadn't had to do in five years.

If nothing else, a small voice in her head told her it would be another fresh start. Her contacts, photos, files, videos, and voice recordings were all backed up to the cloud. The only thing she would have to worry about would be the tedious task of installing apps and trying to remember all her passwords.

Which was a chore and a half.

The ground beneath her suddenly changed to something more solid—she could tell by the difference in the movement and bumping of the stretcher.

Well, that and the surroundings.

She was at another resort. Which one she didn't know. She hadn't taken any time to see what others were in the area and didn't know what was around. It appeared to be adult in nature—for the entire trip from the beach and into the resort grounds, there hadn't been a single child in sight. No branding had given away the name of the place, but from the finishings she could see, everything looked expensive.

"Ms. Ryder—."

Chloe turned to look at Dr. Vargas.

"We're going to take you into our first aid room to get some of your vitals."

Chloe nodded as best as she could while lying down. She noticed that Jack and his friend were still hanging around.

Dr. Vargas turned to them: "Mr. Fraser, Mr. Silverberg— you're welcome to wait outside while I check Ms. Ryder and to make sure she doesn't need to go to a hospital."

Jack looked at his friend: "If you don't mind, I'd like to stay to make sure she's okay."

His friend nodded his head.

"Of course. I'm going to get a drink—do you want anything?"

"A Scotch would be great, thanks."

Chloe watched Jack's friend—Mr. Silverberg or Mr. Fraser, she wasn't sure which—head off in a different direction.

The inside of the resort was expansive and airy with neutral tones and warm lighting; natural elements like lush potted plants, stone accents, and gentle water features dotted the inside, and she saw well-dressed guests and polished, professional-looking wait staff. Her travel editor experience told her it was a five-star resort. She would bet her career on it.

She snorted quietly. She had just escaped death but was already back in work mode and curious how a nudist resort ended up next door to something so high-end. It wouldn't surprise her if she learned that this resort had waged an unrelenting campaign against having a nudist resort being built next door to them.

Or maybe they hadn't found out until right before it had opened. Either way, she couldn't see them being too happy about their new neighbours. She was hoping it wouldn't cause them to have any ill will towards her. Toss her back out into the ocean, they might, if they got wind that she was staying at Costa Morpho.

She wondered if the guests at this resort had any idea what was just around the corner from them. Not that Costa Morpho was something scandalous. In the Western world at least. She could see how it wouldn't fly in some of the more conservative countries.

Inside the first aid room the walls were white with typical doctor's office human anatomy posters and medical accessories decorating the space: tongue depressors, a blood pressure monitor, an uncomfortable-looking plastic bed with white roll-paper covering. She was starting to feel more alert and was fully able to appreciate the battering her body had been through. It felt like she had been thrown into a washing machine, and someone had set the dial to heavy duty.

Fortunately, Dr. Vargas seemed to be aware of how she was feeling and told her he was going to run some pain medication directly into her IV.

"It will take a few minutes, but it will dull anything you're feeling," he said without a glance.

Chloe was grateful. She just hoped the medication wouldn't send her into la-la land.

"Don't worry," Dr. Vargas said offhandedly, "it's just extra-strength Tylenol. It will stop the pain for a few hours, and I'll prescribe you some pills for when it wears off."

"Thank you," Chloe mumbled gratefully.

"Are you a guest at the resort?"

"No." Chloe shook her head slightly. "I'm at the one next door—Costa Morpho."

If Dr. Vargas was surprised, he didn't show it.

"Are you here with anyone? Is there an emergency contact, perhaps?"

"My friend Lala," she replied. "If you call the resort, they should be able to get ahold of her. We're in the Reserve Suite. I think I lost my phone in the ocean."

Dr. Vargas nodded and went to the phone sitting on the counter. He punched in a few numbers, held the receiver up to his ear, and seconds later was speaking in Spanish to the person on the other end of the line.

"Gracias," he ended before placing the receiver down in its cradle. "The front desk is going to call the resort to get ahold of your friend. How are you feeling now?"

"A bit sore. Something tells me I'm really going to feel it in the morning."

Dr. Vargas nodded again.

"You've had a traumatic experience but fortunately no broken bones or major lacerations. You should take it easy the next couple of days. You don't seem to have a concussion, but someone should keep an eye on you all the same. And make sure you have the doctor at Costa Morpho see you tomorrow for a checkup," he directed. "Actually, leave that with me. I'll call and arrange it and send them over my notes."

"Thank you," Chloe said gratefully. It was a miracle she had survived, and she was fortunate that she would walk away entirely unscathed. Well, maybe not entirely; her mind went back to the superficial injuries she had sustained. Another thing she was walking away with was a much healthier appreciation for the ocean. From now on, without a life jacket, she would be steering clear of the water.

"I'm going to keep you here for another half an hour for observation. I'm just going to step out to my office and make a call to your resort. If you need anything, use this phone to call the front desk and they will have a nurse or myself come and assist you."

"Thank you, Dr. Vargas," she repeated.

He opened the door and stepped out with his hand still holding it open. Chloe could hear voices, but she was too tired to strain to hear what they were saying.

"Ms. Ryder," Dr. Vargas appeared in the doorway once again, "Mr. Fraser wanted to know if you would like company?"

"Yes," she nodded enthusiastically.

"Okay," the doctor motioned to Jack who, apparently, was standing off to the side.

A millisecond later Jack, with a look of concern on his handsome features, walked into the room.

Chloe was glad she wasn't currently hooked up to a heart-rate monitor or a blood-pressure cuff. Even in her dazed and injured state Jack was enough to get her heart rate up.

"Hey," he said softly as he approached the stretcher. "How are you feeling?"

"Better now that you're here." She had said it before she could stop herself and then blanched when she realized what she had said.

Fortunately, Jack seemed to take it well and a large, easy smile blossomed across his face.

"Well, in that case, maybe I should pull up a chair and make myself comfortable."

Chloe smiled back. "That would be nice."

Jack did just that.

"Are you staying at the resort?" he asked.

"No." Chloe shook her head and twisted her face a bit knowing what was coming next.

"Where are you staying?" he asked.

"Costa Morpho," she said with a bit of hesitation.

Jack didn't give any outward appearance of knowing what the place was.

"Costa Morpho?"

"Yes." Chloe paused. "It's just around the corner." She paused again. "It's actually a nudist resort."

She wasn't quite sure what had made her blurt out that last part.

Jack looked lost for words.

"Naturist resort, I mean. But I'm not a nudist," she said quickly. "Not that there's anything wrong with that. To each their own. I'm a travel editor and I'm on an assignment. I didn't actually know I was going to a nudist resort . . ." Chloe trailed off.

"Travel editor." He looked impressed. "That's a pretty cool job. But didn't you Google the place beforehand?" He seemed a bit incredulous.

"No." She paused. "I've had a lot going on in my personal life. And I also try and avoid looking up any resort or hotel I'm going to be staying at. That way I don't show up with any bias and I experience everything for the first time. I'm not tainted by any TripAdvisor or Google reviews. You can imagine the shock when I walked into the lobby and everyone except for the staff was naked."

He laughed out loud at that.

"I imagine that was quite the scene."

"Oh, it was something." She snorted at the memory. "I almost thought I was being pranked. But it's not so bad once you get used to it. If you want, you could come check it out sometime?" she raised one of her eyebrows in question.

Good Chloe, she thought, patting herself on the back. Lala would be proud. She had come within seconds of death and now she was hitting on her savior. Maybe it was some sort of trauma response?

"I'd like that." Jack smiled at her.

"I would give you my number, but Poseidon is currently in possession of my phone," she said wistfully.

"How about your email?"

"That I can definitely give you. My laptop is sitting safe and sound and, more importantly, dry in my hotel room."

Jack pulled out his phone.

"It's Chloe, C-H-L-O-E-R-Y-D-E-R at gmail dot com."

"How long are you here for?" Jack asked.

"We're here for another six days."

"We?" Jack asked.

"My friend Lala," Chloe explained. "My best friend. She sometimes joins me if she can make it work with her schedule."

"Ah, okay," he nodded. "Well, I'd love to meet her."

"She might actually be in worse shape than me," Chloe trailed off.

A look of curiosity crossed Jack's face, and he raised one of his eyebrows in question. It was a good eyebrow. Framed his eyes to perfection.

"Lala got ahold of the cocktail menu this morning and made short work of it."

"Ah," he said with understanding.

"She went back to our room for a nap. That's why I was out on the rocks—I wanted to see what was on the other side of them."

"So, you have your best friend to blame for nearly drowning," he pondered. "But you also have her to blame for meeting me."

"You know," she said pensively, "I might have to send her a fruit basket."

"Or maybe you should send one to the bartender," he teased back.

They exchanged flirty smiles.

"Are they keeping you here for a while?" Jack asked.

"Dr. Vargas said he was going to call Costa Morpho to try and get ahold of Lala. But I have a feeling she's gone full Sleeping Beauty 'til at least this evening."

"What did she drink?" He sounded interested.

"All of the drinks."

"All of the drinks?"

"Yes," Chloe snorted. "One entire side of the menu."

"Is she not coping well with the nudity or something?" There was a teasing tone to his voice.

Chloe giggled.

"No, she usually has at least one day when we're away that she goes full-out."

"Ah, well, good that she's getting it out of her system early," he said reasonably.

"What about you?" Chloe asked. She was more than curious about Jack, her knight in patterned board shorts.

"I'm here for another eight days. I came down here with my friend Daniel. He just went through a messy divorce and needed some time away to reset."

"Where do you live?" she asked. She hadn't pegged him for an American, but she could be wrong.

"Canada. Toronto," he added.

"Me, too!" she said enthusiastically.

"What are the odds?" He grinned, following it up by asking which part of the city she lived in.

"I'm in the financial district. My office is downtown. I

work for *Strut*. I don't know if you've heard of it?"

Jack looked surprised. "Magazine? I have. Surprisingly. I'm not up on my fashion but I know that's a popular fashion magazine. Good for you."

Chloe felt strangely happy. Who would have thought that being hooked up to an IV in a doctor's office after nearly drowning could be such an enjoyable experience?

Jack opened his mouth to say something but was interrupted by a soft knock on the door.

"Come in," Chloe said loudly.

Dr. Vargas stepped into view.

"Ms. Ryder, we contacted your resort, but they were unable to get ahold of your friend."

Chloe exchanged a humourous glance with Jack.

"I thought that might be the case," she replied.

"We've arranged to have one of our vans transport you next door whenever you're feeling up to it. Please take your time, we're in no rush. Your health is the most important thing."

"Thank you." Chloe was grateful. "I think I should be okay to go back now. I'm just really tired."

Dr. Vargas had removed her IV and given her a bottle of Tylenol 3s with instructions on how to manage her pain. Jack, bless his heart, offered to accompany her. She protested at first, not wanting to impose on him or interrupt his vacation with his friend, but he insisted.

Her first steps off the examination table were a little wobbly and Jack offered up his arm to steady her.

"Thanks," she said shyly. She grabbed ahold of him, and they slowly headed for the lobby. Chloe was feeling better than when she had first come to, but she still wasn't back to normal. Jack had noticed she wasn't wearing any shoes and had her sit and wait in the lobby for two minutes. A little while later he had returned holding a brand-new pair of hot-pink Havaianas flip-flops.

A smile broke out on Chloe's face as he kneeled down and slid one of the flip-flops onto her left foot.

"Not quite a glass slipper, but the shoe fits . . ." He trailed off.

Chloe's smile widened.

"Cinderella's soggy sister—the one with flip-flops and PTSD," she teased.

In the vehicle, Jack sat next to her and brushed her hair back from her face. Butterflies danced in her stomach. It was a pleasant feeling that was so unfamiliar, it almost felt foreign. Thinking back, the last time she had felt butterflies was when she had started dating Liam.

When they pulled up to Costa Morpho, which was less than a two-minute drive, a first aid attendant who was, mercifully, fully clothed was waiting. Chloe was gracious but waived off his concerns and accepted his contact card in case she needed anything.

"Thank you," Chloe smiled. "I'll call you if I need anything."

Jack insisted on walking her back to her room and Chloe felt a twinge of nervousness mixed with another mass of butterflies. She wasn't used to being vulnerable and letting someone take care of her.

"Remember," she whispered to Jack as she leaned on his arm for support. "This is a nude resort. So, brace yourself."

"Got it—poker face on," he said in mock seriousness.

The lobby was mostly full of staff but there were a few people hanging around. There was a couple sitting at the lobby bar with only their backs visible to her and Jack.

"Does the bar supply the towels?" Jack whispered, clearly noticing the couple had draped a white towel over each of their seats.

Chloe stifled a giggle and nodded.

"They have some behind the bar if a guest forgets to bring one from their room."

"Well, thank god for that," Jack said with mock relief. "At least you know the seats are clean. The things you need to know when it comes to visiting a nude resort . . .," he trailed off.

"Oh, it's definitely been an educational experience," she grinned.

As they made their way past the restaurants and out of the lobby, Chloe steered them towards the pool.

"Get ready," Chloe whispered. "We're taking a shortcut."

Jack walked in stunned silence as they approached the outer perimeter of the pool. Latin dance music emanated from the speakers as they walked past the other guests who were sunbathing, swimming, and saddled up to the bar. There was a raucous game of water volleyball going on and she noticed Jack's eyes grow bigger when he saw it.

"Is it strange I'm having a hard time keeping my eyes above their necks?" Jack said in low tones. "It's the strangest thing. I don't normally pay attention to what people are wearing, but there's something about everyone being naked that's making it hard for me not to look."

Chloe shook with laughter.

"I had the same problem. Once you get used to it, you stop noticing. It's actually kind of surprising how quickly you forget about it. At first I thought I was going to have to wear sunglasses for my entire stay."

"Ola!" Juan, the bartender who had served Lala one entire half of the menu that morning, waved to Chloe when he saw her approaching the pool bar.

"Ola." Chloe waved back.

"Can I get you a drink, señorita?" he asked.

"No, gracias," she said graciously. Maybe tomorrow if she was feeling up to it. Although she had a feeling that tomorrow she would be in a world of pain.

Past the pool they came to a pathway lined with palm trees and foliage that led to the guest rooms. The resort did have a couple of towers above the lobby that contained standard guest rooms, but there were also individual stand-alone suites situated in a lush area beyond the pool. Chloe and Lala were in one of the most opulent suites the resort had to offer—a perk the general manager had probably provided in hopes of impressing her. Golf carts were used for transportation to get around the grounds. She and Jack could have taken one, but she opted not to as walking gave them more time to spend together. There was also something about being in a golf cart next to naked people who jiggled with every bump, turn, and acceleration that she thought might make her feel worse than she already did. She had a feeling that Jello was going to give her serious Costa Morpho flashbacks the next time she encountered it.

"This is a nice resort," Jack remarked as they walked down a set of steps flanked by tall, swaying palm trees.

"It is," Chloe agreed.

"Is your near-death experience going to sour any part of your review?" he asked with curiosity.

"No—I could hardly let something I stupidly got myself into affect my stay. That wouldn't be fair to the readers. Although I'm not sure if or how I will work my misadventure into the article."

They approached one of the largest bungalows—a wooden structure with one wall of sliding glass doors, a cement patio with a lounge set, and landscaped greenery surrounding the space.

"The curtains are closed." Chloe glanced at the sliding glass doors. "I don't know if that means Lala is still sleeping."

She reached into her back pocket, and it dawned on her that she didn't have her room key. Another thing, in addition to her phone, flip-flops, and her dignity, that the ocean had stolen.

"I don't have my key." She turned to Jack. "Hopefully Lala is inside. I'm exhausted. I don't know if I have the energy to walk all the way back to the lobby."

She rapped heavily on the thick wooden door and waited.

There was no response.

Chloe groaned. Mentally, she had been holding up pretty well, given everything she had been through. But the prospect of having to trek all the way back to the lobby in her injured and exhausted state left her feeling mildly upset.

She rapped again and waited.

"I can go get you another key?" Jack offered.

Chloe looked at him gratefully.

"Wait here and I'll sort it out."

"Thank you." She sank down onto the linen couch and closed her eyes.

Tens of minutes later she awoke with a start to the sound of Jack's voice.

"Hey," he said softly.

She couldn't believe she had fallen asleep. Her ocean experience had taken more out of her than she had thought.

A manager, a security guard, and the first aid attendant accompanied Jack. Her identity was verified with a series of questions and, after she was given a quick once over by the medic, she was let into her room. The trio left with a "thank you," and Chloe invited Jack inside.

It was quiet in the bungalow and the door to Lala's room was closed.

"She must still be asleep," Chloe said in a quiet voice.

"That's okay," Jack said. "What's her phone number? I'll send her a text asking her to call me and I can explain what happened when she wakes up."

She gave Jack Lala's number, and he sent her a quick text.

"I'm going to head back now. I know you're tired and I don't want to exhaust you any further. Are you going to be okay?" he asked.

Chloe nodded. "Yes. Thank you. For everything," she said gratefully.

"I'll email you to see if you're up for company tomorrow?" One of his eyebrows was raised in question.

"I'd like that," she smiled back.

He answered her with a grin. "Okay. Sweet dreams, Chloe."

She walked him to the door and stretched her arms out for a hug. Jack's arms went around her and he gave her a substantive but gentle squeeze and a quick peck on the cheek.

"Bye." She grinned with pleasure as he turned and walked away. She closed the door and turned the lock before letting out a big sigh. What a day. And it wasn't even over. Although for her she had a feeling it would be soon. Sleep was coming for her and she couldn't see herself waking up before tomorrow.

She contemplated running a hot bubble bath but the concerns about the scrapes on her body and drowning after falling asleep in the tub won out. She was sticky with salt water and her hair felt knotty, but that was nothing she couldn't deal with tomorrow.

Stepping out of her clothes she pulled on a fluffy white bathrobe, closed her bedroom door, and fell into a deep sleep.

Past

Chapter 9:
A Waking Nightmare

Opus—it was where they always went for special occasions. Since it was neither of their birthdays, not their anniversary, and nor were they celebrating any achievements, Chloe had a sneaking suspicion that tonight might just end with a ring on her finger.

They had passed the five-year mark two weeks ago and, while she wasn't desperately waiting for Liam to pop the question, she knew that at some point it was coming. Sure, things hadn't been great between them the past six months, and Liam had completely forgotten about their anniversary and bungled Chloe's surprise, but he had made reservations this evening at their special dinner spot.

In Chloe's mind, that could only mean one thing.

Still, she tried to temper her expectations—she didn't want to get her hopes up and then be disappointed. If nothing else, she knew she was in for a great meal. It would make up for Liam's massive screwup around their anniversary dinner.

She pulled a new dress out of the closet—a pretty, red mini done up in delicate lace with a high neckline and short lace sleeves. She'd grabbed it from one of the racks at the office. It was a Prabal Gurung piece that was going to be used in an editorial they were shooting next week.

Not that she was in the habit of taking clothing from work. All of them had done it on at least one occasion— sneaking out with an item and then returning it a few days later with the dry-cleaning tags taken off.

No harm, no foul.

The red lace was soft between her fingers as she held up the outfit in front of a mirror. She reconsidered wearing it when she realized that if Liam *was* going to propose to her that evening, lots of photos would be taken. He might even have hired a photographer to capture the whole thing. Which might present a problem when it came to showing her coworkers photos from her engagement.

All her concerns washed away after she slipped on the dress—it was too stunning. If it came down to it, she would just leave out any pictures when recounting the engagement to her coworkers.

"Ready?" Liam's voice came from the living room.

"Almost!" Chloe called from their bedroom. She applied a quick swipe of lipstick. She had put her hair in hot curlers earlier and opted for a dark, smoky eye.

"You look great," Liam said when she emerged from their bedroom.

As far as looking great, she could say the same about him. His salt-and-pepper hair had been cut a few days before and he was wearing a sharp black suit with a white shirt—leaving the top two buttons undone and giving a hint of his hard chest underneath.

Things had finally gotten steamy in the bedroom a few days after the failed anniversary dinner, and although Liam had seemed distracted, it had put Chloe's mind at ease. He had initiated it after she told him how hurt she felt over his absence the last several months. Because of that and in addition to the special dinner he had booked for this evening, she was feeling optimistic. The six months of insecurity, disconnection, and lack of sex was just a blip. Something all couples went through. Liam was almost done the deal he was working on and, soon enough, their relationship would be back on track. After all, they lived together, they were close to each other's friends and families; they vacationed together, made goals together, loved each other, and supported one another through thick and thin. If that wasn't the makings of a solid, lifetime relationship, she didn't know what was.

Along the snow-covered streets of Yorkville, Opus, a knock-out food and wine establishment, occupied an ordinary brick building. Under the dim lights, soft music, and low-toned chatter of fellow diners, she and Liam enjoyed appetizers, mains, and a bottle of wine while they talked about Chloe's work and her upcoming assignments.

Liam ordered dessert for Chloe and poured the remainder of their wine into Chloe's glass before taking a deep breath and uttering four horrible words.

"We need to talk," he said, fixing her with an inscrutable stare.

At first, Chloe wasn't concerned. After all, they rarely fought. And if there was an issue that they needed to talk about, she was sure it would be something they could easily resolve.

Still—there was something about the look on his face. It was an expression that she couldn't quite place. A mixture of hesitancy and concern. And something else. He looked uncertain. Scared, maybe.

It was odd and she didn't know what to make of it. Maybe it was just nerves due to the prospect of proposing?

She gave her boyfriend a quizzical look and took a drink of wine. After putting the glass down, she gave Liam an expectant look.

"Okay—talk about what?"

Liam swallowed.

"You know that I love you, Chlo?"

Chloe nodded, puzzled that he was starting off a discussion this way.

"These past five years together have been great."

That's odd, she thought to herself. Why did it sound like Liam, her boyfriend of five years, her future husband, the father of her future children, the man she would grow old together and die with, was prepping her for an 'it's not you, it's me' type of conversation? It sure was a weird way to start out his 'asking for her hand in marriage' speech.

"Sorry?" Chloe said, struggling to process the words and expression on her boyfriend's face. She suddenly had a sick feeling about what was coming; she wasn't so sure she wanted to hear what he had to say.

"I said," Liam sounded exasperated, "these last five years have been great."

"Sorry?" she said again, this time sounding desperate. She was beginning to suspect that something sinister was coming. If she didn't actually let him get the words out, maybe what she was beginning to suspect was happening wouldn't actually come about. Like avoiding collections. They can't force you to pay if you don't answer their calls.

Liam gave her a guilty look and a sinking feeling came over her.

"That's why this is so difficult," he said barreling ahead.

Oh god. It was happening. He wasn't going to propose to her. He was going to break up with her. At Opus. At their special restaurant. After their five-year anniversary. After they had built a life together.

Over the next five minutes, Chloe had an anxiety black out. Six months after the fact, there would still be a hole in her memory. She didn't know the exact words that he had used, but she knew that they all boiled down to one thing: Liam didn't want to be with her anymore.

She wept openly at the table—composure and meticulously applied makeup be damned. Tears streamed down her face as he talked, but what he said, she couldn't recall. All she knew was it was bad.

She became vaguely aware at one point of their waiter placing a dish of crème brûlée down in front of her while trying his best to be discrete. She felt someone's eyes on her and noticed the woman at the table next to theirs. She was definitely eavesdropping. A dinner roll had been hovering three inches away from her mouth for the past few minutes and Chloe finally turned and gave her a teary glare.

Abashed, the woman quickly peeled her eyes off of the decoupling couple while Chloe turned her attention, but not her memory, back to her, apparent, former boyfriend.

It took her a second to realize a few moments later that he had stopped talking and a sudden rage swept over her.

"Are you fucking Sophia?" she asked, her eyes trained on Liam as she picked up her napkin and dabbed at the tear streaks on her face.

"What? No." Liam looked stunned.

He was denying it, but there was something in Liam's eyes that she didn't quite trust.

And she thought she knew why. Those late nights he had spent slaving away at the office? Sophia had been right there beside him. Liam had told her as much. It occurred to her then that Dasha, her boss, had been right.

"I just think we've grown apart," Liam said lightly, not meeting her eyes.

Chloe was astonished. *Grown apart?* she thought angrily. *How the fuck do you grow apart when you live together?* She realized she already knew the answer. *You grow apart when a certain blonde investment banker starts working overtime hours with your boyfriend.*

"Grown apart!?" she blurted out angrily. "Grown apart? Liam, pardon my language, but how the fuck do you think we grew apart when you've been spending every waking hour at work without me?"

She reached for her wine. From the look on Liam's face, he was gearing up to respond but Chloe was having none of it. She raised her finger and wagged it at him as she drank from her glass.

"No," she said determinedly. "You don't get to respond. You don't get to sit there and brush it off or try and justify breaking up with me on the grounds of 'growing apart'." She raised one hand in air quotations. "When you're the one who has been absent for the past six months."

Liam said nothing. She had told him he didn't get to respond, and it seemed he was taking it to heart.

But toss it. She did want him to respond. She just didn't want to hear what she knew he was going to say. She wanted him to respond by telling her that it was just an awful joke. That he wasn't actually breaking up with her. She didn't want him to respond by telling her he was sorry.

"Say something!" she said angrily.

"I'm sorry, Chloe," Liam said softly. "I really am."

Big fat tears welled up in her eyes and spilled down her cheeks.

Chloe. He called her Chloe. He hadn't called her that since the first month they had started dating. She was always Chlo. His Chlo. His honey, his baby, his babe. Now she was Chloe.

It was odd, but his use of her first name was what really drove it home for her. Hearing that Liam didn't want to be with her anymore hurt, yes. But there was something about the use of her first name that made it seem so final. As if things could have gone back to normal, like they had been six months ago, if he had only called her Chlo.

The crème brûlée, her favourite dessert, which Liam had insisted on ordering, sat cold in front of her.

Fuck the crème brûlée. She stared at it miserably as if it was the source of her discontent. Had he actually thought that ordering her a dessert would somehow soften the blow?

Liam opened his mouth, but Chloe had had enough. Sitting in the restaurant was starting to feel suffocating.

Without a word to her former boyfriend, she pushed back her chair, grabbed her purse, stood up, and headed for the exit while trying to avoid everyone's stares.

It wasn't that she and Liam's breakup had been loud and dramatic. No, that wasn't it. Despite the fact that it was a small restaurant, Chloe was confident that the only other people who were aware of her relationship demise were the nosy woman who had been sitting next to them and their waiter.

And while their conversation hadn't drawn attention, Chloe's post-breakup appearance had. Not knowing that her boyfriend was going to torpedo their five-year relationship that evening, she had put on regular mascara and eyeliner, not the waterproof kind. She could feel everyone's eyes on her—a vision in red lace and Halloween makeup. *Oh god*, she thought to herself; she would never be able to come back here.

"Are you okay, miss?" A hesitant voice broke through her musings.

She looked to her left. A busboy, bless his heart, was concerned about the deranged-looking woman in high heels and a cocktail dress. Given the way she looked, he probably didn't know whether to offer her help or holy water.

"I am not," she said kindly. "But thank you for asking."

She grabbed her phone out of her purse and pulled up her Uber app. No way was she taking the subway looking like this. Murphy's Law dictated that this would be the time she would run into someone she knew. Then word would be all over the street that she and Liam were over and that Chloe had come apart faster than a Shein sweater.

Devastation washed over her, but it was interrupted by a sudden thought.

What the fuck was she going to do about their living situation?

That, she decided, was to be determined, but one thing she knew was that Liam was absolutely, positively not sleeping at their condo tonight.

At home, still sporting tear-streaked mascara and the pretty red dress, she had Googled Sophia. It took her less than two minutes for her to find the woman she was looking for. Sophia Sullivan was a tall, lithe, tanned-to-perfection blonde bombshell. The kind of woman who seems to have effortlessly perfected the sexy, tousled-curls style and who looks like a model in every photo. Her smile revealed a perfect set of perfectly proportioned pearly whites, and her cheekbones were as sharp as knives.

Chloe felt like she was going to be sick and a new wave of anguish washed over her as she pictured Sophia cozied up to Liam during one of their late nights at the office. Then an image of Liam and Sophia banging on his desk flitted through her brain.

She should not have Googled Sophia. She should really *not* have Googled her.

Sobs wracked from deep inside her, and she emptied a tissue box trying to dry the flow of her tears. Finally, she went to the bathroom, wiped off her makeup and snatched an entire roll of toilet paper out from under the sink.

Liam texted her shortly after and said he would spend the night at Karam's—his close friend from university—to give Chloe some space.

She hadn't replied.

She was in a nightmare. A waking nightmare. One that wouldn't go away when she woke up the next morning. That was—if she was even able to get any sleep. How she was going to walk into *Strut* on Monday morning and keep her composure was beyond her. How was she going to be able to concentrate on her work? How was she going to be able to do anything?

A myriad of thoughts flashed through her mind as she lay awake in bed that night. Sadness, sorrow, anger, and everything in between. Scenarios of revenge raced through her head—everything from throwing Liam's clothes off the balcony to showing up at his office on Monday morning and causing a scene.

She had never had a breakup like this before and as she tossed and turned that night while thoughts raced through her head, she came to understand what 'coming unglued' really meant.

*

Her eyes were glassy the next morning as she had coffee and contemplated the previous evening. Her hair was wild and unruly, and she felt dehydrated from all the tears; her emotional hangover was helped along by a couple of hours of restless sleep.

What had Liam been thinking? Taking her to their special dinner spot only to drop terrible, life-shattering news? Had he done it in an attempt to sully all the great memories they had shared there?

No, she realized. Liam was more practical than that. He had taken her there because he thought that if he broke up with her in a fancy establishment, she wouldn't cause a scene.

Well, she reflected, he'd been right on that account. Her behaviour hadn't drawn any attention. Her post-breakup makeup, however, had.

Out of nowhere a fresh set of tears spilled out of her puffy eyes and onto her housecoat.

How could this be happening to her?

She and Liam had been so happy together. Hadn't they?

All the great times they had shared whirred through her

mind like a photo album. Liam getting promoted at the bank. Going on their first vacation together. Family Christmases, birthdays, anniversaries. The years they had spent building a life together. Her partner. Her best friend.

All of it was gone.

Because of some stupid blonde bimbo named Sophia.

She should have seen it coming, she scolded herself. Maybe if she had been more aware—had asked more questions when Liam started mentioning the new woman at his office.

Sophia Sullivan had been hired as an investment banking associate with Liam's team six months ago. When he mentioned that there was a new girl on his team, there hadn't been anything that initially gave her pause.

But a few weeks later, she noticed he was talking about his new coworker a lot. Sophia was mentioned so often, in fact, that it had taken her a bit aback. Liam had other female coworkers, but they rarely came up in conversation.

Twice she had caught him texting with a curious smile on his face and when she asked him about it, he had brushed it off as a funny meme from one of his group chats and quickly pocketed his phone.

It struck her as suspicious and didn't do anything to calm the concerns that lurked in the back of her head. But she didn't press him on it.

Until one evening when Liam mentioned how he and Sophia had tried out a new restaurant for lunch that week.

An alarm bell had gone off in her brain.

His usual lunch partner was his coworker Adam. But the way that Liam was talking, it sounded like Sophia had taken over Adam's place.

"Does Adam join you?" she asked, keeping her voice light.

"Yeah," Liam had responded, shifting his gaze to the T.V.

Unsatisfied, Chloe, trying to maintain an air of

nonchalance, asked what Sophia looked like. At that, Liam's ears went pink—a telltale sign that he was uncomfortable with the conversation—and he shrugged.

"I don't know. Blonde. Tall."

"Does she have a boyfriend or a husband?" she asked, struggling to keep her tone neutral.

"I don't know." Liam shrugged, his attention still focused on the television screen, which was showing an infomercial for a kitchen gadget.

Chloe had pursed her lips together. Tall, blonde, someone he was spending a lot of time with and who he kept talking about, and he didn't know if she had a partner.

A couple of weeks later she had broached the subject of Sophia again. Under questioning, Liam had blown a fuse and stormed out of their condo. He slept over at Karam's place that night.

After that, Liam stopped talking about his coworker, and Chloe, too afraid of setting him off, didn't bring her up again until the night of the failed anniversary dinner. And while Sophia's name was kept out of Chloe's mouth, that woman's presence weighed heavily on her mind.

Of course, she still didn't have any proof that Sophia was the cause of Liam's sudden change of heart. But she didn't know what else it could be. The timing seemed suspicious— she had started working with him six months ago, which was right around the time his physical and emotional absence had started.

She thought back to Opus and his response to being asked about whether he was sleeping with Sophia. He had denied it, but Chloe didn't believe him. What else could have happened six months ago to have caused such a change?

One week later, Chloe had called Liam's friend, Karam. The dark-haired banker worked at a boutique wealth-management firm in a building close to *Strut*. One thing she was thankful for was that the bank Liam worked for had changed office buildings a little over one year ago. This, at least, ensured that she wouldn't have to worry about seeing him in her work lobby or in the elevators.

"Chloe." Karam sounded hesitant. "Hi."

Of course he wasn't thrilled to hear from her. He was Liam's friend. And Liam was where his loyalty lay. Still, she wanted to talk to him. If Liam had been cheating on her, she wanted to know. And besides, Karam could have let her call go to voicemail. The fact that he had picked up gave her the tiniest bit of hope that he would honestly answer her question.

"Hi," she said back, her voice wobbly.

There was silence on the other end of the phone.

"Karam, I have to know. Please tell me. Is Liam with Sophia? Is that why he broke up with me?"

The silence from Karam's end was deafening.

"Karam?" she said, her voice breaking.

"Chloe, look . . ." he said after a second, sounding uncomfortable. "I—it's not any of my business. I'm sorry. It's not my place to tell."

"Oh my god." Her heart dropped as water welled up in her eyes. "He is. I knew it. Oh my god. How could he do this to me?" She started sobbing.

"Wait! No!" Karam sounded panicked. "I didn't say that! They aren't together . . . I don't think they're together."

Hearing that didn't buoy her feelings like she had hoped. It just caused her to ruminate for different reasons. Was Karam telling the truth? He had primarily been Liam's friend, yes. But five years of birthdays, barbeques, and forced group chats had to count for something.

Right?

And if Liam hadn't dumped her for Sophia, then what was the real reason behind it?

She believed he had broken up with her due to 'growing apart' about as much as she believed that Elvis was alive and running a Tim Hortons in Ontario.

Present

Chapter 10:
Dinner with Jack

"Are you okay!?"

The sound of Lala's panicked voice jolted Chloe out of her slumber.

"Mmm?" she responded sleepily, her eyes still closed. It felt like she had just had the best sleep of her life. She was still wearing the fluffy robe and, from the Dracula sleep position she was in, it appeared that she hadn't moved a muscle all night.

She stretched out her legs and winced in pain. Well, *that* would certainly explain why she had stayed stationary all night—her muscles hurt like hell. And it wasn't the good kind of pain. Like the kind you feel the day after going to an intense exercise class. It was a 'what happened to my body, how is it that even my pinky hurts' kind of suffering.

She chided herself.

Yes, she was banged and bruised, but upon further reflection, it *was* a good pain. Because pain meant she was alive. When she thought back to her harrowing experience yesterday, she knew that things could have gone much differently.

The bed beside her depressed suddenly and she was aware that Lala was sitting next to her.

"Chloe," Lala whispered, putting her arms around her friend. "Jack called and filled me in on everything. I can't believe I almost lost you! You are so lucky that he saved your life. Are you hurt? Are you okay?"

"Mmm," Chloe, her eyes still closed, mumbled again. "I'm okay. Everything hurts, but I'm okay," she said sleepily. "I have some cuts and bruises, but the doctor said otherwise I'll be fine."

"Thank GOD!" her friend exclaimed. "And to think— you were on the verge of death while I was passed out after too many cocktails. That's terrible. *I'm* terrible."

Chloe opened her mouth to respond, and Lala cut her off.

"Actually, *you're* terrible," she said in an accusatory tone. "If you had joined me on my quest to drink all the cocktails you wouldn't have gone out on the rocks. You would have been passed out in bed next to me," she said practically before switching gears. "I hope you know you're not leaving my sight the rest of this trip," she said matter-of-factly.

"Thanks, La," Chloe said, finally opening her eyes to find her best friend staring at her.

"How are you feeling?" Lala asked her again.

"I'm feeling like I need a bath and breakfast, stat."

"Say no more!" Lala jumped off the bed and ran into Chloe's bathroom. The muffled sound of running water filled the room and seconds later so did the scent of lavender.

"Lavender bubble bath coming right up." Lala appeared in the doorway. "You get in the bath, and I'll order room service," she commanded. "Can I offer you some in-room drip-coffee to start?"

"Please! Thank you!" Chloe said gratefully.

Lala swept out of the room and Chloe gingerly stretched

out. She wasn't sure if it was the scent of the lavender bubble bath that had her feeling so relaxed or the apparent eighteen hours she had spent sleeping. She listened to the sound of the running water for a few minutes and then slipped out of bed to go check on it. A mound of frothy white bubbles was almost flowing over the top of the porcelain tub. She turned off the tap, pulled off her robe and gently stepped in. An involuntary groan of pleasure escaped her as she sank down into the warm water and pain shot through her as the water reached the cuts on her skin. Steam rose around her and the fizzing sound of dissolving bubbles broke the silence. She kept her eyes closed as she sank farther into the water and her thoughts went back to the day before. It seemed so long ago and almost like it had been a dream—the water, the waves, Dr. Vargas, Jack.

She was so grateful to Jack. It wasn't every day that you were rescued from certain death. Rarer still was it to be rescued by a man who looked like he had just stepped out of the pages of GQ.

She winced as she adjusted her limbs in the water. It felt like her body had been tossed around in a washing machine yesterday and now she was reaping the consequences of it today. Which, when she thought about it, was kind of accurate. The ocean swept away debris, churned water, and kept sand clean. It was nature's washing machine but, unlike the one at home, it didn't come with a safety setting.

Powering through the aches and stings, she washed her hair and gently scrubbed her skin, being careful of the cuts and mindful of her bruises. Consequently, when she emerged from the tub she felt like a new person. It was amazing what a hot bath and some soap could do for you.

"Chlo!" She heard Lala yell from the living room. "Breakfast is ready!"

"Thank you!" she answered back. "Give me a few minutes."

"Take your time," Lala called. "And let me know if you want me to bring it to you in bed."

She grabbed the other bathrobe from the back of the door and wrapped her hair up in a towel. Glancing in the mirror for the first time since the previous afternoon, Chloe was surprised to see that nothing appeared to be amiss. Despite the bruises and scrapes, there was nothing different about her face. It was weird how you could go through something so harrowing, but it didn't leave any outward signs. (Well, cuts and bruises aside.) Inside, something felt different, and it seemed to her that there should be something transformational about it on the outside too. Looking at her, no one who met her would have any idea that the day before she had almost died.

She glanced at her nightstand where the coffee Lala had brewed for her sat—lukewarm by now, she imagined—and went to join her friend.

The round dining table had a heavenly looking spread sitting on top of it and the smell caused Chloe's stomach to growl. She realized she hadn't eaten since the previous morning. Lala was already digging into an omelette with a side of bacon.

"Coffee?" Lala asked as she picked up the silver coffee craft from room service. "Not drip coffee. This is the good stuff."

"Yes, please." Chloe took a seat as Lala poured her a cup.

"Oh god, this smells amazing," Chloe moaned as she took the proffered mug.

In addition to the eggs and bacon she had ordered for herself, the table was laden with French toast, hashbrowns, sausages, fried mushrooms, pastries, and fruit.

"This looks so good, La. Thanks for ordering."

"Please," Lala said through a bite of bacon. "It's the least I can do. I woke up around 6 p.m. last night with a raging headache and saw a text from an unknown number. I thought it was a scammer, but when I read it, I nearly dropped my phone. I called Jack immediately and he told me everything. You are so lucky he saved you. I checked on you throughout the night, but you were snoring like a grizzly. Seriously, Chlo—did the doctor give you sleeping pills? I have never heard anyone snore like that before."

"No. No sleeping pills," Chloe said as she cut a piece of French toast. "I think it was from all the adrenaline. I honestly thought I was going to die," she said seriously. Her memory of the incident had come flooding back to her last night. "My life literally flashed before my eyes. My last thought was how distraught you and my mom and dad were going to be and how stupid it was of me to go out on those rocks." She shook her head at the thought.

"Ugh, I can't even imagine." Her friend looked upset. "That must have been terrifying. I am so glad Jack saved you. We should send him a thank-you card or something. If it wasn't for him, you wouldn't be here right now."

"That's a good idea." Chloe popped the syrup-coated French toast into her mouth.

Lala looked hesitant for a moment.

Chloe, still chewing, raised one brow in question.

"Not to change the subject or anything, I know you almost died. But—," she hesitated, "what's Jack look like? He sounded hot on the phone."

Chloe choked on her French toast and started coughing.

"Sorry! Don't choke and die on me now!" Lala said in a panic.

Chloe let out a few more coughs and cleared her throat with a drink of coffee.

"Don't make me laugh!" Chloe squealed. "But since you asked, not only does he sound hot, *he is* hot. Like, incredibly hot."

"Yesssss!" Lala raised her fist triumphantly before stabbing a piece of her omelette and popping it into her mouth.

"He's here on vacation with his friend who just went through a divorce," Chloe continued. "He said he would email me to check in and see how I am today. I lost my phone in the ocean," she added with a grimace.

"I've already given him a full report," Lala confessed. "He asked me to let him know how you were when you woke up this morning. He's very concerned about you. He seems like a good guy."

Chloe was pleased to hear that Jack had asked about her and that Lala, even though she had never met him, seemed to approve.

"I think so too," Chloe agreed. "He waited while the doctor took care of me, and he brought me back to the resort. We talked a bit when the doctor was out of the room, and I really enjoyed his company. I like him," she added as if it wasn't already obvious to her friend.

"I love this," Lala declared. "You go to a nude resort for work, nearly drown, and get rescued by a hottie. Did he give you mouth-to-mouth? Is he going to be your hot vacation fling?"

Lala might be getting just a little ahead of herself, Chloe thought, but she did appreciate her friend's enthusiasm.

"No mouth-to-mouth," she snorted. "And I don't know about a vacation fling, but I hope I see him again. Did he tell you he lives in Toronto?"

"No way—what are the odds?"

Chloe smiled.

"I know. I don't know much about him, but I'd like to see him again."

They spent the rest of breakfast chatting before deciding on what to do for the day. The resort, aware of what had happened to Chloe, had canceled their itinerary that day—a tour of a nearby town and beer-and-rum tasting. Lala was cognizant that Chloe was probably in a fair amount of pain even though she insisted the Tylenol the doctor had given her would take away the worst of it, and she insisted they spend the day at the spa.

"Manicures, pedicures, facials, massage—" Lala paused. "Actually, you're pretty bruised and banged up," she said glancing at Chloe's legs. "Maybe raincheck on the massage?"

"I think I could go for a light one," Chloe said. "As long as they work around the bruises. It might actually help."

They booked a several-hours-long spa session for the two of them and spent the afternoon experiencing all that Costa Morpho had to offer in terms of relaxation. When they made it back to their room around mid-afternoon, Chloe went straight for her laptop.

She didn't even pretend that she was checking her work email because Lala would see right through it. She was hoping to hear from Jack, and she found an email from him waiting in her inbox when she logged onto her personal account. She giggled at the subject line: *Soggy Cinderella.*

Dear Chloe, his email began. He asked how she was feeling, told her that he had spoken to Lala, and asked if she wanted to get together that night if she was feeling up to it. The aches were still there, but the marathon spa session had left her feeling as limp as a cooked spaghetti noodle; she was definitely feeling up to getting together with Jack.

"Lala," she asked her friend. "What would you say to meeting up with Jack and his friend for dinner tonight if they're free?"

"Yes, yes, and yes," she said enthusiastically. That was Lala—always up for adventure. Especially if it involved an attractive man. Chloe had filled her in on Jack's friend, whose name she didn't know but whose face she had gotten a good look at. It was weird what adrenaline did to you—Jack, his friend, and Dr. Vargas's faces were all etched in her mind as if someone had taken a photograph of them and placed it in her brain.

She fired off a quick email to Jack asking if he and his friend would like to meet her and Lala for dinner. To bypass her lack of a phone she asked him to text Lala.

Not ten minutes went by before a message popped up on her bestie's device.

"They're in!" Lala exclaimed. "He wants to know if we'd like to go to their resort. Apparently, they have five different restaurants. What do you think?"

"Let's do it," Chloe replied.

Lala typed out a text and confirmed a time.

"I said we would meet them in their lobby at six," she said, tossing her phone on the couch.

"Careful!" Chloe teased—if something happens to your phone, we're back to communicating like it's the nineties."

"Not landlines and letters?" Lala said in a mock horror.

"Yes, Lala," Chloe deadpanned. "Landlines and letters."

*

At quarter to six, Chloe and Lala were waiting in the lobby of Costa Morpho for a house car to drive them next door. It was a short walk, but given they were both wearing pumps and had spent a large portion of time on their hair and makeup, hoofing it to the resort was out of the question. Not to mention, Chloe was still a hurting unit.

Lala's red locks were done up in sexy curls that made it look like she had just left a salon, and she wore a fire-engine-red mini-dress and 'barely there' makeup that took just as much time to do as makeup that's 'very there'. Chloe, for her part, had opted to pull part of her hair back with a clip and had put on layers of mascara, a swipe of eyeliner, and a hefty helping of blush. Her black linen gown had a thigh-high slit, a fitted bodice, and an off-the-shoulder neckline.

When Chloe had looked in the mirror, she felt good about herself. Despite the assortment of black, purple, and blue bruises she was sporting, she felt confident. It had been a while, she realized, since she had felt that way. The last six months of dating Liam had done a number on her self-esteem. Which hadn't improved after being broken up with. But, she questioned, had her confidence been all that high when she was with Liam to begin with? It was one of the things she had been thinking about now that she had the benefit of time and distance.

The van pulled up to the familiar—to Chloe—vaulted-ceiling lobby of the Four Seasons and the duo stepped out of the car and into the warm evening air. They were only a few steps inside when Chloe spotted Jack and his friend sitting on cushioned chairs just to the left of the concierge. A grin spread across Jack's face as he stood up to greet them, and his friend followed behind.

"Hi!" Chloe smiled. "Lala, this is Jack." She gestured to her rescuer who was handsomely clad in blue cotton pants and a white button-up linen shirt. It offset his perfect tan, and Chloe felt her stomach do flip-flops.

"Jack, nice to meet you." Lala shook his outstretched hand.

"Likewise." He grinned at her bestie. "This is Daniel," he nodded his head towards his friend. Daniel was in gray slacks, a white button-up shirt and a gray linen sports jacket. He looked just as handsome as his friend and Chloe could see the spark of interest emanating from Lala.

They shook Daniel's hand and Chloe thanked him for coming to her aid the previous day. Daniel shook it off and insisted that it was all Jack.

For Chloe, it *was* all Jack, but not in the sense of being rescued.

"For dinner, we have a couple of options," Jack told them. "I made reservations at the seafood, Italian, and Asian-fusion restaurants—what are we thinking?"

"I vote Italian," Lala said automatically.

"A woman who knows what she wants," Daniel teased.

He was already flirting with her friend and that was before any kind of liquid courage. Maybe Chloe wasn't the only one who had found a potential vacation romance.

Lala shot Daniel a flirty smile and turned to Chloe. "What's your vote, Chlo?"

"I'm good with Italian," she nodded.

"Italian it is," Jack declared.

The foursome walked through the lobby and onto the grounds of the resort exchanging small talk as they went. Jack naturally ended up beside Chloe while Daniel and Lala walked just ahead of them.

"You look stunning," Jack remarked as they headed towards the restaurant.

"Thank you." Chloe smiled shyly. "At any rate I imagine I look better than the soggy sea creature you pulled out of the ocean yesterday."

Jack laughed before Chloe added: "By the way—you look pretty good yourself."

The Italian restaurant was situated near the beach and had an expansive, open patio that overlooked the water, several palm trees, and the surrounding shoreline. They sat outside next to a stone wall, the men on one side of the table and Chloe and Lala on the other. Soft Italian music emanated from the dining room indoors, but it couldn't drown out the rhythmic crashing of the waves. A candle sat in the middle of the table and lanterns provided soft light that competed with the pink, purple, and orange streaks in the sky that followed the sun's descent. It was a beautiful view and ambience, and a perfect way to top off a relaxing day.

"This is gorgeous." Chloe motioned towards the scenery. "Thank you for inviting us."

"My pleasure," Jack replied. "Although I have to admit it may have been out of a bit of self-preservation on my part."

Chloe gave him an inquiring look.

"If we went to your resort for dinner, I thought I might

have to eat in the nude. I figured that sight would probably put people off their meal," he teased.

The girls laughed, and Daniel interjected.

"I might have changed my hotel reservation had I known there was a nude resort next door," he joked.

"You would be surprised," Chloe remarked. "I was horrified at first, but you get used to it pretty quickly. Although Jack does have a point about the restaurant thing . . .," she trailed off.

"Yeah," Lala added, "It's one thing to walk around naked, go for a swim, or have a drink at the bar, but it's something entirely different to sit in a restaurant and eat a meal in the buff." She made a face. "We weren't sure what the protocol was and thought maybe clothes would be a requirement, but that did not turn out to be the case. I don't know if I'll ever recover from what I witnessed at the breakfast buffet yesterday. I can't believe they even *have* a buffet at a nude resort. Who thought that was a good idea? You go in for a sausage and the next thing you know, you've accidentally tried to dish up Albert from California's sausage. It's not good," she added to resounding laughter.

"But seriously, you guys should come over for dinner one night," Chloe followed up. "If nothing else, it's an interesting experience. One you'll probably never get otherwise. Unless you get into the whole naturist thing. Apparently, it's very liberating."

"We'd like that," Jack nodded. "It would be a nice change of pace to not have to dress up for dinner."

Lala chimed in: "Honestly, I've never felt fancier wearing flip-flops.

"That seals it," Jack said confidently. "I'm showing up in a bathrobe."

Chloe smirked. "And you'll *still* be overdressed."

Their dinner was companionable, and they chowed down on appetizers followed by mains. Lala, Daniel, and Jack went through two bottles of wine while Chloe stuck to sparkling water. She had taken Tylenol a couple of hours earlier and knew the pharmaceutical and alcohol didn't mix. Despite that, she had a warm glow inside that was entirely owing to the intoxicating effects of Jack.

After dinner they ordered dessert and then headed for a late nightcap at the lobby bar. Lala, Chloe was happy to see, had gotten on with Daniel famously. They exchanged warm hugs before they headed back to their resort with Daniel and Jack promising to join them at Costa Morpho the following day for dinner.

"Fuck," Chloe exclaimed when they reached their resort.

"What?" Lala asked.

"I forgot that the hotel arranged for us to go out on a catamaran tomorrow. Do you want to text Jack and see if he and Daniel want to join us?"

"Abso-fucking-lutely!" her friend exclaimed.

A few minutes later Lala's phone beeped.

"They're in!" She sounded excited. "This is going to be so much fun. Sea, sun, and sexy men!"

Chloe was equally as enthused. She couldn't wait to see Jack again. The spark between them was electric. Despite her best friend's teasing, she wasn't looking for a vacation fling. Nor was she looking at Jack as a potential partner. She enjoyed his company—immensely. And he had saved her life. But they had only spent a handful of hours together. On top of that, she was terrified at the prospect of opening herself up to the possibility of having her heart broken. Again.

Chloe relayed the details to them via Lala and then they went to bed. Meeting-time at the catamaran was at an ungodly 7 a.m., which despite being two hours behind the Eastern Time Zone they lived in would still make for an early morning. There was something about the fresh air and warm weather that left them feeling zonked.

Chapter 11:
Out to Sea

The catamaran that Costa Morpho had booked was taking them on a sightseeing tour. The concierge had promised them a day of snorkeling, swimming, sightseeing, and snacks. The only thing he said he couldn't guarantee was sun; that was in the hands of Mother Nature. But fortunately for them, the sky was clear and the water was calm.

Despite having nearly drowned two days before, Chloe was feeling okay about being on a boat. Although it might have had something to do with the 'boat' being a sixty-foot catamaran, which, owing to its structure, would sail through choppy waters like a hot knife going through butter.

As a precaution, Chloe was outfitted in a bright-orange life jacket even though she and Lala were still on the shore waiting. It was probably overkill, but she wasn't taking any chances. Even with her feet firmly planted in the sand.

The beach was empty, aside from she and Lala and a woman, wearing only a hat, who was combing for seashells.

The smell and sounds of the ocean invaded their senses and they watched the catamaran's crew launch their tender towards the shore. Lala and Chloe hadn't quite made their 7 a.m. call time that morning but, then again, neither had Jack and Daniel. Daniel texted Lala—she had exchanged numbers with him the night before—to let her know they would be a few minutes late. The two of them showed up carrying backpacks just as the small, motorized boat rode the waves onto the shore. The two-man crew pulled the boat farther ashore and the four of them threw their bags into the craft.

Daniel helped Lala into the boat before climbing in himself and, while the water was calm, Chloe was dismayed to find that she was hesitant to climb in.

Jack noticed and offered her his hand.

"You're okay," he said quietly, placing his hand on her arm in reassurance. "I won't let anything happen to you."

She grasped his outstretched hand, using it for balance as she stepped into the boat. He gave her hand a squeeze as he climbed in himself and took a seat beside her. With the life jacket and Jack's presence, Chloe felt reassured and the panic that had started rising in her chest settled down.

Daniel and Lala were busy flirting; Daniel scooped up a handful of ocean water and splashed Lala with it as the boat rocked with the motion of the waves.

"You'll be okay," Jack leaned in and repeated to Chloe while giving her a soothing pat on her hand.

In that moment, she felt relaxed.

Seconds later the motor rumbled; salt water splashed over the bow as the tender cut through the waves and headed towards the catamaran. Which could more accurately be described as a huge yacht.

From the shoreline it had seemed pretty big, but up close and meters from it, it looked positively massive. Of course, she knew it was all part of the resort's attempt to woo her and, in turn, result in them getting a good review. As she did every time she was on a luxury vacation, Chloe felt a sense of gratitude for her good fortune. She would never be able to afford luxury vacations like these on her editor's salary. But as an editor who exclusively traded in travel, the perks were incredible.

"Ola, señors and señoritas!" they were greeted by the captain, who introduced himself as Captain Ronaldo, once they were aboard the yacht. He gave them a tour of the catamaran and explained what they would be doing for the day. In the main interior the on-board chef presented them with a spread of fresh fruit, juice, bacon, eggs, and assorted bread and pastries. It was enough to feed a football team, and the four of them eagerly dug in.

"Mimosas?" the chef asked, to which Chloe and Daniel enthusiastically accepted.

The cork popped and bubbles started fizzing as the captain started up the yacht and they began a smooth glide across the water.

One of the crew members, who introduced himself as Carlos, put on some salsa music and after they finished breakfast, they headed for the front of the yacht with towels, drinks, and sunscreen.

"This is the life," Lala remarked, splayed out on a towel in her bikini.

The sun was already heating up the air, promising a sweltering afternoon, and they were intermittently misted with water as waves crashed against the boat. There hadn't been any wind on the beach that morning, but it was hard to tell if there was any out on the ocean, given the speed with which the catamaran was sailing.

The four of them chatted amiably while sitting on the front of the yacht with Chloe still wearing her life jacket. Before she knew it, they were pulling into an area that Carlos told them was called Monkey Head Rock. He pointed to the large rock formation that jutted out from the ocean. Chloe had to admit it was aptly named—it did bear an uncanny resemblance to a primate's head.

"It's a good place for snorkeling," Captain Ronaldo told them, maneuvering the catamaran close to a cove.

Chloe wasn't sure she was feeling up for snorkeling—the thought of putting her face in the water and relying on a plastic tube to keep her alive made her heartrate increase—but paddleboarding struck her interest.

The captain turned the engine off which allowed for the slapping of the waves and screeching of the seagulls to be fully heard. The sky was crystal clear and a bright, exuberant blue; Chloe watched as pelicans soared above the ocean and dove into it periodically to scoop up fish.

She closed her eyes and took a deep inhale, holding her breath for a few seconds before letting it out. She had never meditated before, but she imagined that this was the feeling that practitioners were talking about when they mentioned getting into a Zen state.

Her travel assignments were rarely stressful, but there was something lighter about this one. Notwithstanding the fact that two days ago she had almost died. Or maybe the lightness had something to do with that?

Carlos and the other crew members assembled snorkeling gear at the back of the boat and Daniel and Lala donned fins, goggles, and snorkels and jumped into the ocean. Jack had held back, cognizant that Chloe might not be feeling comfortable with the prospect of going into the water.

"I think I'm going to try the paddleboard," she told him.

Jack offered to join her.

"It's okay, you don't have to," she said, feeling self-conscious. "You can go snorkeling if you want, I'll be fine."

"I want to go with you," Jack said. "If you wanted to stay on the catamaran and not even go into the water, I would be okay with that too."

Chloe smiled as Carlos unhooked two blue paddleboards

and put them down on the platform.

Jack helped Chloe onto one of them and passed her a paddle. She stayed on her knees and waited for Jack to get on his before they began to paddle towards the cove where she could just make out Daniel and Lala's snorkels.

Ocean water splashed over her knees and Chloe squealed at the coldness.

"How are you doing? Are you okay?" Jack asked, aware that she might be having second thoughts.

"I think I'm okay." She sounded surprised. Which she was. Nearly drowning had been traumatic; she almost couldn't believe that just two days later she was already back in the water. "The water is just really cold."

"Good." Jack smiled. "Should we try to stand up?"

Chloe nodded. "Let's do it. I'm not sure if I have my sea legs though."

Jack stood up effortlessly as his paddleboard crested over the water and Chloe slowly maneuvered into a crouch, wobbling to try and keep her balance as she finally stood up.

She was surprised to find that it wasn't too difficult.

"Well done!" Jack clapped.

"I guess all of those yoga classes Lala dragged me to have paid off," she said wryly.

The water beneath them was crystal clear and they could see the sandy ocean floor, which was littered with rocks, seaweed, and coral.

"Look!" Chloe pointed excitedly. "A turtle!"

She was delighted to see the hard-backed creature glide through the water beneath them.

"He's pretty fast." Jack followed her gaze.

"He's pretty cute," she said happily.

They paddled around for a bit before pulling their boards together and linking up by holding onto each other's oars. Jack dangled his legs in the ocean while Chloe sat down with her knees up and wrapped her arms around them.

"Thanks again for inviting us today," Jack said. "We would probably be sitting at the pool for the fifth day in a row if you hadn't."

"I'm glad you and Daniel could come." She sounded sincere. Which she was. "It's great to be able to share the experiences."

There were a few moments of silence before Jack interjected.

"So," he said, sounding inquisitive. "Not to be too forward, but what's your story?"

"My story?" Chloe inquired.

"Yes—you work at a popular magazine; you're here on a work assignment with your best friend. You're smart, cultured, pretty—are you single?"

"Very," Chloe replied a little too quickly.

One of Jack's eyebrows raised in question.

"I got out of a long-term relationship seven months ago," she admitted. "Not by choice," she added by way of explanation.

"Ah, that explains it," he said regretfully. "I'm sorry. And I'm sorry I brought it up."

"No, not at all," Chloe brushed it off. "I was pretty broken for the first few months." She glanced over to the area where Daniel and her friend were snorkeling. "But Lala put me back together."

"She seems like a really good friend," Jack said sincerely. "When I talked to her on the phone, I thought she was going to have a breakdown she was so concerned about you."

"She and I have been through a lot together," she replied. "We've been friends since university. Her parents are both gone and she lost her brother to a drunk driver six years ago," Chloe twisted her mouth at the memory. "It was devastating for her. So you can see why she was so upset to hear that I almost drowned."

Jack looked shocked. "I'm sorry. That's horrible."

Chloe nodded in reply.

"What about you?" She shifted the subject.

"Me?" Jack paused. "Well, I was in sort of a similar situation to you actually," he said ruefully. "Maybe not quite the same. But a similar outcome. I was with someone for three years and had already proposed," he said wryly, "and then I caught her cheating on me with her ex-boyfriend."

Chloe's mouth dropped open in horror.

"Oh my god," she said with a grimace. "How awful."

Jack shook his head. "It was," he said dryly. "We'd already booked the venue, but I was able to get the deposit back. Fortunately. It destroyed me for a bit, but I've come out of it with a healthier outlook on things."

They sat there for a beat with their paddleboards following the motion of the ocean.

"And besides," Jack continued, "look at it this way—if all that hadn't happened, we wouldn't have met and I wouldn't have been there to save you from drowning."

Chloe smiled back. "Silver linings."

They held eye contact for a bit until Chloe looked away. She suddenly felt shy.

"Should we head back to the boat?" Jack asked, not wanting her to feel awkward.

"Yeah, let's," she said. "I think I'm ready for a cocktail."

She had forgone any Tylenol that morning despite the lingering pain. Whether it was the spa day, the great dinner, or just the effects of being almost two days out from the incident, she had woken up feeling much better this morning.

Daniel and Lala were still out snorkeling as she and Jack paddled back to the boat.

"How was the water?" Carlos asked as he grabbed their gear and pulled it back onto the catamaran.

"Gorgeous!" Chloe remarked. "We saw a turtle!"

"Lots of tortugas in this area," Carlos replied and asked if they had seen any fish.

"No," Jack replied. "I think we were too distracted talking to each other."

Carlos grinned.

"Are you ready for some drinks?" he asked.

"Definitely!" Chloe replied.

In the cabin Jack grabbed a beer while one of the crew members made Chloe an Aperol spritz. They were just tucking into some of the snacks that the chef had laid out when they heard Daniel and Lala laughing.

The sopping wet duo appeared in the cabin moments later, towels wrapped around their waists and dripping with water.

"You should have seen the fish!" Lala exclaimed. "They were so pretty! We even saw a puffer fish!"

"Ah, I'm so jealous," Chloe said, feeling genuine envy despite having no regrets about her choice to opt out of snorkeling. "Did you see the turtle?"

"Yeah, he swam right past us," Daniel chimed in. "Cute little guy."

They took a seat in the cabin and drinks from Carlos, after which the four of them clinked their cocktails together and toasted to adventure and new beginnings.

Chloe liked that. It sounded promising.

The afternoon was spent chilling on the front of the catamaran, having drinks, sightseeing, and talking. Lala took photos and video for Chloe who had remembered that morning that she was in Costa Rica for work and needed photo and video content for Instagram. Unable to document her trip without a phone, she had asked Lala to step in as her official photographer.

By the time the catamaran started its journey back to their resort, Chloe was feeling content. More than content, if she admitted it to herself—she was feeling exhilarated.

This is what life should be, she thought. This was what life *had* been before the breakup. Despite feeling like Liam had done irreparable damage to her, several months later she was happy to find that she was able to enjoy life. It was an easy promise that people had made to her during her spiral into depression, but it wasn't something that, at the time, she could either comprehend or believe.

They four of them parted in the lobby of Costa Morpho that evening with hugs all around. For Chloe, it also ended with a promise from Jack to spend the next day at her resort. There were things she still needed to see and experience in order to write up a proper review and Jack, ever the gentleman, offered to join her. Even after she reminded him that he may be subjected to some sights he didn't want to see.

"Naked yoga," Chloe had warned, "is not for the weak of heart."

He had pondered that for a second.

"That doesn't seem too bad," he said reasonably, before his face changed to mock alarm. "Oh wait, I didn't take into account the downward dog. On second thought," he said dryly, "maybe naked yoga isn't for me."

Chloe giggled.

"There's always naked water volleyball or naked aerobics," she suggested helpfully.

"I'll take either one over naked yoga. But, if you *have* to suffer through it, I'll happily suffer through it too."

In their room later, Chloe asked Lala if she was going to join them. She happily declined, knowing that Jack would be coming to spend the day at Costa Morpho.

"I mean, if you had to do it all alone, I would come with you, but since Jack's joining, I think I might go spend the day doing . . . something else . . .," she trailed off.

Chloe had a bit of an idea as to what that something else might be.

"Would that something else maybe be named Daniel?" she asked innocently.

Lala let out a laugh.

"Guilty as charged. He invited me to come over to their resort when he found out Jack was coming to ours. Bit of a partner swap. It actually seems pretty fitting really, given where we're staying."

"La, our resort is for naturists, not swingers," Chloe snorted. "Big difference."

"Minor details." Lala waved her hand. "All I know is that Daniel is shredded like a bag of lettuce, and I have a sudden craving for a salad."

Chloe burst out laughing. Lala wasn't exaggerating. She had gotten a good look at Daniel when he had come in, shirtless, from snorkeling. The phrase 'sculpted like a statue' came to mind.

"Just promise me you won't elope," Chloe teased. "He did *just* get divorced."

"Please," her friend brushed off Chloe's comment. "I'm impulsive, Chlo, not insane."

"I seem to recall someone wanting to marry the bartender after one sip of his drink," Chloe said thinking back to the other morning.

"I was dehydrated," Lala said slyly. "Speaking of—Daniel is a walking thirst trap." She fanned herself with her hand.

Chloe laughed.

"You are impossible."

Lala winked. "And you love me for it." She stood up and headed for her bedroom. "Night, Chlo!"

Past

Chapter 12:
A Friend in Need

"Jesus."

That was the first word out of her mom's mouth when she saw her.

Chloe wasn't sure if it was a comment on her appearance or an urging for her to find him. Although given what had greeted her in the mirror that morning, she was pretty sure it was the former. Her appearance could accurately be described as *The Walking Dead* meets *Rocky*.

In addition to being unable to catch any restful sleep, she also hadn't found the motivation to shower. Which wasn't doing her hair or her face any favours. Her outfit didn't help anything either. A large coffee stain spread across the front of her gray sweatshirt and her similar-coloured sweatpants were tinged with flecks of food.

The look on her mom's face said everything her one-word utterance didn't, and she immediately gathered Chloe into the kind of hug that only moms are capable of. The all-consuming, all-loving, safety-filled kind that really lets you know just how much they care.

"Honey," she said softly, "I am so sorry."

Chloe collapsed into her mom's arms and cried while her mom comforted her. The next thing she knew a steaming mug of tea was cupped in her hands and she was sitting on the couch in her living room.

Her mom asked questions about the breakup, but Chloe brushed them off—she had discussed it ad nauseam with her friends that week and wanted to take her mind off it. The scene at Opus was on constant replay in her head and the last thing she wanted to do was to spend the next few hours wallowing in it again.

Which was easier said than done.

Her mom graciously acquiesced and, sensing that Chloe didn't have the mental capacity to respond in anything more than an affirmative 'hmm', 'no way', and 'that's funny' manner, she talked. And talked. And talked.

Two hours later, Chloe was all caught up on the gossip about the neighbourhood, friends, family, and work. Her cousin Tracey, she was not surprised to hear, was engaged for the fourth time in almost as many years.

"We're placing bets as to how this one pans out," her mom said conspiratorially. "So let me know if you want in on the pool. Grandma Ryder has $100 on them not making it 'til Easter."

Normally, Chloe would have eaten it up. She loved hearing about the goings-on in other people's lives, especially Tracey's. As much as she liked her cousin, she was a bit deranged when it came to her love life. But the fog of despair that had settled over Chloe made it difficult for her to focus on much of anything.

Liam was still staying with Karam, but Chloe knew that it was only temporary. Technically, Liam owned their condo so she would have to give it back to him at some point. They hadn't communicated since the breakup, with the exception of Liam telling her via text a few days after he had dumped her that he was coming over to pick up a few things over his lunch hour.

Not that he had gone to Karam's with only the clothes on his back. No, no. Liam was smarter than that. He had packed a few things into his gym bag and had apparently dropped it off at his friend's place several days before he had dumped her.

Bastard.

How could he, she wondered, spend those few days sleeping next to her when he had every intention of breaking things off? Or maybe it had been going on for longer than that. Maybe he had been planning to break up with her for months. Had he just been keeping Chloe, his girlfriend, on the back burner while deciding if he wanted to pursue things with Sophia instead?

It hurt to think that her ex-partner might have been so Machiavellian towards her. So cruel.

Which was life, really. But that didn't mean she liked it.

Unwilling to leave her condo and not wanting to face the world, she had hidden in the bathroom before noon. When Liam came to grab his things, he had noticed the closed bathroom door with light peeking out from under it and he had given a hesitant knock on the door.

"Chloe?" he asked.

Her stomach had clenched and her throat tightened before she replied in a scathing manner.

"Go to hell."

Her voice was full of venom.

Present

Chapter 13:
When in Rome

"I wasn't sure what to wear," Jack said wryly. "But I figured the Four Seasons wouldn't take too kindly to me showing up in the lobby naked. I came to Costa Rica to see the sights. Which does not include the inside of a jail."

Chloe giggled.

"Don't worry, they don't force you to take your clothes off here."

Although, she thought to herself, she wouldn't much mind if they implemented a mandatory no-clothes rule just for Jack. She had had a good look at him the day they went out on the catamaran and his body was, in a word, banging. He was muscled, but not overly so, with the lean build of a soccer player and abs you could clean clothes on.

Lala had gone over to Daniel's resort for the day after double checking first to make sure Chloe would be okay.

"Of course!" Chloe said brightly. "I'm glad you're getting on with Daniel. We're here to relax and have fun so go and have some fun!"

"Will do, Chlo! As long as you take some of that advice for yourself." She sounded happy as she set off towards her salad.

Chloe smiled. She was sure she was going to have a fun time with Jack.

It was so pleasant, she thought, to feel that flicker of interest in someone. She had known, of course, from previous breakups that while the heartbreak felt like it would last for an eternity and that she would never be attracted to another man again, that time would pass and there would be someone who would ignite that fire. She had just been with Liam for so long that she had thought it might take years for her to feel that spark again.

"So, what do you have planned for us today?" Jack said lightly. "I know I said naked yoga isn't my thing, but if it's important for your work assignment, I'm in."

She smirked in reply.

"No yoga. But we do have lunch reservations, an aerobics session, and entertainment we need to check out tonight. Aside from that, I figured we could grab a cocktail and head down to the beach. Maybe play a bit of volleyball?"

"Sounds good," he said lightly. "I love volleyball. Just one question," he asked sounding a bit uncertain. "Do I have to take off my shorts?"

She patted him on the arm reassuringly.

"No." She smiled. "I promise you can keep your shorts on. Best to keep your sunglasses on too," she warned. "Even if you're not trying to stare, it takes your eyes a bit to adjust to all of the . . . exposure. It's a bit of a shock to the system."

"Noted," Jack nodded. "I will keep my sunglasses glued to my face. Hopefully I've gotten used to it by dinner, otherwise I'm going to look like a creep."

"Just remember rule number one," Chloe said in mock seriousness. "No gawking."

Jack shook with laughter.

"They actually have rules against perverts? This place really has thought of everything."

"It's a very classy resort," Chloe teased. "Nudity notwithstanding."

They grabbed two bottles of water from the bar at the pool, ordered a drink, and made their way down to the sand where the volleyball game was already underway.

Chloe's experience that everyone at the resort was very friendly was also borne out by the people who invited them to join. She and Jack wound up on opposite teams, which made for a fun competition. The players, with the exception of one man, skewed older and the atmosphere was gregarious. Players high-fived each other and gave teammates claps of support.

It didn't take long for Chloe to discover that Jack was vicious on the court—he looked like he could have played Olympic-level volleyball.

Okay, that might be a bit of a stretch, but she was thrown off by how athletic he was. She, on the other hand, was less coordinated and much less skilled. But that didn't stop her from getting in a few good hits.

When the game ended, 15–21 for Jack's team, the players lined up and shook hands at the net. A big grin spread across Jack's face when he reached Chloe.

"You didn't tell me you were a world champion volleyball player!" she hissed jokingly.

"I didn't want to spoil it for you." He laughed. "I thought I might be able to impress you with my ball-handling skills."

"I'm not touching that one," she teased back.

They headed for the beach chairs where Jack and Chloe had left their things.

"Do you want to relax out here for a bit?" she asked.

"I'd love to," Jack nodded. "Let me just go up and get a couple of towels. And a refill?" He gestured to Chloe's empty glass.

"Yes, please!"

Relaxing in the sun for a 'bit' turned into two hours. It wasn't the typical sleep, read, or listen to music kind of relaxation. They spent the entire time turned towards each other, talking.

On the yacht the day before, she had found out that Jack was a lawyer who specialized in finance. Jack regaled her with stories of crazy clients and Chloe responded with tales of work trips gone awry.

"I missed two days of an assignment I was enroute to Croatia for," she told him. "My connecting flight in London got delayed so they sent me to Germany. I had to stay there overnight and was just about to board when they shut down the airport because of climate activists." She paused for dramatic effect. "They had glued themselves to the runway."

Jack laughed.

"Inconveniencing thousands of travelers. Not the best way to win people over to your way of thinking," he chortled.

"Not at all," Chloe agreed. "Not that I have much to complain about. There was one person on my flight who was trying to get to his mom who was in hospice. If that was me," she continued, "I think I would have marched down to the tarmac and ripped them off the runway myself."

Their talk soon turned to their families.

"My mom was a single parent, so we were pretty poor growing up," Jack said offhandedly. "She did the best she could, but we had to rely on foodbanks and charities to get by. It's something I've never forgotten. We were lucky there were people and places we could go to when things were tough, and money was tight." He shrugged. "So, I give back now by donating a few hours of legal work every month at a community clinic."

"I love that!" Chloe said with genuine admiration.

She really did. Jack was handsome and intelligent, he had a great sense of humor, he had saved Chloe's life, and he was *also* kind?

There was no way any man could be so perfect. What was he hiding? Were all of his exes 'crazy'? Did he leave toenail clippings all over the floor? Did he cry over dish soap commercials? The man seemed almost too good to be true. Or maybe, she thought, she had found one of those proverbial diamonds in the rough; a pearl in the sand, as the scenery would have it.

By noon, there was a marked feeling of intimacy between the two of them. It was funny how that sometimes happened. You meet someone new and unexpectedly hit it off; the next thing you know, it feels like you've known them your entire life. That was how it felt with Jack.

Not that she was fooling herself thinking that it might turn into anything. If there was one thing she had learned from her relationship and subsequent breakup with Liam, it was not to daydream and posit about the future. It was more important to appreciate things for what they are and not for what they could be.

And appreciate Jack and the time they were spending together, she did. If his attentiveness and happy demeanor was anything to go by, it seemed he was having just as much fun as she was.

Their lunch reservations were for Costa Morpho's American restaurant, Oak. To outsiders it might have seemed like an odd type of cuisine to be offering, but when one took in the proximity of North America to Costa Rica, it made a lot of sense. Especially given most people Chloe had spoken to or heard talking seemed to be American or Canadian, which had even included a few French-Canadians.

"What's the protocol?" Jack whispered conspiratorially as they walked inside. "Surely they don't allow people to eat in the nude?"

Chloe smirked in reply. Allow people to eat in the nude Costa Morpho did, as Jack was about to find out.

After they were seated, she looked across the table at Jack and was pleased that he seemed to be taking it in stride. She had a chicken salad with a side of fries, while Jack had a burger. The food was just as good as their conversation, which was to say—it was great.

The waiter cleared away their plates and Jack leaned back in his chair.

"That hit the spot," he said appreciatively. "What's on the agenda now?"

"Well," Chloe said mischievously, "I hope you're ready to work off that burger."

"Aerobics?" Jack grimaced.

"Aerobics," she grinned and nodded.

The group workout session was held on the cement pad near the pool where Chloe had seen guests taking salsa lessons earlier in the week. There were five other people aside from her and Jack as well as an instructor who was wearing black shorts and a resort-branded t-shirt.

"I have to warn you," Jack whispered as the instructor turned on some dance music, "I'm coordinated when it comes to sports, but I'm hopeless when it comes to choreography."

"Two left feet?" Chloe teased. She couldn't wait to see him in action.

"Two rights," he shot back. "And they're both wrong."

The instructor introduced herself as Maria and started barking instructions while moving her body. The handful of participants followed Maria's movements which amounted to some warm-up stretches.

"Arms way up high," Maria commanded. The seven people did as they were told.

As expected, everyone aside from Jack, Chloe, and the instructor were not wearing clothes. She glanced over at Jack as Maria barked at them to lunge and saw a twinkle of humour in his eyes.

He hadn't been joking when he said he was uncoordinated Not that aerobics was exactly dancing, but the movements did require you to pay attention to choreography. It wasn't so much that Jack lacked rhythm—he seemed to have that in spades. It seemed more like he lacked the ability to follow the sequence of steps.

Chloe giggled to herself as she followed Maria's movements and tried to keep her eyes off the other participants. If her mind had been boggled at the way salsa dancing caused a naked body to move, her mind was blown by the movement induced by aerobics. Despite her horror at the nudity earlier in the week, which she was now putting down to a serious case of culture shock, she was starting to have a new appreciation for the folks who went to these kinds of resorts. With the constant bombardment of impossible beauty standards, weight-loss adverts, and flawless bodies, there was something refreshing about being surrounded by people who were, literally, comfortable in their own skin.

Which was also ironic given where she worked. *Strut* tended to deal in curated perfection and tall, nary-an-ounce-of-fat-on-them types of models. It might be something, she reflected, she could touch on in her article. While she had been seriously gobsmacked for the first twenty-four hours at the resort, Costa Morpho would be getting a glowing review.

"Gracias, señoritas and señor!" Maria thanked the participants who were now all hot and sweaty. Jack suggested a dip in the pool to cool down and, in spite of Chloe's earlier reservations about sharing the same water as a bunch of skinny dippers, she happily agreed.

Jack changed into the swim shorts he had brought along and Chloe took off her dress to reveal a bright-pink bikini.

She was surprised to find that once she and Jack were in the water, she didn't give the people around them a second thought. Jack, in fact, and despite his teasing, had seemed to adjust to the environment far faster than her. He seemed to have a 'go with the flow' type of personality, which she really liked. It occurred to her that Liam would not have taken to the resort so easily. In fact, she could have seen him abandoning her for the resort next door and refusing to spend any time at Costa Morpho.

Not that she was comparing Jack to Liam. It was just one of many interesting observations that had popped into her head over the past couple of days. Both men were handsome, smart, and successful, but they were also very different in a myriad of ways.

She and Jack swam around and cooled down for a bit before getting out of the water and drying off in the sun. Jack's wet muscles glistened in the lounger and Chloe found she was having a hard time adhering to Costa Morpho's number-one rule—no gawking.

As the sun began to set, she and Jack shared cocktails in the lobby. They found a corner with squishy furniture and soaked up the air conditioning while they continued getting to know each other. Jack asked her so many questions— about her work, her life, her childhood, her friends, her family. How did she come to be a writer? What were her hopes and dreams? Her values and her beliefs?

There seemed to be a genuine interest on his part in truly understanding her and it was a feeling that was entirely mutual.

It occurred to her as she was telling him about how she hoped to one day write a book about all her funny travel stories, tips, and tricks that Liam had never asked her some of those things.

Odd, she thought, how something can seem so perfect when you're together, but perceptions can change with the benefit of time and distance.

Had her and Liam's relationship really been all that great?

Not that she was deluding herself into thinking that a

relationship with Jack was where things were heading.

Quite the opposite, really.

She was enjoying getting to know him and spending time together, but what it was, in her estimation, was two individuals finding themselves brought together by happenstance who also happened to find that they liked one another's company.

For right now, that was enough for Chloe.

"You said earlier we had to check out some entertainment tonight," Jack said a little while later. "What is it?"

Chloe twisted her mouth to the side.

"Believe it or not," she said wryly, "but it's actually a talent competition."

Jack snorted and shook his head in good humour.

"Remember," Chloe teased, "it's important for my work!"

"It's all good, Chlo," he smiled.

Her stomach tightened at his casual use of her nickname. Something about it gave her a happy feeling inside.

"I can't wait to tell Daniel about our day." Jack shook his head. "My friends are never going to believe me."

Privately, Chloe thought her friends were never going to believe her either. About Jack, her near drowning, or the resort.

Twinkle lights spiraled around the trunks of the palm trees that lined the darkened path to the pool. The cement pad where Chloe and Jack had taken the aerobics class earlier was now outfitted with rows of chairs that reached all the way to the bar. Almost all of them were occupied with people who had drinks in their hand, and fanny packs, purses, and bags hanging from their chairs. One woman, Chloe noticed, was wearing a bright-pink wig, and one man was wearing a top hat.

Facing the chairs was an elevated stage that had black fabric curtaining the bottom and a tall red-velvet curtain that provided a backdrop for the performers. A spotlight flooded the empty stage with bright light, and loud salsa music pumped through the air.

Jack and Chloe grabbed two seats at the bar and ordered up a drink.

"I can't tell you the last time I took in a talent show," Jack said after taking a drink of his beer. "I think it might have been in sixth grade. I don't go to a lot of resorts—is this typical?" he inquired.

"No," Chloe shook her head. "I saw one at a family resort in Cabo, but that was years ago. They usually offer some kind of entertainment—cultural shows, singing, dancing—those kinds of things. I was in Panama one year over Christmas and got to see a *very* saucy version of *The Nutcracker*," she trailed off.

Jack raised an eyebrow. "Do tell."

"Picture this—Clara in a red sequin thong bikini gyrating on the Rat King like it was Saturday night at a strip club."

Jack started laughing. "Sounds like quite the cultural experience. Kind of like how we put our own spin on Chinese and Mexican food in North America. They gave *The Nutcracker* a Latin twist."

Chloe smiled and had a sip of her drink.

Suddenly, the salsa music stopped, and a voice came from the speakers.

"Bienvedidos damas y caballeros!"

She and Jack turned towards the stage where a Costa Morpho staffer in a black suit stood with the microphone.

"Welcome, ladies and gentlemen!" he repeated in English. "To Costa Morpho's talent night! How's everybody doing?!" he said enthusiastically. There was a smattering of clapping and a few hollers from the crowd.

"Tonight," he continued in accented English, "we have some very special talents to show you from Costa Morpho guests. So, please sit back and enjoy the show! For our first act, I would like to call up on stage a Señor Diego Guzman!"

The audience clapped and a heavy-set Latin-looking man stood up from his chair and ambled onstage. The MC handed him the microphone and Diego Guzman stood in the spotlight in all his naked glory. His black hair and mustache looked like they had been combed with grease, and his girthy midsection covered up his groin.

For that, Chloe was thankful.

Seconds later a song that sounded classical in nature started playing and Diego, quite unexpectedly, accompanied it with his baritone voice. His opera singer's vocals cut above the music and his body tensed and quivered as he hit different notes. It was actually pretty impressive.

Chloe, who had no idea what to expect from Costa Morpho's guests, clapped along enthusiastically when Diego took a bow.

She looked at Jack; he was also clapping.

"I have to say," he said in a low voice. "Opera isn't my thing, but he has a great voice."

A middle-aged woman took to the stage next with a flute and played a Top 40 song mash-up from the previous decade. Following her, a bald man juggled oranges while delivering a monologue from *Hamlet*. That one was a little weird, but at the end, Chloe clapped politely along with the rest of the guests. Following that, a trio of ladies showed off a salsa dance they had learned earlier in the week.

She and Jack applauded politely along with the rest of the crowd and chatted between performers. Just as the woman wearing a pink wig stepped on stage, Jack leaned over to Chloe.

"I'll be right back," he said, setting down his beer. "I have to run to the washroom."

"Okay, but hurry back!" Chloe implored. "You don't want to miss the guy with the top hat—I think he might do some magic tricks."

Jack shot her a grin and headed out.

Three performances later Jack still hadn't come back, and Chloe was starting to worry. He should have been back by now—the bathrooms were just around the corner. Had he gotten lost or had something happened? Her mind wandered and it popped into her head that there was also the possibility that he hadn't really enjoyed their day, and he had decided to ditch her. The cringeworthy talent show might have just been the final straw.

She dismissed the thought as soon as it entered her brain, but there was a small feeling of unease in her stomach. She hadn't known Jack very long and she didn't know him very well. She thought she had known Liam inside and out and look what had happened with him. People were full of surprises.

If Jack had ditched her and gone back to his resort it would sting. But she also knew she could deal with it. After all, if she could make it through a devastating heartbreak and have the courage to venture out into the ocean two days after nearly drowning, she could handle being stood up.

She was pulled from her thoughts when the MC walked on stage and took the microphone from a gray-haired lady.

"Let's have a round of applause for Señora Bridges," the MC said, clapping as best as he could with one hand. Chloe joined in the applause with the rest of the audience. "Gracias Señora Bridges!"

The lady returned to her seat and the MC continued.

"Up next, we have a very special performance," the MC said playfully. "A last-minute entry from a Señor Jack Fraser!"

Chloe gasped as the audience burst into applause again and the MC went behind the curtains. The giant spotlight was trained on the empty stage and there was silence as the crowd waited for the next act.

Jack had signed up for the talent show? Her Jack? He was seriously going up on stage?

Suddenly, Jack's voice, amplified by the microphone, came from somewhere behind the curtain.

"Testing, testing," he paused. "Can everyone hear me?" The crowd responded with a muttered "yes" and Jack continued.

"Alright," he said lightly. "I'd like to dedicate this performance to the beautiful and captivating Chloe Ryder. Chloe," he continued, "this one's for you."

The crowd let out a collective "oooooh" and a deep blush blossomed across Chloe's face.

The music started up and her jaw dropped open. He *wasn't*. Jack absolutely was *not* doing this. Was he?

The opening bars of Right Said Fred's "I'm Too Sexy" started playing and Chloe burst into a fit of laughter.

Jack, still hidden behind the curtain, sang the opening line then flung it open and strutted on stage in a mock sexy walk. Chloe nearly fell off her barstool. Blue, red, and yellow lights came to life and bathed Jack in a disco of colour—it almost looked like a professional pop performance.

"I'm too sexy for my shirt, too sexy for my shirt," Jack crooned while playing to the audience. They whooped, cheered, and catcalled, with their support growing louder as Jack undid the buttons on his shirt with one hand.

Chloe could not believe what she was seeing. Jack, with the swagger of a Bachelorette contestant, was fully committing to the bit—stripping on stage in front of sixty or so strangers without any hint of self-consciousness or shame.

"I'm too sexy for your party," he sang while he waved his shirt around his head before casting it off into the crowd.

The audience roared and she heard someone yell, "Take it off!" Chloe was laughing so hard she could barely breathe.

As the chorus started, Jack strutted around the stage, swiveling his hips in an exaggerated manner as he belted out the lyrics. God, she wished she had her phone right now to record this. Lala would be so pissed to have missed it.

"I'm too sexy for my car, too sexy for my car," Jack sang seductively.

Out of nowhere, a bright-blue feather boa sailed onto the stage from the audience and Jack picked it up and put it around his bare shoulders. He gave it a shimmy and then twirled one end dramatically in his hand.

Mercifully, he kept the rest of his clothes on, and Chloe, between laughs, joined in the chorus of cheers. On the final verse, the lights went up and the audience gave him a standing ovation. Tears of laughter streamed down Chloe's face, and Jack, with a large smile on his face, caught her eye and took a theatrical bow.

A short woman walked up to the stage and Jack handed her the boa before he jumped off and headed towards Chloe. It took a minute for him to work his way back due to the number of people trying to chat with him, and him trying to find his shirt.

"I cannot believe you did that!" Chloe squealed with laughter as he eased onto the bar stool beside her.

Jack, with his shirt back on and buttoned up, shot her a grin. "Ah, I figured I'd have some fun and liven things up a bit."

"That was hilarious." Her eyes twinkled. "I would never have the guts to get up there in front of a group of people and sing like that."

Jack grabbed his beer and leaned back in his chair, totally at ease.

"It's nothing really. If you can't laugh at yourself, how can you laugh at anybody else?"

He had a point.

"You'll miss out on so many things if you let feelings of self-consciousness get in the way. You are funny, beautiful, totally fun company, you have a kick-ass career, and you're smart. You are the last person who should be feeling self-conscious about anything."

He clinked his glass against hers and maintained eye contact. Inside, Chloe felt a tug deep in her stomach. It wasn't butterflies this time, nor was it flip-flops. It was impossible lightness and a heavy dose of adrenaline. A feeling of electricity; it felt like something invisible was tethering them together and Chloe didn't want to look away.

"Refresh your drinks?" The bartender's voice cut through them and their gaze broke apart.

Chloe smiled and shook her head while Jack ordered another. When the bartender left there was an awkward silence and Chloe wondered if, like her, he was grappling with the electricity she had felt between them moments before.

She broke the silence first.

"I have to admit, I was starting to get worried about you," she said lightly. "I thought maybe you had gotten lost or hurt or something. It crossed my mind at one point that maybe you'd ditched me . . .," she trailed off. "I'm glad you didn't."

Jack chuckled.

"Trust me, the last thing I want to do right now is ditch you," he said sincerely.

They parted ways a short time later in Costa Morpho's lobby. There was laughter on their lips, a glint in their eyes, and before Jack left, he gave her a deep, heated kiss. It was exactly what she had hoped for and better than she could have anticipated.

Before Jack got into his Uber, he cupped his hand around her face.

"Thank you, Ms. Ryder," he said in mock formality, "for the unbelievable day." The smile on his face reached his eyes. "Seriously, Chloe. Thank you. It was one of the best days I've had in a while."

Chloe beamed back at him.

"Thank you for coming and for being such a good sport. I don't know if I'll ever be able to get the picture of you shirtless and gyrating on stage with a feather boa out of my head," she teased before giving him a hug goodbye. "I really enjoyed myself too."

"Listen," Jack said, "I know it's last minute, but would you be game for going to Coco Beach tomorrow?" he asked. "I keep hearing that it's a cute little beach town and I thought we could check it out."

"I would love to," she replied immediately. There was nothing more she wanted than to spend another day with Jack.

Past

Chapter 14:
Chloe's Terrible, Horrible,
No Good, Very Bad Day

It had been two months since the breakup and Lala was on her way over. She had been a bastion of support for Chloe, suddenly single, who was eternally grateful for it.

The night the breakup had happened Chloe didn't tell anyone. Emotional devastation aside, she also had feelings of extreme embarrassment to contend with. She had kept the state of her and Liam's relationship a secret for several months, sweeping her worries and concerns under the rug while projecting to friends and family that everything was rosy. Perhaps most embarrassing of all was that she had actually believed that Liam might propose to her that evening. That belief had been so strong that she had hinted to a few of her friends that there was a good chance there would be a change in her relationship status that night.

Which there had been. Just not the kind she had been hoping for. Instead of being upgraded to fiancée and future wife, she had been downgraded to Chloe, party of one. The embarrassment was almost too much for her to take.

Her first phone call the next morning had been to Lala. Her friend had barely been able to understand her on the phone and she had come by quickly afterwards. Alejandra and Opal had shown up a little while later and they supported Chloe during her emotional breakdown.

A hurried knock at the door alerted Chloe, wearing the same pajamas she had gone to bed in two nights ago, that her friend had arrived. She went to open it.

The minute she saw the look on Lala's face she knew something was wrong.

"What is it?" Chloe looked at her with caution. She didn't know what Lala was going to tell her, but she knew it was going to be bad.

"Give me a second," Lala said, stepping inside to give her friend a big hug. "How are you doing?"

Chloe's eyes began to mist. What was it about people expressing concern about her that made her want to cry?

"Oh, you know . . .," Chloe trailed off noncommittally.

Lala stepped back for a second and furrowed her brow.

"Um, Chlo?" she said hesitantly. "I don't want to judge you or anything, but have you changed out of those pajamas since Thursday?" She glanced at the clothes that Chloe had not, in fact, changed out of since Thursday. Lala had come over that night with Häagen-Dazs and a board game.

Chloe grimaced and Lala shot her a pitying look.

"Okay, I'm not going to judge, but I will implore you to consider the benefits of a shower and clean clothes." She paused. "Or at least rotating out your pajamas."

Lala headed for the fridge and pulled out a diet soda before taking a seat at the dining table. Chloe followed and took the seat beside her. She wasn't onto the wine yet as, despite being in a hole of depression so deep she couldn't see sunlight, she had made it a rule for herself that she was not to indulge in any alcoholic cocktails before 5 p.m. Unless, of course, it was a statutory holiday or a weekend. Then she relaxed this rule to 1 p.m.

"What is it?" Chloe, again, asked cautiously.

The diet soda tab opened with a metallic click and Lala took a sip.

"I don't even know how to tell you this," Lala said with trepidation. "I feel *awful* telling you this." She paused a beat. "But I don't want you finding out from someone else or finding out when you're alone." She took a deep breath.

Chloe's heartbeat sped up and she braced herself for what was coming. She was pretty sure at this point that she didn't want to know.

Lala continued.

"I have it on good authority, and by 'good authority', I mean I saw it with my own eyes and then confirmed it with one of Liam's friends."

Chloe's stomach turned in knots.

"What did you see and what did you confirm?" Chloe's voice shook. She didn't want to know what Lala saw and confirmed. She *really* didn't want to know.

"Do you really want me to tell you?" Lala looked concerned.

"He's with Sophia, isn't he?" Chloe's heart beat loudly in her ears.

A pitying look crossed her friend's face, and she nodded.

"He is," Lala sounded pissed. "That total trash monster of a man. Moved in with her, the bastard."

Chloe said nothing for a minute and then she burst into tears while Lala leaned over and comforted her friend.

Hearing that Liam no longer wanted to be with her, that he didn't want a future together had been brutal. It had kept her in an emotional spiral for more than two months. But somehow, hearing that her suspicions had been correct and that he was with the woman she had spent so much time concerned about made it that much worse.

They were living together.

Two months after breaking up with Chloe, her ex-boyfriend was actually living with another woman.

Her heart, which was already broken into a million pieces, turned to dust.

Present

Chapter 15:
Life's a Beach

Lala was lounging on the couch when Chloe emerged from her room the next morning. She hadn't seen Lala before she went to bed, but she looked refreshed and perky despite having come home later than Chloe.

"Morning, La." Chloe yawned as she headed to the coffee maker.

"Morning!" Lala sounded happy.

"How was your night with Daniel?" Chloe raised her voice above the loud grumbling of the coffee machine. She frowned at it. It was really something—they could put a man on the moon, but they couldn't figure out how to design a quiet coffee maker.

Lala let out an exaggerated, dreamy sigh.

"My night was great. Spectacular. Fantastic," she said in earnest before dropping her head back dramatically. "All of the above. We had an amazing day in Coco Beach and then went back to his resort for dinner. The highlight of the night was dessert. Which we had in his room. He's delicious by the way."

Chloe snorted.

"I knew you two would get on. Did you and Daniel make any other plans?"

Lala shook her head. "No. He's coming over today for a few hours, but we don't have anything planned. I like him. Grade-A vacation fling. I'm sorry to say it, Chlo, but I am so glad you almost drowned," she said matter-of-factly before pausing. "Wait, I don't think that came out right." A befuddled look crossed her face.

Chloe laughed. "No, I get what you're saying. I feel the same way about Jack. Who knew that doing something so stupid could result in something so good."

"Amen." Lala leaned back on the couch. "So, what happened with you and Jack?"

Chloe knew what Lala was really asking. She told her friend about what they had done the day before and how it had ended with a kiss and the two of them making plans to go to Coco Beach.

"Well, if you end up anything like Daniel and me last night, I'm going to start using 'Coco Beach' as a euphemism for 'between the sheets'."

Chloe laughed. She had no expectations of anything happening between her and Jack. Not that she would be opposed to it. She was just excited to spend more time together.

"Coffee?" she asked her friend, who nodded eagerly in reply.

Chloe poured out two cups before opening up her laptop where she found an email waiting from Jack.

Coco Beach, the subject line read. She smiled as she skimmed the first line of his email which thanked her for "a truly amazing day and kiss I can't get out of my head." He proposed a 10 a.m. meet-up time and Chloe sent back a message confirming and letting him know she would pick him up. As a special guest of Costa Morpho, she had access to a car and a driver, which she was going to make full use of that day.

She and Lala went for a quick breakfast where they agreed to meet up for dinner that night with their vacation dates. It was their last night in Costa Rica and Lala wanted to make the most of it.

"I have a feeling I might stay over at Daniel's tonight," Lala said casually. "So, you'll have our little bungalow all to yourself." She raised her eyebrows suggestively.

"La!" Chloe chided her.

"I'm just saying!" Lala said defensively. "If you want to take advantage of the space, it's all yours."

She left Lala at the entrance to Costa Morpho and gave her a hug before getting into the car. As the door closed behind her she heard Lala yell, "She's going to Coco Beach!"

Chloe smiled and shook her head.

Several minutes later she and Jack were in the back of the car, enroute to the town. It was a twenty-minute drive, which gave them time to chat.

"Lala had a great time with Daniel." Chloe smiled. "She told me all about it over breakfast."

The vehicle dropped them off at the farthest point of the town—the beach—where the main road ended. Like the other beaches she had seen in the Central American country, Coco Beach was beautiful. It was also much busier than the ones at her and Jack's respective resorts. Here, locals mingled with tourists—laying on the beach, building sandcastles, snacking, drinking, and swimming as the sun beat down above them.

Like all the days she had experienced in Costa Rica so far, she couldn't have asked for a nicer one.

They grabbed a coffee at a quaint outdoor restaurant just steps from the sand and spent the next couple of hours wandering around the tourist shops and checking out various trinkets, clothing, and souvenirs.

Chloe picked out a couple pairs of earrings and Jack bought a shirt before they found themselves amongst a slew of restaurants and bars on the main street.

"Lunch?" Jack asked as they approached the line of noisy establishments.

"Good idea." Chloe nodded. She was famished and feeling just a bit dehydrated from a combination of the sun and all the walking around. They stopped into the oddly named Z-Lounge, which appeared to function as an open-air restaurant during the day and a nightclub in the evening.

A ping sounded on Jack's phone, and he glanced at the screen.

"It looks like Lala and Daniel are out for dinner," he chuckled. "She just texted me that they've decided to eat in."

Chloe snorted.

"Well, I'm glad they're getting on," she shrugged.

"It's funny." Jack furrowed his brow. "I've known Daniel since high school and Lala is much more his type than his ex-wife. Strange how things happen. He goes away on vacation to celebrate being single—a few days later he meets your friend, and, boom, he's smitten."

"Smitten?" Chloe was taken aback. She thought Lala had been exaggerating with her description of her and Daniel's day, but maybe she was being serious. Goodness knew Lala was never one to dip her toe in the water. When it came to men, she went full cannonball, all the way.

Jack looked a bit abashed.

"Well, he hasn't come right out and said it, but I can read between the lines. And his eyes."

That *was* interesting. Lala's vacation fling might want something more. Either way, Chloe wasn't worried about it. When it came to men and matters of the heart, Lala could handle her own and then some. But Daniel's interest in Lala was definitely something Chloe would be passing along.

They passed the afternoon by walking through the town and stopping into little bars along the street. When the sun began to go down, they headed for The Lobster House restaurant which was on the main street.

The hostess seated them at a corner table that provided privacy, quietness away from the busy restaurant, and a phenomenal view of the setting sun.

The smell of ocean air coursed through Chloe's nose as the twinkle lights strung above their table swayed in the wind. She zoned out thinking about what a great day she had had when her gaze found its way to Jack's face.

A playful grin was tugging at the corners of his mouth and there was a twinkle in his eye.

"What?" She smiled at him.

"You." His smile widened.

"Me?" Her brow furrowed momentarily.

"Yes, you," Jack replied. "You look beautiful sitting there with the sun setting behind you and total contentment on your face."

Chloe instantly felt her skin flush. "You're making me blush," she said shyly.

He smiled even wider.

"Besides," she teased, her face still flushed red, "how do you know I'm totally content?"

Jack tilted his head.

"I don't know," he said thoughtfully. "There's something about how your shoulders seem relaxed, and the calm look on your face. It seemed like something was weighing on you before and whatever it was isn't anymore."

She smiled gently. He wasn't wrong.

Their meals came a short time later and the seafood was divine.

"This lobster is amazing," Chloe sighed. "This day has been amazing."

Jack reached over and gave her hand a gentle, reassuring

squeeze. He echoed her thoughts. "It really has been."

On the car ride home, Chloe asked Jack to come to Costa Morpho for a drink.

"I'd love to," he grinned, and they had a late-night nightcap at the tiki bar.

Chloe, exhausted by the sun and all the walking they had done, started yawning.

"You're tired," Jack said softly. "Let's get you back to your room."

Chloe happily accepted.

Their footsteps echoed on the ground over the sound of insects chirping, and tall lamps lit the way down the darkened path. When they reached her villa, she turned to Jack to thank him for such a wonderful day.

He leaned in for a kiss—a phenomenal one at that—and Chloe melted before she pulled away with a smile.

"Do you want to stay over?" she asked shyly.

Jack kissed her again.

"I'll take that as a 'yes'," she grinned as she unlocked the door to her bungalow and led Jack inside.

Chapter 16:
What Dreams May Come

Soft snores broke through Chloe's dream and she opened her eyes slowly. A feeling of relaxation washed over her as she reflected on the previous day. She and Jack had had an absolute blast. There were no awkward moments, no moments where she felt ill at ease; for whatever reason, the two of them just worked.

She rolled over, knowing full well she was a mess of makeup, having not washed it off before she fell asleep. Jack, who appeared to have a smudge of lipstick on his cheek, was snoring peacefully beside her.

The night had been nothing short of electric. And while she knew that the butterflies she felt could signal a warning— they usually came about when people met someone they were crazy about—she was enjoying the feeling.

Her mom's cringe-worthy advice to get over someone by getting under someone else did have an element of truth to it, Chloe acknowledged. Although she knew it wouldn't have worked the same way if she had gone out to a bar and picked up the first man who looked her way. For her it took time, and healing. Not to mention meeting the right person.

She took a deep breath, and a small smile spread across her face as she listened to the soft snoring of the handsome man beside her. They had ended the night in bed after a wine-fueled bubble bath. Fluffy bathrobes lay discarded on the floor on either side of the bed and half-full wine glasses sat on their nightstands. The high thread-count sheets and velvet-soft blanket made her feel like she was lying on a cloud, and suddenly she was transported to a different time.

Liam was there, cuddling with Chloe on the couch in their condo. There was a ring on her finger and a baby girl in the next room.

She awoke with a jolt, her heart beating wildly.

It had been two months since she had had a Liam dream.

Nightmare, she corrected herself.

Although this nightmare had her feeling anything but bad. In fact, she was unhappy to find that the dream brought back a deep feeling of yearning, which gave her an entirely new set of issues to process. It was funny how your subconscious could do that to you. It could take one perfectly happy moment and throw a wrench in it.

Although, she reflected, maybe it had more to do with her mind further processing the breakup. Jack was the only person aside from Liam she had slept with in more than five years.

She fell asleep again and woke up a little while later to find Jack watching her sleep.

But not in a creepy way. In a sweet "I'm really into you and think you look adorable when you're unconscious" kind of way.

"Hi," he said softly as she breathed in deeply, a small smile playing around her mouth.

"Hi," she whispered back.

"You were snoring like a freight train," he said teasingly.

"Noooo," Chloe said in embarrassment.

Jack chuckled.

"You weren't. You were quiet as a church mouse," he said. "You look very sweet when you're sleeping," he observed.

Chloe blushed.

"Come here." He reached his arm up and she crawled over and nuzzled herself into the crook in his shoulder. Jack put his arm around her and planted a kiss on top of her head.

"Yesterday was great," he said.

"I had such a fun time," Chloe agreed.

There was a pause, and she could tell that Jack wanted to say something

"Listen, Chloe," he hesitated, "the last few days have been amazing. I don't know where this is going, but I really like you."

The butterflies in Chloe's stomach started to flutter.

"I really like you too," she said sincerely. "I'm so happy we met. Even if this is all it ends up being, I've had such a great time getting to know you this week."

"Well, I promise you I'm not going to ghost you." He squeezed her closely. "I want to see you when we're both back home."

Chloe smiled and snuggled in closer.

She suddenly heard the door to their bungalow open, which was followed by Lala's voice.

"Chlo?"

Chloe didn't respond for a second, unsure of what to say.

"Um, I'm in here—don't come in!" she added sounding guilty.

"Ohhh!" Lala's voice suddenly took on a playful tone. "I see a man's shoes. You went to Coco Beach!" she exclaimed loudly.

Chloe slapped her hand to her face and shook her head.

"Lala?" Chloe raised her voice through the door.

"Yes, Chlo?"

"I love you, but could you kindly fuck off for thirty minutes?"

There was a short burst of laughter before Lala replied.

"You got it, Chlo. I'm just going to grab my bathing suit. If you need anything, I'll be at the pool."

Several seconds later, Chloe heard the door to their villa close.

Jack left shortly after that with Chloe's number in his phone. She didn't have a phone to text him with, but that would be remedied as soon as she was back in Toronto.

"Have a safe flight, Chlo." He gave her a warm hug and a quick kiss before heading out.

"Thank you." She smiled. "I hope you and Daniel enjoy the rest of your trip."

He grinned back. "Something tells me we're going to enjoy it a whole lot less without you and Lala around."

Afterwards, Chloe packed up her bags, dropped them with the concierge, and headed to the pool.

She and Lala were stretched out on loungers soaking up their last opportunity to grab some rays. Chloe's carry-on bag sat beside her, and they both had lime margaritas.

Lala had given her a proper ribbing about Jack and then pressed her for all the details. She had also dished on her day with Daniel.

"This has been the best trip ever." Lala raised her glass in toast. "To best friends, beach days, and hot men!"

"Ladies," a sixty-something-year-old man walking by shot them a sexy smile, "I'm flattered."

The girls looked at each other in horror and then burst into giggles when the man, who was now walking with a lot more swagger, was out of sight.

They lay back down and Lala started scrolling on her phone.

Chloe's mind wandered to when she and Lala had first

arrived at the resort. A smirk came to her lips at the memory of how she and Lala had reacted upon realizing they were staying at a naturist resort. Despite initially being more than a little freaked out, Chloe had quickly gotten used to it and found all the other guests to be friendly and, surprisingly, pretty normal. Aside from the whole no-clothes thing. She still didn't understand their lifestyle but, she realized, she didn't have to. It all boiled down to respecting other people's choices even if they weren't her thing.

A thought suddenly struck her.

It was their last day at the resort, and while she had experienced most of what Costa Morpho had to offer, there was still one thing left.

"Lala?" She sat up and looked at her friend.

Lala turned her head and pulled up her sunglasses.

"What's up?"

"It's our last day here and all." She took a moment. "And I feel like there's still one thing we have to do."

Her friend gave her a quizzical look.

Chloe reached behind her back and undid the bow holding her bikini ties together before reaching for the tie around her neck.

"Yesssssss!" Lala said loudly. She pumped her fist in victory as Chloe pulled off her top and held it in the air. "She did it!!!"

This was it. She had done it. She was naked from her bikini bottoms up. She was Chloe—unbound and unwound—and she was feeling exhilarated.

She became aware all at once of people around her clapping and hollering in support of her carpe diem moment. Chloe blushed at the attention before taking a seated mock bow as Lala pulled her top off too.

"That's the spirit!" someone yelled from the pool.

"Solidarity, my friend," Lala said with a grin. "Fuck. When I think back to the state you were in in February, if someone had told me seven months later you would be topless at a nude resort after having a hot vacation fling, I would have called the psych ward."

Chloe smiled.

"It's thanks in no small part to you, La," she said gratefully. "Seriously. And I'm so happy you could come on this assignment."

"Hold on!" Lala said, struck with sudden inspiration. She unlocked her phone and then trained it on Chloe. "Smile, Chlo! For The Gram."

Chloe, sunglasses on her face, smiled wide and held her bikini top up high again as Lala clicked away.

"The girls are never going to believe this," Lala said. She turned the camera to selfie mode and snapped a topless pic of the two of them together. "Say 'no tan lines!'"

"No tan lines!" Chloe beamed.

*

Their flight left late that evening and as they waited for their car to the airport, Chloe felt a sense of melancholy. Being able to get away with her best friend, almost drowning, meeting an amazing man, and experiencing a naturist resort for the first time—it had been an unbelievable week and had given her a new lease on life. So why did she feel so sad?

The week had been transformational. That was exactly what she had hoped for but hadn't really believe would happen. Still, it was undeniable she was leaving Costa Rica as a different person than she had been when she arrived.

Maybe that was the reason for the melancholy, she thought. She was in mourning. For the old Chloe.

On the plane ride back in the nearly pitch-black cabin, Lala snored beside her. Soft rock emanated from her AirPods as she reminisced about the week. She was so grateful about the way things had turned out, both with her work assignment and with regards to her relationship with Liam.

Somehow, despite months of feeling hopeless and burdened by the knowledge that the future she had envisioned for herself was gone, she felt lighter.

Which seemed very odd.

But maybe it was a part of reaching acceptance. She had zero control over how things had panned out with her ex. The only thing she had control of was herself.

She was still living in Liam's condo as per the terms of their agreement, which Karam had negotiated on his behalf. Liam had agreed to let her stay there until she was able to secure something long-term and, truthfully, she hadn't been looking. Her ex hadn't made an issue of it, which she assumed was due to a guilty conscience, but Chloe finally felt like she was ready for a change. Whether that meant evicting her current tenant and moving back into her old condo, continuing to rent out her place while renting a different condo, or selling her condo altogether, she didn't know. But one thing she *did* know was that it was time for her to move out and move on.

Past

Chapter 17:
Cleaning out the Closet

"Open up, bitch!"

Chloe was startled by the expletive that accompanied the aggressive knocking on her door. Of course, she would recognize the voice anywhere. And it didn't tell her that she was the sudden target of a home invasion. The voice told her she was the sudden target of Lala.

Which was somehow even scarier.

"Coming!" Chloe yelled, unsure if her friend would be able to hear her.

She frowned as she looked at the space around her. Her condo, well, Liam's condo—he was still living with Sophia and hadn't been in any rush to evict his former-girlfriend-now-turned-tenant—wasn't giving shabby-chic so much as it was giving shabby. Cups sat on the table, the counter, the side tables. Fast-food wrappers and empty ice cream cartons littered the space. A layer of dust was visible to the naked eye on every wooden surface, and the bird-of-paradise plant she had so diligently taken care of since bringing it home two years ago was looking as sad as she felt. A glance at the living room couch revealed a perfect outline of her body, which was surrounded by crumbs she hadn't bothered to clean for—oh, well—weeks.

She had been wallowing in filth for four months and it was just hitting her now what a state of disgrace her home was in. How she had managed to avoid attracting cockroach and mouse roommates was nothing short of miraculous.

She turned the lock on the door with a 'click' and heard more voices—Opal and Alejandra. The door swung open, and she was greeted, as expected, by the trio.

"Surprise!" yelled Opal.

Lala gave her a sideways look.

"Really, Opal?" she said in judgement. "It's not a party."

Opal looked momentarily offended.

"It's not a party, Lala," Opal retorted. "But it *is* a celebration—of new beginnings, and of Chloe," she finished off smugly.

Lala considered that for a moment.

"Hi, guys," Chloe said with as much enthusiasm as she could muster. It had been one month since Lala had staged her ice cream and yoga intervention, and Chloe had been on a slow and steady upward climb. Despite that, it was still difficult sometimes for her to put on a happy face. She noticed that her friends' arms were full of bags and bottles. Additionally, on Alejandra's part, she carried a bouquet of brightly coloured lilies, peonies, and posies.

"Well—are you going to invite us in?" Lala mock demanded.

Chloe gave a short, humorous snort.

"Of course." She opened the door wide and stepped out of the way. The trio bustled inside, took off their shoes, and then took in the state of Chloe's condo. It had been several weeks since anyone but Chloe and Lala had seen the inside of it.

"Jesus Christ, Chlo," Alejandra remarked. "We came to clean, but at this point I think your condo might need an exorcism."

Lala took in the view and concurred.

"Call us Sisters Lala, Opal, and Alejandra," she nodded before handing Chloe one of her bags. "Our Holy Lady of Perpetual Cleanup. Secret keepers of Clorox and multi-purpose cleaner."

Alejandra interjected, "We brought stuff to make dinner and do some meal and freezer prepping for you. We've also brought drinks, snacks, and board games. Most importantly, we've brought cleaning supplies. This place needs a love scrub."

Lala gagged.

"A *love scrub*, Alejandra?" she said in mock disgust. "Please never use that term again."

Chloe felt slightly embarrassed.

"Thank you," she sounded sheepish. "I have cleaning supplies. I've just lacked the will to use them."

Opal, who had dropped her bags on the counter, somehow managing to find space between the dishes, wrappers, and empty containers, was already rummaging in the cupboard under her sink for cleaning products.

"Right," Lala said, taking charge. "First, we'll put away the perishables. Then, we'll pour some drinks and get to cleaning."

The next forty minutes saw the foursome scrubbing, polishing, Windex-ing, and sweeping for their lives. Alejandra had taken the liberty of putting on some upbeat pop music that was a throwback to their early twenties and they chatted, sipped, and cleaned like crazy. Chloe was surprised at what a difference it made to have the three of them there and something to do. She was so occupied by the cleanliness mission that she didn't have the time to be sad.

The whirr of the dishwasher sounded off in the background, giving the promise of clean cutlery. It was a godsend, from the looks of how much food her friends had bought, that it didn't look like she would be eating takeout for a while. The rest of the dishes sat in the sink, waiting their turn for the tableware equivalent of a carwash. Just on the other side of one hour, her counters were sparkling, her floors were clean, four bags of garbage had been thrown down the chute, and her bird-of-paradise plant had been fed and watered.

The place even smelled clean. Which, Chloe supposed, it was. But it was also owing to the scent of Windex mingled with the vanilla bean candle Alejandra had brought and lit before they got to work. The number of garbage bags they removed was a real testament to Chloe's state of mind, and their removal, along with the cleanliness of her condo, raised Chloe's spirits and left her feeling lighter.

After a quick post-clean toast, Chloe's kitchen counter was once again covered, but this time by all the groceries.

Opal got to work on making a hearty stew and the comforting scent of rosemary, thyme, and sage filled the air.

Chloe felt her stomach rumble. She had been eating exclusively takeout the past few weeks, yes. Just like she had been for the past four months. But in the last month, with Lala's encouragement, she had mostly switched to the salad, hummus, and chicken kind of takeout. Despite that, her friends had removed several empty containers of Chinese food and other kinds of fast, deep-fried, and carb-heavy items during their cleaning spree. Noodles, egg rolls, sweet and sour sauce, and rice. Her diet for several months had not been designed to make her feel any better, but it had brought her some level of comfort. It had also been interspersed by pizza, burgers, fries, and Thai.

They spent the rest of the evening playing board games, drinking rosé and gossiping. Well—Opal, Alejandra, and Lala did, at least. Chloe tried to keep up with what they were saying, but the rosé was causing her to feel a bit weepy. Which was a shame because while she might be appreciating the fact that her girlfriends had come through for her in her time of need, she knew that when the sun came up tomorrow, she would be all alone again with nothing but her feelings. They carefully avoided any mention of her ex and any relationship-related talk, for which Chloe was grateful.

By the time her friends packed it in for the evening at a staggering 1:43 a.m., Chloe was exhausted. She hugged each of the girls and tried to find the words to tell them how appreciative she was, but nothing she said seemed sufficient. They hugged her back and told her how much they loved her and how happy they were that she was starting to come out on the other side.

Before she went to bed that evening, Chloe cried.

But it wasn't for the death of her relationship. This time it was for a different reason. They weren't tears of sadness. They were tears were of gratitude. For her friends.

Present

Chapter 18:
Back to Reality

They were sitting in their weekly Tuesday-morning work meeting. It was Chloe's first one since her jaunt to Costa Rica and, by this point, everyone at *Strut* knew that Chloe's assignment had revolved around a naturist resort.

She had fielded questions about the sights she had seen at Costa Morpho in addition to questions from those curious as to just how those types of places worked. Which was something she would definitely be covering in the feature. Her coworkers wouldn't be the only ones curious about the ins and outs of an upscale naturist resort. Which was what she now exclusively referred to Costa Morpho as, and she found herself correcting her colleagues when they used the term 'nudist'. Amongst the things she had learned during her stay was that 'nudist', due to its supposed negative connotations, was out, and 'naturist' was in.

As a lover of words and the English language, Chloe was fascinated by how lingo fell in and out of usage. It was a bit like fashion, she supposed. One day Madonna's cone-shaped bra and Millennial ankle socks were in, the next day, they were out.

After her return, several of her colleagues remarked on how relaxed Chloe seemed. It brought back memories of her first encounter with Aurelie, her travel editor predecessor.

"I could only get that kind of a glow with self-tanner!" Shai, *Strut*'s assistant beauty editor, moaned to Chloe in the staff kitchen. "I want first dibs on your next trip," he said seriously. "Sea, sand, sun, shirtless men, and margaritas."

Chloe smiled in reply.

"My next trip is to an igloo resort in Finland—you're welcome to tag along."

Shai's face scrunched up in disgust.

"Not for all of the La Mer in Sephora."

She had left Costa Rica with the promise of seeing Jack when they were both back in Toronto, and while Chloe had hoped that would be the case, she hadn't been entirely sure if it would happen. On her part, the intentions were there, but she also knew that the best of intentions and the greatest of connections sometimes couldn't withstand the rigours of actual, everyday life.

Vacation life was one thing—wait staff there to do your every bidding, maid service, gourmet meals, sand, sun, and cocktails. Reality was another.

And while she wanted to continue seeing Jack, it was without a specific goal in mind. Just enjoy his company, really. Which she had in Costa Rica, immensely. Still, there had been no way to know if Jack, upon returning to Toronto, felt the same. So, it was a pleasant surprise when, four days after she had arrived back, Jack sent her a text with an invitation for dinner.

Over a meal at a downtown bistro, she was even more pleasantly surprised to find that their easy banter and conversation hadn't just been a vacation thing. On some level, their dinner together felt even better in Toronto. It felt more like a real date and not a romance-novel vacation fantasy. Which, if Chloe was honest, was kind of what her trip had felt like the entire time. Although, while Jack had a toned body and a handsome face, there hadn't been any open-shirt oiled-up abs, and the Fabio-esque long, golden locks hadn't been Jack's, they had been Chloe's.

Jack was actually coming over for dinner that evening. It would be his first time seeing her place and she wondered whether he might feel uncomfortable being in her home. Granted, Liam hadn't lived there for seven months, but it was still his condo and some of his belongings were still there.

As for all the things that had made her and Liam's condo a home—smiling photos on the fridge, cute mementos of their time and travels together—she had removed all of it and put it into the building's storage locker. Other things, like his ugly Kansas City Chiefs blanket, she had stuffed in the back of the closet. Horribleness—from being punted to the curb by her long-term boyfriend—aside, she was grateful that he at least hadn't done it at the start of the football season. The Chiefs were one of the top teams in the NFL and she wouldn't have been able to turn on the T.V. or even glance at a newspaper without being smacked in the face with a reminder of her ex.

As for Liam, she hadn't seen or heard from him since the day he had told her he was coming over to pick up some of his things. All other communication had been through his friend Karam. Lala, at one point, after a pitcher of Aperol Spritz, had encouraged her to stop paying Liam rent and start squatting on his property.

"Would serve the fucker right!" she declared while swirling her glass of orange liquid in the air.

Chloe had chuckled. While thoughts of revenge were fun fuel to ponder, revenge wasn't her style. Sometimes she wished she had more fight in her, like her friend. Lala didn't take shit from anyone and there was never a man who had crossed her who had come out on top.

But that wasn't Chloe. Her method of dealing with things included curling into herself, licking her wounds, and suffering in silence.

One thing her travel assignment had brought her, aside from a new love interest and a sense of peace, was the knowledge that she needed to move out. Liam's place was in a better location than her old condo, but she needed a fresh start. Even if that fresh start was back there. And so, one week after she arrived back in Toronto, she issued an N12 to her tenant and prepared to move back in.

A knock at her door alerted her that Jack was there, and when she opened it, she was greeted with a kiss and a bottle of wine.

Soft Jazz played in the background and the lights were dimmed for the evening. Above the chit-chat about their days, Chloe poured them both a glass of wine. She loved how easy it was—conversation with Jack. It flowed like they were longtime friends.

"What's for dinner?" he asked, eyeing the assorted pots on the stove.

"Roasted veggies, saffron rice, and salmon," she said proudly. "Oh, and French bread," she added. "I made apple pie for dessert."

"Sounds great," he said, looking impressed.

Chloe beamed.

"We'll see how well my cooking skills stack up against yours," she teased.

"My cooking skills? You mean my ability to order in from Uber Eats?" he teased back. The night he had had Chloe over for dinner he had realized too late that he had forgotten to pick up the main ingredient for beef Wellington—the beef— and had ordered in takeout instead.

She giggled.

"I think you can probably outdo Pizzaiolo, but if not, I still appreciate the effort."

Jack helped set the table and they had dinner and companionable conversation. Afterwards, they headed for the couch with dessert.

Chloe was just laughing at a story about work Jack told her when there was a knock at her door.

Her face scrunched up in confusion.

"Are you expecting anyone?" he asked.

"No." She shook her head as she got up and went to answer the door. "It's probably just a newspaper salesman. One came by a few weeks ago after someone let them into the building."

She swung the door open and her heart nearly stopped. She was standing face-to-face with Liam Hollingsworth.

Her jaw dropped and she was momentarily struck dumb. What was her ex-boyfriend, the man who had dumped her at Opus seven months ago, the man who had left her for his coworker, doing on her doorstep?

Okay, to be fair, it was actually his doorstep.

But still.

Liam looked both uncertain and confident at the same time, and in one of his hands he had her favourite bottle of wine. Her heart skipped a beat at his appearance. He was still her Liam. The same handsome, salt-and-pepper-haired Liam she had met and fallen in love with.

Only, he was no longer hers.

It was surprising for her to find that even now, half a year later, she had a feeling in the pit of her stomach at the sight of him. It was also confusing. She thought she had gotten over him. Perhaps, a thought flitted through her mind, the feeling was just due to the shock of not seeing him for seven months and the sudden and unexpected appearance of him on her doorstep.

"Hi," he said with a smile.

"Hi," she replied after a beat.

"Can I come in?" He tried to peer around her.

"Umm," she hesitated, "now's not a good time."

"Oh," Liam suddenly looked a bit put out.

"Are you okay, Chlo?" Chloe heard Jack's voice behind her, and she turned to him with the same stunned expression on her face.

"Yeah, I'm okay," she said breathlessly. "Give me a second."

Liam spotted Jack behind her and his face fell.

"Sorry," he said sheepishly. "I didn't think . . . I should have thought . . .," he trailed off.

"It's fine," Chloe said dismissively.

"Can we talk?" he asked.

She shook her head. "No. I mean, yes. We can talk. But not tonight."

"Okay," he sounded resolute. "I'll text you in the morning."

Chloe nodded and Liam thrust the bottle of wine at her.

"Take this," he insisted. "I bought it for you."

She hesitated a second before taking the bottle and issuing him a "thanks".

Moments later the door was shut, and she was walking back to the couch where Jack was sitting.

Still feeling stunned, she dropped the wine onto the table in front of them and took a seat. She was dismayed to see that her apple pie was no longer steaming.

Jack watched her carefully.

"Are you okay?" he asked her again.

She nodded in response.

"Was that Liam?"

She nodded again.

"Yes." Her voice sounded a little hoarse. "That was Liam. I haven't seen him in seven months. I have no idea why he just showed up like that."

Jack took a drink of wine and leaned back on the couch. He looked like he might have a pretty good idea as to why her ex-boyfriend had suddenly appeared on her doorstep, but he kept quiet.

"He said he wants to talk to me." She turned and looked at Jack.

"Do you want to talk to him?" he asked.

Chloe shook her head.

"No. I mean, yes. I mean, not *talk* talk to him. I only want to find out what he wants to talk to me about."

Jack nodded in understanding.

"I get it." He looked at her with resignation and then drained his glass of wine. "Listen," he said, placing his empty glass on the coffee table, "I'm going to call it an early night and give you a bit of space to process. I know we aren't committed or anything, but I really like you and I really like where things between us have been heading. I also know what happened between you and your ex and I can tell what a shock tonight was for you. It's probably best if I give you some space while you figure things out."

That snapped Chloe out of it.

"No!" she protested. "I don't want any space," she said sincerely. "I'm over Liam. Honestly, Jack."

"I believe you." He nodded his head. "I just know that when things are unresolved, that's where problems can creep in. And I wouldn't want to keep you from any resolutions."

"Please," she pleaded. "You're not keeping me from anything. I love spending time with you and I'm over the moon with how things have been going between us."

He looked reassured at that.

"I believe you," he said again. "Why don't you sleep on it and text me in the morning."

Chloe nodded. She could live with that.

Jack stood up and brought his glass and plate to the kitchen before heading for the door.

"Thanks for dinner tonight, Chlo," he said as he was putting on his shoes. "It was great."

She went in for a hug when he stood up and she kissed him on the lips. Softly at first and then harder. He kissed her back with just as much enthusiasm and planted a kiss on her forehead before he walked out the door.

Left with her own thoughts, she went directly for the apple pie before finishing off the remainder of her glass of wine. With her belly full and a lubricated mind, she went to bed and spent an hour tossing and turning before she fell into a deep slumber.

*

Beep!

Chloe blearily reached around on the bed beside her, searching for her phone.

Her alarm hadn't gone off yet, which meant it was before 6:30 a.m. She berated herself for forgetting to turn off her ringer. Who could possibly be texting her at such an awful hour?

Her hands connected with the rectangular object and as she clicked it on, she squinted her eyes: 6:14 a.m. Damnit. She could have slept for another sixteen minutes.

A jolt went through her when she saw who the text was from—Liam. Unable, according to him, to stop himself from messaging her so early because she was on his mind.

What in the everloving fuck, she thought.

Was this some kind of sick joke? Some cruel irony the universe or Jesus or her ancestors were playing on her? She was finally over her ex and had moved onto someone new and *now* Liam decided to make an appearance?

She took a few deep breaths to calm herself. After all, she didn't actually know what Liam wanted. And just because he had reappeared, it didn't mean she had to let him back in her life.

It was ironic, really. When she was going through the misery of their breakup, she had fantasized about him appearing on their doorstep, begging for her back and apologizing for breaking up with her.

She snorted to herself. Good lord, she really had been in a sorry state back then.

Clicking her phone back off she closed her eyes and savoured the comfiness of her mattress.

Last night Jack said he was going to leave her alone to process her thoughts, but all she seemed to have processed that night was the wine. A breakfast of coffee perked her up and she sat there in silence with the lights dimmed and a candle burning. She thought, she thought, and she thought again.

At work that day she was distracted and had finally texted Liam back around noon. She had texted Jack first thing in the morning, and he had responded back within the hour.

Liam, in stark contrast to what his pattern of communication had been in the last six months of their relationship, messaged her back in three minutes.

It was unnerving.

Meet me for dinner this week? he asked.

She pondered.

Dinner with him hadn't gone so well last time.

She still hadn't found it in her to go back to the restaurant she had walked out of looking like she had been on an all-night bender.

But things were different now. Sure, his appearance last night had shaken her, but that was mostly because she had been so shocked. No matter what Liam had to throw at her, she was confident that this time, she would walk out of the establishment with her head held high and her mascara intact.

She texted Liam and agreed to meet him for dinner.

In another surprise, he responded by asking Chloe where she wanted to eat. It was a sign that he was trying to make up for his behaviour.

Poor effort, really.

If he wanted to make up for what he had done, he really had a lot of work ahead of him. Not that she wanted flowers and chocolate and groveling. Although, it might help. Not in the 'getting back together' department, but in the 'I was a total asshole, I apologize and plead with you to forgive me for being such a jerk' department.

If she had been feeling in the punishing mood, she would have chosen Don Alfonso, Nobu, or St. Thomas. Trendy, hard to get into, and sky-high prices. Instead, she opted for Toca. Fine dining for sure, but not something out of the ordinary or something that screamed 'special occasion'. It was one of her go-to restaurants when she was in the mood for familiar and fancy food.

You're sure? Liam texted in reply. *You don't want to go somewhere nicer? Nobu or Butcher Chef?*

Chloe texted him back and told him she was sure. But his question did make her curious. If Liam was offering to take her to Nobu, she didn't need to be in the punishing mood—it seems he was flagellating himself.

Chapter 19:
The Unexpected

Toca was housed at the Ritz-Carlton. It was in close proximity to Chloe's home, and unless there was a conference in the hotel, it was usually quiet. It also had phenomenal mushroom ravioli and a glass-covered cheese cave. Which was exactly what it sounded like—a cave in the middle of the restaurant that was full of cheese. Chloe had checked it out one night and consumed so much dairy she went home feeling like a wheel of brie.

The hostess showed her to the table—a chic curved booth where Liam sat with his back to her. She was a bit surprised at the table he had chosen. The seating arrangement would require them to sit next to each other in a cozier position than she would have liked.

"Chloe." Liam looked relieved when he saw her.

She had a sneaking suspicion that he thought she might stand him up tonight. It would have been well within her rights to do so, but it wasn't the way Chloe played.

"Hi," she said casually. To her surprise, her voice didn't

have any hint of bitterness or a nervous catch. If they had done this six months ago, she reflected, she would have shown up looking like something the cat dragged in and, tears in her eyes, would have begged him to take her back.

Now, though? She was happy and content. Both with life and her budding new romance. She wasn't showing up tonight out of desperation and hope. She was showing up out of curiosity. And she wasn't dressed up to the nines like in the movies when the main character goes to meet her ex. From her hair to her outfit, Chloe was totally casual.

She took a seat next to Liam and put her purse down between them.

Why, several months after breaking up with her for another woman, did he want to see her? She had told Jack about Liam's request to meet for dinner and he had seemed cautious but supportive. He had questioned her about it—not anything like giving her the third degree but just trying to suss out her feelings about Liam.

She had allayed Jack's concerns without him voicing them, and she truly believed in what she said. Jack had respected her decision and just told her that he was there for her if she wanted to talk afterwards and to let him know if she needed some space.

The waitress put a menu down in front of Chloe and she requested tap water and a pilsner. Tonight, she wanted to keep her wits about her.

The gentle glugging of water into her glass punctuated the silence between her and her ex.

"So," he turned to her after the waitress walked away. "Thanks for coming, Chlo."

She raised an eyebrow in response. The last time she had seen him in person, he had intentionally not called her by her nickname. He had used her full name. A strategy, she was certain, to hammer home the fact of how his feelings towards her had changed.

Why was he suddenly calling her Chlo?

"Oh, it's fine," she said in response before pausing. "I was a bit confused as to why you wanted to meet for dinner."

"Ah," he leaned back self-assuredly. "Why don't we save that conversation for when we get our mains."

She shrugged in reply: "Okay."

They passed the time engaging in small talk until their meals arrived. Liam, careful to avoid any mention of work, likely owing to the fact that he was dating one of his colleagues, had asked about her work, family, and friends.

"You look great," he said sincerely. "I mean that."

Chloe, mid-drink of beer, snorted into her glass.

"If I remember correctly," she said after taking a drink, "the last time you saw me I was crying my eyes out and had mascara, eyeliner, and tears running down my face." She paused to let that fully sink in. "It's a low bar in comparison to that, so it doesn't take much to look great," she said dryly.

Liam hung his head.

"I really am sorry about that." Remorse was evident in his voice. "Do you—." He was cut off by Chloe raising her hand in a 'stop' motion.

"Let's wait until after dinner, shall we?" she said eyeing up her mushroom ravioli. "This is one of my favourite meals and I don't want it being ruined by whatever it is you're going to say."

He considered this for a moment and then nodded before tucking into his Cornish hen.

Several minutes later Chloe leaned back in the booth, her stomach full of ravioli. She dabbed at her lips with her napkin before setting it back down in her lap.

"Dessert?" Liam offered.

She shook her head no.

Even if she had been in the mood for dessert, there was no room for it after the ravioli.

"Okay." He put his fork down and fortified himself with

a drink of wine.

"Listen, Chlo," he began as she reached for her beer.

Her stomach immediately tightened in anticipation. Not knowing why he wanted to meet for dinner had been bothering her for the past few days. Now that the moment of revelation was at hand, she was apprehensive.

"I want to apologize, from the bottom of my heart, seriously, for what I did to you seven months ago." He looked into her eyes. "It was wrong, it was stupid, and to date, it is the biggest regret of my life."

Chloe felt the wind rush out of her chest.

He was doing this? Liam was *actually* doing this?

"I think just with the pressures at work and everything, and approaching such a milestone anniversary, I panicked. I know it was wrong. I *knew* it was wrong. I treated you badly the last six months we were together, and I'll never forgive myself for it."

Chloe struggled to keep her expression neutral.

It really was wild how life worked. She had spent months pining and tens of hours daydreaming about the very thing that appeared to be happening right now. Daydreaming that Liam would come to his senses and realize that he made a huge mistake. Realize that he loved her and that he wanted to be with her. Grow old with her, have a family with her.

And now, it appeared her daydream was coming true. Several months and one Jack later.

"I've thought a lot about our relationship and what I did wrong and about how much I regret letting you go," he said sincerely. "And I want you back. I want another chance. I love you, Chlo. I want to marry you. I want to go back to the way things were, but I want to make them better. I want to make up for the way I treated you and spend the next fifty years of our lives making you happy. Kids, adventure, growing old together—I want it with you, Chloe. I want it all and I want it with you."

Chloe sat there, too stunned to speak. It wasn't often she found herself stunned into silence, but Liam had managed to do it to her twice in the span of a few days.

"I—I . . .," she stammered. "I need to think about this," she said desperately. "I need some time."

"Of course," Liam soothed. "Of course you need time. Take some time and get back to me. I love you, Chlo. You know that."

Chloe couldn't respond. She didn't know what to say.

"I don't expect you to accept my apology or trust me right away," he said with understanding. "But I'm hoping with time we can build that back up and you can work towards forgiving me. I know I hardly deserve it, but I'm hoping you'll give me a second chance."

It was almost too much for her to take in.

"I need to think about this," Chloe repeated. "I don't know what to say."

There was a moment of silence between them and thoughts raced through Chloe's mind.

If she was honest with herself, she still loved Liam. There was some small part of her that felt she always would.

Could she go back to him? Go back to the way things were before? With Liam working late nights on deals while he made bank and excelled in furthering his career?

Twenty years from now, dumping Chloe for Sophia would be seen as a blip in their relationship; a minor bump in the road. It's something that happens to the best of couples. After all, people aren't perfect. People are human; they slip up. They make mistakes. Even in relationships. Even when they love their partner more than anything else on Earth.

She and Liam hadn't taken a walk down the aisle and made vows and commitments to one another in the presence of friends and family, but Chloe had been excited to marry him one day. And she knew the vows—everyone knew the vows.

It was 'for better or worse'. It wasn't 'for better or better'. And situations such as your long-term boyfriend dumping you for a woman he worked with during a mid-life, late-thirties crisis before realizing that the grass wasn't greener on the other side? That, Chloe suspected, was exactly what the 'for better or worse' vow was made for. *Exactly* what that part of the vow was made for. Richer or poorer was covered. So was sickness and health. What else could better or worse be referencing?

She supposed it was kept as vague as possible because no one wanted to be smacked in the face with 'for commitment or affairs' when they were standing up at the altar.

For monogamy or innumerable side pieces, went through her head.

Nothing romantic about *that*. It would put even the staunchest of romantics off marriage.

But—she and Liam had never made it that far. Not that it really made much of a difference. Only legally, she mused. The two of them were as good as married in every other aspect of their lives. They were each other's contact in case of emergency, they were each other's financial beneficiary should anything happen to either of them. They had plants together. And they shared a home together.

Well. They had once shared a home together. Now it was just a condo in which Chloe was temporarily staying.

But Liam was asking for her back.

She could take him back. Take him back and rebuild everything. Rebuild the life they had created and that had been burned down by a bitch named Sophia.

Okay, that wasn't fair.

Sophia definitely knew about Chloe, but she also knew that it took two to tango. If Liam hadn't wanted to try and pursue someone else, Sophia, the physical embodiment of temptation, wouldn't have pulled him away from Chloe.

Still—they could rebuild. Like that Japanese art form, the

one where they take broken pieces of pottery and piece them back together by filling the cracks with gold—kintsugi. Their relationship wouldn't be the same as it was before; it would be something different. But it could transform into something beautiful; something better than it had been.

Although, given Liam had strayed from her in the first place, didn't it stand to reason that the strong, resilient relationship she thought they shared didn't technically exist? It was a bit depressing to consider. But that was the crazy thing about relationships. The crazy thing, really, about people. You never could be too sure about them or about what was going on in their head. Never be quite too sure about how they were experiencing something or felt about it.

Unless of course the person was totally honest.

Honesty was a trait she valued, and Liam hadn't been honest with her about his feelings. As devastating as the breakup had been for Chloe, it could provide her and Liam with the opportunity to rebuild things, starting with a stronger, more open and honest and structurally sound base.

And if she was honest with herself, she could kind of understand why Liam had strayed.

Understand, yes. But not quite forgive.

The concept of marriage, even if one has been in a committed relationship for several years, is scary. Aside from being legally bound by one person for the foreseeable future, there was also the possibility of a nasty, financially ruinous divorce.

A case of cold feet on the part of one partner before they realized that the grass isn't greener on the other side could do a lot to a person. It could make them realize the error of their ways. And now that Liam knew the error of his ways, he knew for certain that he should not have dumped Chloe for Sophia. There was a good chance that he had learned his lesson. That he would be content and happy with what he had with Chloe.

Or would he?

Another cliché that always rang true was that people often don't know what they have until it's gone. She had always felt that the cliché needed to have a second part added onto it. Something about trying to appreciate what you have while you have it.

To Chloe, it seemed that oftentimes when people stop appreciating what they have, when they take what they have for granted, that's when they lose something they didn't fully appreciate in the first place. And the regret sets in later.

She held all the power in this situation. Which was not something she took lightly. She and Liam had had their entire lives mapped out together. They knew they would get married, knew they would have kids, and they knew, barring any kind of horrific accident or disease, they would grow old together. He had thrown that all away on a hot (Chloe was objective enough to admit it) coworker before he had come crawling back and begged for another chance.

Even as recently as one month ago she would have loved nothing more than for Liam to realize his mistake and beg her to take him back. She would have done anything to have him back. Dignity momentarily abandoned, she would have immediately jumped into his arms—the hurt he had caused her would have been instantly forgotten

But that was one month ago.

And this was now.

He had blown up their future together because of someone he met at work. Who was to say he wouldn't do it again?

Chloe loved Liam, yes. But something in her had fundamentally changed since her trip. Lala had dragged her out of her depressive state before that, yes. But the change of pace and scenery of Costa Rica had done wonders for her perspective and inner peace. And while she was enjoying the time she was spending getting to know Jack, she knew he wasn't the sole source of her feelings.

She had realized something.

Inner peace and happiness couldn't come from another person. It had to come from within.

She didn't know where things with Jack were going, but she was sure of one thing—if she managed to find love again, she would approach it from a much different perspective.

The love of her life might be hit by a bus when crossing a street one day. That could just as easily put an end to her happily-ever-after the same as an affair could. It was one of the infuriating things about life—you never know just what curveball it was going to throw at you.

Liam looked at her expectantly.

"Chlo?" he said softly, shaking her out of her reverie.

She shook her head.

"Look, Liam," she began. "This is a lot. This is a lot to drop on me out of nowhere. Umm . . . I need time to process this," she said seriously.

"I understand." He nodded. "That's why I hoped to talk to you the other night at our—your—condo."

Chloe glanced at her beer.

"Not to pry," he said tentatively, "but who was that guy who was there with you? It's been eating me alive," he confessed. "The thought of you with someone else. Knowing that I let you get away and that someone else found you."

"He . . .," Chloe began. "His name is Jack. I met him on my last work assignment." She paused. "He's a lawyer."

Liam looked stone-faced.

"I can hardly blame him," he said with regret. "I had the best thing that ever happened to me and I let her slip through my fingers."

Chloe took a deep breath.

"Do I have a chance, Chlo?" He looked at her with pleading eyes. "I just need to know. If there is even a one in a billion chance, I want to do everything I can to get you back and to make it work."

For the umpteenth time that night, Chloe was dumbfounded.

Things like this happened in movies and romance novels. Things like this didn't happen in real life. Things like this didn't happen to normal, everyday girls like Chloe.

"I don't know," she said regretfully. "I need to think about all of this. You need to give me some time."

Liam nodded—he looked resolute.

"I understand," he said. "Is it okay if I check in with you every couple of days?"

Chloe nodded. "Yes. That would be okay."

He offered her another drink, which she declined, and the cheque came shortly after.

Outside the restaurant the two of them stood there awkwardly. They weren't friends, they weren't lovers, they weren't a couple. What was the proper parting protocol for two people who knew one another inside and out but who were now almost strangers?

Liam took care of the awkward moment by reaching out for a hug.

"Just a hug, Chlo," he said. "I'm going to respect your space and boundaries until you make up your mind."

Her heart fluttered and she gave him a genteel hug that was just short of affectionate. Her Uber pulled up seconds later and she got in without a backwards glance to her ex-boyfriend.

Chapter 20:
A Pinch of Salt

She had been contemplating what her ex-boyfriend had said; his words roiled around in her head the whole week. Jack, cognizant of what a tailspin Chloe must be experiencing, had tried hard to give her some space.

Space, however, wasn't what Chloe wanted.

She had told Jack that Liam had asked her to go for dinner in the spirit of transparency. Transparency, she had learned a long time ago, was key to any kind of relationship. And a lack of it was what led to issues. And although she didn't know where things with Jack were headed, she was committed to being honest with him about everything.

He hadn't asked what she and Liam had discussed during dinner and Chloe hadn't found it in herself to tell him. She knew if the shoe was on the other foot, the last thing she would want was for someone to leave her hanging while they figured out their feelings.

And figuring out her feelings was exactly what she was trying to do.

It was quite the conundrum. One week ago, she would have said with 100 percent, absolute certainty that she would never be interested in her ex-boyfriend again. That nothing could or would ever make her want him back. That ship, she was certain, had sailed.

But that had been before Liam had done his apparent about-face and thrown her feelings into turmoil.

It was agonizing.

Of course, her group chat with Lala, Opal, and Alejandra had exploded when she texted to tell them about Liam's unexpected appearance. Their opinions had been just as different as themselves.

Lala suggested she go to dinner at Nobu, order the most expensive things off the menu, including wine, and then tell him to go fuck himself at the end of the night.

Alejandra was in favour of not giving him the opportunity to even talk. *I don't know, Chlo*, she had written. *He dumped you without warning, without the opportunity to even talk about things to try and fix whatever the problem was, and he moved on with his coworker so quickly that it's insulting. I'll support you with whatever you choose to do, but if it was me, I wouldn't give him the time of day.*

Opal, on the other hand, encouraged her to meet up with him for dinner and hear him out. Sure, how he had treated her was dastardly, but people do make mistakes and sometimes they come to regret and rectify those mistakes.

When she had told her mom that Liam had reached out to her, her mom had talked her through her feelings and let her know that she was there for her no matter what.

In the end, Opal's advice won out. And while there was a certain feeling of satisfaction she derived from hearing Liam apologize and beg her to get back together, there was also a twinge of regret.

If she hadn't given him the time of day like Alejandra had suggested, she wouldn't be in this predicament now. She would be blissfully unaware and happy with Jack and the way that things were progressing.

If she had shut Liam's request down, would there ever have come a time where curiosity would have gotten the better of her and she would have wondered what it was that he had wanted to talk to her about?

She supposed the answer to that had been yes, which was why she had ultimately decided to meet him. And now that she had, she was more confused than ever.

He had checked in with her a couple of times that week like she had said he could. It was nothing heavy—all light conversation, supportive, and memes.

It was jarring when she found herself laughing out loud at work after opening up a meme he had sent her that was so dad-joke bad it was funny.

The realization that she could potentially fall back into things with Liam so easily scared her. And she knew that what she was doing wasn't fair to Jack.

*

"I don't want to tell you what to do, Chlo," Lala said seriously. "But holy hell, what a fucking predicament."

It was six days after her dinner with Liam and her besties had assembled at her place to go over the latest development in her love life.

She had texted the group chat after her and Liam's dinner, but she hadn't gone into detail. She had just sent them an *S.O.S.* message. And then, realizing that they might interpret it as her being in danger, she followed it up with a short note letting them know she was in a major, but not life-threatening, predicament—that Liam had asked her to get back together.

She had sent it after 10 p.m., but their group chat exploded and a flurry of messages populated the chat well into the next day.

That bastard! Alejandra had written. *Just when you've moved on, you were over him, and you're happy, he comes crawling back into your life!*

Opal, as supportive as ever, became the textual equivalent of Switzerland. Supportive of both parties but ultimately staying neutral. One thing she did tell Chloe to do, however, was to tell Jack.

In true Lala fashion, her friend encouraged her to agree to get back together with Liam, punish him and make him work hard to atone for his terrible behaviour, and then dump him in a humiliating fashion after he thought he was back in for good.

The advice of her friends had merit (okay, maybe not Lala's idea of punishing Liam by making him buy her a G-Wagon), and Chloe felt as lost as ever.

It was only after a one-on-one meeting with Dasha that she really felt some clarity.

After going over her budget for the upcoming quarter and pitching a few travel features to her boss, their conversation turned personal.

When Chloe had arrived back from Costa Rica, she had been careful not to tell everyone, her friends and mom excluded, that she had met someone while she was away.

She knew how that usually went. Telling people that you had met someone special was akin to getting a love interest's name tattooed on your body—it was one of the fastest ways to jinx things and send a potential relationship to a watery grave.

Goodness knew Chloe had seen enough of that with one of the junior interns at the office. It seemed like every other week Alisha was meeting a special someone whom she thought she was going to marry. When a colleague would ask her how her romance was going a couple of weeks later, she would scrunch up her face and announce that she was dating someone else. Eventually, *Strut* staff learned to stop asking.

"How are things outside of work?" Dasha had inquired.

"I must say, I know you were getting back on track before you went on your last assignment, but that trip seems to have really been beneficial for you."

Chloe had beamed.

"But I have noticed the last few days you've looked a little stressed and sleep deprived," she trained her piercing blue eyes onto Chloe's. "Is everything okay?"

How *did* her boss have such a knack for reading people? Chloe wondered. She couldn't imagine Dasha as a parent. Her poor kids wouldn't be able to get anything past her.

"Everything is . . .," Chloe searched her mind for the right words, "complicated."

She briefly explained the predicament she was in, including the fact that she had met someone special when she was on her latest assignment. When Chloe finished the story, which ended with her getting in an Uber after dinner with Liam and feeling incredibly confused, Dasha leaned back in her chair and said nothing.

A mild bout of anxiety overcame her as she waited for her boss to respond.

"What do you want to do about it?" Dasha asked bluntly.

Chloe thought for a good few seconds and realized she didn't have an answer. She shook her head.

"I honestly don't know," she said quietly.

"I'm not going to tell you what to do," Dasha said practically. She picked up the sparkling water she had on her desk and took a drink. "But let me tell you a little story."

Chloe's curiosity was piqued.

"A scorpion," Dasha began, a serious look on her face, "asked a turtle for a lift across a river. The turtle was concerned but the scorpion assured him that he would be okay: *why would I sting you?* he said. *It would kill us both.* So," Dasha continued, "the turtle agreed to give the scorpion a ride and halfway across the river the scorpion stung him." Her boss fixed her with that piercing stare again. "The turtle drowned, and the scorpion drowned along with him."

"Do you know, Chloe, what the moral is of that story?"

Chloe thought for beat.

"Don't trust a scorpion?"

Dasha tilted her head. "Don't trust someone when they are, by their nature, untrustworthy."

"Liam is the scorpion," Chloe replied.

Her boss took a deep breath.

"When someone shows you who they are, when they show you what their nature is, believe them," she advised. "I said I won't tell you what to do and I won't. I will just say that Liam has shown you who he is. I would tread cautiously and really think about how he treated you and the months of misery he put you through. Think about how he broke up with you, how you felt, and what he did in the aftermath," she paused.

"Nothing is guaranteed in life. People do make mistakes, but people are who they are, and they rarely change. If it was me, I would think long and hard about that before you make any decisions, and I wouldn't let daydreams of the future or of what could be cloud your thoughts and feelings."

Chloe nodded and thanked her boss.

Once again, it was so strange to Chloe that her boss, whom she didn't spend time with outside work, who she relied on for a pay cheque, was able to get to the root of the issue and provide her with the most valuable insight.

*

Chloe's friends were spread out in the living room, with she and Lala on the couch and Opal and Alejandra occupying the two accent chairs. A massive charcuterie board sat on the coffee table in front of them and deep house music played softly in the background.

"If you do decide to give things with Liam another go," Opal counseled her, "you would need to have all the information."

Alejandra nodded. "Agreed. You need to know everything. Every dirty little detail. How he moved on so quickly, if he was having an affair, why he broke up with you in such a bad way, what made him realize he made a mistake. Everything."

They gossiped over drinks and snacks well into the night, and a good portion of it was about Chloe and the situation she was in. By the end of the night, she was exhausted, and her friends left just before 11 p.m. Which was far past her bedtime.

She would be spending the next day writing. She was on a deadline for her Costa Morpho article, and she hadn't even started it.

Which was strange in a way because of the phenomenal time she had had there. She supposed her procrastination likely had something to do with her current situation.

The next morning, she brewed herself a cup of strong coffee and sat down at her laptop.

She stared at the screen for an hour, unsure of where to start, when a text message popped up on her phone from Jack.

Just checking in, Chlo, it read. *I know you're writing today—let me know if you want to grab dinner later x.*

Not wanting to give in to distraction, she turned her phone so the screen faced the desk and, minutes later, a beep indicated she had another message.

She scrunched her face to the side and picked up the device.

I know I said I would give you space, but I wanted to see if I could take you for dinner tonight, Chlo. I'm committed to this. I want you back.

Liam.

She put her phone on silent and pushed it away. Then, she put her hands on the keyboard and started typing.

Two hours later she sat back and read over what she had written. It was a good start, she thought happily.

She picked up her phone and reread both Jack's and Liam's messages before she typed back.

I would love to.

Chapter 21:
The Great Escape

Fall in Love at Costa Morpho. It was the article for the latest issue of *Strut*. She had fallen in love with the resort, yes, and she had fallen in love *at* the resort.

If someone had told her six months ago that she would end up on assignment at a naturist resort and would not only enjoy her time there, but find new love, she would have asked them what they were smoking.

The day she had written the first draft of the feature, she had gone out for dinner with Jack. Liam hadn't taken the news that she already had plans well. The funny thing was, she agreed to go for dinner with Jack because he was the one who had asked her first. If Liam had beaten Jack to the punch, she would have opted for dinner with him—reservations about his character and getting back together be damned.

A few days later, she had gone out for dinner with Liam again. Taking the advice her girlfriends had given her to heart, she had put Liam through the fifth degree.

They had dinner at a little English pub on the east side of the city. It was an inconvenient location for both of them, but it had great food and a cozy environment.

Over appetizers and wine, she questioned him.

"Help me understand," she had started off, "how you moved on so quickly?"

Liam's eyes flicked to the left before he met her eyes.

"I wasn't thinking with my head, to be honest," he said sincerely. "Sophia had been coming onto me for months and because we were spending so much time together, we developed an emotional relationship. She started confiding in me, flattering me, talking about her ex. Saying how she wished she had such a dedicated, supportive, and hard-working boyfriend as me . . ." He trailed off.

"And nothing happened between you two during that time?" she asked pointedly. "For six months before you broke up with me it felt like you were distant and distracted."

"Nothing, Chlo," Liam looked sincere. "I swear on my life."

She thought about it for a second. She was satisfied by his answer. Giving into temptation wasn't something she condoned or something she was thrilled about, but it had never occurred to her that Sophia was coming onto him.

Not that it absolved Liam of any guilt.

"What made you realize breaking up with me was a mistake?" she asked.

He shook his head.

"It was when she and I settled into a routine. It didn't feel right. At first it was invigorating and exciting." He looked sheepish. "But the more time she and I spent together, the more I realized I had made a huge mistake."

Chloe kept listening as she popped a warm olive into her mouth and washed it down with a sip of wine.

"You're supportive and kind. You're not demanding, you're not belittling, not combative. You've stood by me through thick and thin, and you've been my biggest champion." He leaned forward. "I thought about all the great times we shared together. About all the plans we had made for the future. And I realized what an idiot I was to throw that all away just because I was under stress. I lost sight of who I really am and what I really want because of a coworker who I confided in and spent a lot of time with. I realized I blew up my life for nothing. So, I broke up with her in hopes of getting you back."

Chloe didn't know how to respond to that.

It was a small satisfaction to finally receive answers to the questions she had agonized over for several months. But it was also a shock to her system. She thought about Liam's behaviour during their last six months together and realized just how checked out of their relationship he had been.

"I'm sorry, Chlo," he pleaded with her. "I really am. I wish I could take it all back. Everything. I'll never forgive myself for the way I treated you and for how I hurt you."

Chloe worked to keep a neutral expression on her face.

"And what about now?" she asked. "You still work with Sophia."

Liam shook his head. He had told her during their first dinner that he had moved out of Sophia's place and had been living with Karam for the past month. So, while she was no longer his girlfriend, she was still his colleague.

"She recently took a job at Bank of America." He took a drink of his beer. "Her last day at the office was two weeks ago."

A weird sense of relief swept over her. Sophia was gone. The woman she had spent so many hours and days worrying and feeling sick over was gone. Chloe had been unsure as to whether she was going to give things with Liam another go, and the lightness she felt after hearing that Sophia was out of his life was further confusing.

They had finished their appetizers and drinks with a

conversation that was much lighter than before. And outside the pub that evening, Chloe had been the one to initiate a hug.

*

After that evening, Liam had taken to texting and calling her with increasing fervor—asking her to go for lunch, for dinner, for walks. It was, Chloe assumed, because he knew he had competition, but she was still shocked by how determined he seemed to get her back.

With regards to Jack, she didn't know if they would go the distance, but for now, she was enjoying the journey. She was learning to appreciate things for what they are and not dwelling on wild fantasies of the future. More importantly, she had come to appreciate that friends and family are the most important things in one's life. Romantic partners were great, but it was crucial to cultivate a life she was pleased with instead of crafting her life around her partner. That way, if something did happen—infidelity, a breakup, or, god forbid, death—she wouldn't fall apart.

Not that she was falling apart anymore. She was thriving. It had been one month since Liam had come crawling back into her life, and she had done a lot of soul-searching. For the most part, her mind was made up, but there were many 'what if' moments.

What if things didn't work out with Jack?

What if Liam actually was reformed after his stint with Sophia?

What if it *was* a one-off and he would be faithful to her until the end of times?

It was stressful and she leaned heavily on her girlfriends. There were moments she was tempted, that was true. Throwing away the potential life with Liam she had envisioned for herself was hard. But when she really thought about it, Liam had thrown it away first.

Which was a funny thing really.

It was hard for her to believe that this was where she had ended up. She had known with every fiber of her being that she and Liam would have a happily-ever-after and she had been devastated when it didn't turn out that way. For months.

She had sobbed, and hoped, and dreamed that one day he would change his mind and come back to her. That day had come, and it had been followed by many more. But it hadn't turned out the way she had anticipated. It turned out, when she really thought about it, she didn't want Liam anymore. She didn't trust him, and she looked at their relationship through a new lens.

Life was funny that way, she reflected. Sometimes you want something so badly only to realize later on that it wasn't actually for you.

It was only a little over two months since she had returned from her life-changing trip to Costa Rica, and just as long as she had known Jack. But despite the short time they had known each other, Chloe really felt herself falling for him. She wasn't naïve enough to think it was happily ever after for the two of them. She knew there would come a point where things about him would annoy her and the other way around. If they even made it to that point. But she was feeling optimistic. The opportunity to try and make a relationship work with Jack—a man who not only seemed to like her, all of her, but who also made her feel like she was special—was something she didn't want to pass up.

Jack worked just as many long hours as Liam did but somehow always found time for her.

She made up her mind. She had been open with Jack and he had backed off, saying he didn't want to sway her one way or another. But she hadn't let him. "I want *you*," she had said to him firmly. Jack had smiled, but she didn't think he entirely believed it.

She didn't know if she entirely believed it at first, but she was sure of it now. She had made up her mind and closed the door on a future with Liam.

And a good thing too. Only two days later, Lala had called her up to see if she could come over. It was early evening on a Monday and Chloe had just changed into her comfy clothes.

"Totally," she told her friend. "I'll make dinner."

"Why don't I bring dinner over?" Lala suggested.

Chloe had gotten out a bottle of pinot noir and two glasses. Twenty minutes later, Lala was on her doorstep with Thai.

"Hi!" Chloe enthused, grabbing the heavy brown bag from her friend. "Do you want some wine? I opened a red."

"Yes," Lala said emphatically. "I actually think you're going to need it."

Chloe blanched for a second.

"What," she said cautiously. It wasn't so much a question. She was almost afraid to ask.

"Pour me a glass, I'll take out the food. We can dish up and then we'll talk."

"Lala, you're scaring me." Chloe wasn't being dramatic. There was a pit starting to form in her stomach.

She hoped it wasn't something about Jack.

The throaty glug of wine being poured into Lala's glass and then topping off Chloe's was intermixed with the sound of containers being opened and cutlery and plates being pulled out of their respective places in the kitchen. She handed Lala a giant glass of wine and Lala clinked her glass against Chloe's.

"Cheers, Chlo."

Chloe hesitated. She had a feeling that whatever Lala was about to tell her wasn't something she wanted to toast to.

Lala took a drink and set her glass down on the counter with a heavy thunk.

Chloe took a deep breath.

"Lala—what the hell is going on?"

Lala pursed her lips and then took another drink of wine.

"Sit down." The redhead gathered up the Thai containers and brought them to the dining room table before going back for the plates and utensils.

Chloe did as she was told, and Lala soon joined her. The aroma of steaming hot Thai noodles, rice, and chicken wafted through the air as Chloe stared at her friend.

Finally, she couldn't take it any longer.

"Lala—what the hell?"

Lala bit her lip.

"I found her Instagram," she said after a moment.

"Found her—who is her? Whose Instagram?"

"Sophia's." There was trepidation in her friend's voice.

Chloe felt her heartbeat speed up.

"What did you find?"

Lala gave her a wary look.

"Are you sure you want to hear this?"

Chloe nodded. She knew Sophia was no longer in Liam's life, but what could Lala possibly have to tell her? Was Liam lying? Were they actually still together? Had they gotten *back* together in the past couple of days?

"Brace yourself," she paused. "Liam didn't start a relationship with Sophia after he broke up with you. If the Instagram photos are anything to go by, he started seeing her a few weeks after she started working with him."

Chloe felt like someone had punched her in the stomach.

"No," she shook her head. "No. That can't be right. Liam wouldn't have done that to me." There was small beat before she asked in a small voice: "Would he?"

There was no reassurance coming from Lala, and Chloe saw the truth of what her friend was saying written on her face.

"I am so sorry." Lala shook her head. "I thought it was

important that you know. Especially since he's been trying to worm his way back into your life. I have her Instagram account if you want to see it."

She thought for a moment. Lala didn't know that she had already made up her mind about her ex-boyfriend. Chloe had closed that door, but left it unlocked—leaving open the possibility of a friendly acquaintance. But if what Lala was telling her was true, she would be taking a welding torch to the seams to stop the door from ever opening.

"Show me," Chloe said wearily. She suddenly felt exhausted.

"Are you sure?" Lala looked hesitant. "I don't want you to end up back on the couch in your pajamas, waterboarding yourself with wine and ice cream."

"I want to see," Chloe said firmly.

Lala pulled her phone out and pulled her chair closer to Chloe's. She typed 'blonde.banker.babe' in the search bar of her Instagram and clicked on the sultry profile photo.

Chloe couldn't understand it. During some of her lowest moments after Liam had dumped her, she had spent hours going through social media trying to find the workmate Liam had dumped her for. But it had all been for naught. The fact that she didn't appear to have her name in her Insta handle would have made it difficult. Especially because Sophia wasn't one of Liam's 230 followers and Liam followed around 1,200 accounts.

Shamefully, Chloe had made it about halfway through the 1,200 accounts, squinting at each profile photo to see if it resembled the blonde bombshell Liam had left her for.

But blonde.banker.babe had somehow escaped her.

And good thing too. As Lala scrolled down through Sophia's photos—and there were many; it looked like the woman spent most of her day posting on Instagram—she started to feel ill. It had been February when Liam had announced he was leaving her. He had told her emphatically that there hadn't been anyone else, had denied doing anything offside when she accused him of cheating.

And yet, here, here was proof that revealed otherwise staring her in the face.

Of course, it wasn't face shots. No. Sophia Sullivan was too savvy for that. She knew, of course that Liam had a live-in girlfriend. And apparently, she had seen no problem with having an affair. Six months prior to Liam leaving her, Sophia's Instagram feed showed photos of the two of them together. A photo with Liam's hand—she recognized his hand, she knew the freckles and the watch he was wearing. A photo of Liam from behind while friends of hers in the comment section asked who the mystery man was. As she scrolled through Sophia's feed a wave of nausea overtook her. There was a photo posted when Chloe had been away on a travel assignment that showed Liam asleep in bed. In Liam and Chloe's bed.

That bastard had actually brought Sophia into their home. Into their bed.

She thought she was going to be sick.

"Are you okay?" Lala saw the look on Chloe's face.

Chloe shook her head and looked away from Lala's phone.

"I am so sorry to be the one to do this," she said sympathetically. "Seriously, Chloe. I agonized over whether or not to show you. I can't imagine how devastated I would be if I was in your shoes."

Chloe kept shaking her head. She wanted to run, she wanted to scream, she wanted to break something.

"I figured you needed to see it because I know you've been thinking about taking him back. And if you *do* want to take him back, you should at least have all the information."

Chloe took a deep breath and engaged in two rounds of box breathing. It was a technique she had learned in her mindfulness class. Then she took a large drink of wine.

Which was not a technique she had learned in mindfulness class

Lala grabbed the bottle off the counter and sat back down to console her friend.

"He's an asshole, Chloe. A total asshole. For him to put you through this and lie about it while the whole time he was cheating on you with that two-bit whore is unconscionable," Lala paused. "Unless, of course, you've decided to reconcile with him. In which case he is still a total asshole, but I will support your choices."

Chloe let out a laugh despite herself.

"He *is* a total asshole," Chloe agreed. "I just didn't fully appreciate how much of an asshole he is until now. And for the record, I decided yesterday that I'm not going to give him another chance. And a good thing too. That was horrible to see." She motioned towards Lala's phone. "Awful. And I don't even want him anymore. I would have been destroyed by that if I had decided to give things with him another go."

"I am so proud of you." Lala sounded genuinely pleased. "You are stronger than you give yourself credit for and you are absolutely making the best decision. And besides," she added, "Jack is way better looking and treats you way better. The man actually saved your life, for Christ's sake!"

Chloe nodded and took another drink of wine.

Fuck Liam.

"You're not mad at me?" Lala was serious.

"Of course not," Chloe said. "I appreciate you showing me. I kind of wish I hadn't asked to see the photos but I think I needed to. Really validates what I decided yesterday."

"Good. Because I would never want to make you upset. Now," Lala looked at the untouched food containers, "I'm going to dish us up. You need to eat. And I need to eat. Otherwise, I'll end up leaving snarky wine comments on blonde.banker.babe's photos."

They ate in companionable silence as Chloe tried to

process what she had seen on Sophia's Instagram feed. She had gotten over Liam and started something new with Jack. But being hit with the extent of Liam's betrayal had ripped open the scab that had almost fully healed over.

The affair would take a while to process, but she knew she would get over it in time. And in a much, *much* shorter amount of time than it had taken for her to finally get over their breakup.

Later, the two women sat on the couch and had a deep talk about life until Chloe, exhausted, dragged herself to bed. Lala tucked her in and quietly slipped out the door.

She was a great girlfriend. The best.

*

The next morning Chloe's mind was a little hazy. Seeing proof that Liam had lied and cheated on her was painful. Like a knife being stabbed in her heart. But there was also something beneficial about it. It solidified the decision she had made, and it pushed away any lingering doubts she might have had.

That was at least one thing she could see clearly that morning. Better to be smacked in the face with the truth than coddled with a lie.

She had plans with Jack that evening and she was really looking forward to seeing him. Even if it had only been three days since their last date.

When it came to breaking the news to Liam, she hadn't decided how she wanted to go about it. There was the option to take the high road—having a conversation with him and letting him know her decision. There was also the option to ghost him, which was what he probably deserved. There was also the option to let him read about her decision for himself in the next issue of *Strut*, which would be out on newsstands in one week. With the ferocity with which Liam was trying to get Chloe back, she was certain he would read her latest article. And just like that, Chloe decided to go with option number three.

She couldn't deny that part of it came from the bit of hurt she held, reignited, perhaps, by the images from blonde.banker.babe that were burned in her brain.

Liam had crushed her. Left her broken for months and, she now knew, had had no issues with lying to her face and cheating. For Chloe, it was one too many transgressions and what Liam needed was a taste of his own medicine. She knew he would get that after reading her latest travel feature. What he would do afterwards she wasn't so sure of. But for that matter, she didn't really care. For her, it was about showing Liam that she had gotten her glow-up and moved on. Liam breaking up with her had led her to become stronger than ever and ready to take on whatever life would bring. She was in the beginning stages of what had the potential to be a great relationship, but even if it didn't work out, she was whole.

More than that, she was happy.

Which was something that she had discovered over the past seven month came from within. It grew with the people you surrounded yourself with—your friends, your family, your colleagues, and your acquaintances. It didn't come from having a partner, and it wasn't something you could rely on another person to give. It came from being grateful. From appreciating what you have in life and looking for those silver linings. Looking back now, it was so obvious.

It had taken her nearly a year of ruinous mental health to figure that out, and ironically, she now felt grateful that Liam had broken her heart. It had been the catalyst for her transformation; for her own metamorphosis. And she knew that come what may, from here on out, she had the tools to deal with it.

Epilogue

"Good to go, Chlo?" Jack's voice came from outside the door.

"Yes!" she called back.

Chloe gazed around the condo, the place she had called home for almost six years. It was stripped bare of all her belongings and now looked rather sparse. It was sparkling clean and looked sadly empty without all her things. It was no longer a home. It was a place she no longer recognized.

She was moving back into her old condo that day—one month after her article about Costa Morpho had come out. Her tenant had agreed to leave early, and Chloe couldn't wait to get back into her old place and get settled.

Liam, as she had anticipated, had read her article. He had picked up the latest issue of *Strut* the day it had hit newsstands and after he read her article, he went ballistic.

It didn't bring Chloe any satisfaction, and she replied to his multitude of angry text messages and phone calls with her own message.

Liam, she had written, *I am sorry you're unhappy with my decision. I truly loved you and thought we would grow old together. When you broke up with me, I was devastated. My hopes, my dreams, and my future were shattered.*

When you came back into my life, I seriously considered forgiving you and starting over. But then I realized—I'm not the same person I was eight months ago. I realized I want a fresh start and to give things a go with the man I am currently seeing. Maybe it will work out, maybe it wont. One thing I do know is I will be okay either way. I know this because I believed my life was destroyed when you dumped me, but I came out of it a stronger and more resilient person. After I made my decision, I found out you cheated on me with Sophia for the last six months of our relationship. I specifically asked you if that had happened and gave you the chance to come clean. And you lied to me. Again.

I forgive you, Liam. And I want to thank you for helping me to discover what the root of happiness actually is. I wish you all the best in the future and I hope you are able to take something away from this. There are no hard feelings on my part, but I no longer want you in my life. I am moving out of your condo at the end of the month, and I will leave the keys in the mailbox. Have a great life, Liam. C

He hadn't taken that text well either and Chloe had been forced to use the block function on her phone and email.

*

Horns honked and vehicles zipped by as Jack drove them over to Chloe's condo. It was a warm October day and people were enjoying one of the last sunny days of the season. The scent of pumpkin spice wafted from the container in Chloe's hand, and she took a sip of the sweet autumn drink.

"I have a three-day assignment in Houston next month," she said casually, watching Jack's face as he concentrated on the road. "If you can swing it, do you want to come?"

Jack smiled.

"I say—I say—I say," he said in a Yosemite Sam accent as Chloe giggled. "Tell me when and I'll make it happen."

A bright smile spread across her face as he made a

lefthand turn onto Spadina. Chloe leaned back in the passenger seat of his car and a sense of tranquility washed over her.

If you enjoyed this book, please leave a review on your chosen platform. Reviews are helpful to other readers and allow authors to continue sharing their stories. If you would like to know when I release more books, please sign up for my newsletter at jacquelineparrish.com/newsletter.

Acknowledgements

A huge thanks to my sister, Megan, who enthusiastically reads everything I send her. I promise I'll return the favour when you finish your thesis. To my mom, for supporting my aspirations and powering through this one in just a couple of days. To Carlin—the best bestie a person could ask for, and a never-ending source of inspiration and hilarity. Lastly, thank you for reading this book. I hope it brought you a few laughs and a little escape.

Keep reading for a look at

A Fashionable Affair

Chapter 1:
Tinsley

"Name?"

"Tinsley Tomlinson, *Fashionista Magazine*."

"Ah." The headset-wearing clipboard girl scanned the list, flipped past two pages and scrolled through the names.

"Tomlinson, here you are!" She smiled, uncapped the highlighter and crossed off Tinsley's name. "Love your magazine!" she gushed. "Will anyone else from *Fashionista* be joining us today?"

"Ah . . ." Tinsley hesitated. "I don't believe so."

"Perfect." The woman smiled warmly. "So happy that you could join us."

Tinsley smiled back and casually strode past the velvet rope. Her fake magazine persona had surpassed second nature and was currently vying for first—she almost believed that she was the fashion editor of a famous women's magazine herself.

Another headset-wearing woman in a short black dress greeted her just inside of the venue.

"This is Patricia." The woman gestured to the smiling, curly-haired lady to her right. "She's coordinating this afternoon's event."

"Hello, Tinsley." Patricia, also clad in black, thrust her hand forward. "So lovely to meet you! Can I get you anything to drink?"

"Oh! Yes, thank you," Tinsley replied, shaking Patricia's hand. "Lovely to meet you as well."

"We've created a line of custom cocktails for this afternoon's event." Patricia turned to the bar beside her where a framed list of drinks and their accompanying descriptions sat. "The orange creamsicle martini is one of my favourites. It tastes just like a popsicle."

"That sounds good." Tinsley smiled, watching as the bartender poured an orange liquid into a stainless-steel cocktail shaker.

Patricia disappeared while Tinsley waited for her drink—a neon-orange concoction that came rimmed with sugar and garnished with a slice of orange. She thanked the bartender before adjusting her suit jacket and taking in the room. It was a gathering of empowered women in art and fashion. Or at least that's what the invitation had promised. Looking around she saw a room of mostly familiar faces. It hadn't taken her long to realize that when it came to the art and fashion industries, social circles were very small indeed. She was on her second orange creamsicle martini, waiting for the presentations to begin, when she spotted Patricia walking towards her.

"You were right." Tinsley smiled and raised her glass. "These martinis are fantastic."

"Tinsley," Patricia began, looking uncomfortable. "I was curious how someone so young managed to snag such a prestigious job, so I went and checked your name on the *Fashionista* website."

Oh fuck. Tinsley's heart stopped. *She knows I'm not an editor.*

"Patricia!" Tinsley said, her stomach twisted in knots. "I can explain! I know what you're going to say and I'm so, so sorry!"

Patricia looked at her uncertainly.

"How could you do something like this?" she asked, sounding disgusted.

"I didn't mean for it to go this far," Tinsley pleaded. "It just . . . kind of happened."

"You're promoting designer diet drinks and trophy wife T-shirts?" Patricia interrupted. "I cannot believe that you've given that misogynistic company your endorsement! And to think that we invited you here today as one of our empowered women." She paused, shaking her head. "What the hell is wrong with you? Endorsements like that set back the women's movement."

Tinsley's heart started beating again. Diet drinks and trophy wife T-shirts? Patricia was right—what the hell was wrong with this Tinsley woman? She's a total weirdo.

Chapter 2:
Tori

Tori sat at the tiny desk in her fourteenth-floor cubicle sorting through the new marketing material that she would be using to question consumers with. Her firm, Staten, had a handful of big company clients but as an entry-level marketing assistant, Tori was on the bottom of the totem pole. She was the coffee runner and consumer call girl for the company's smallest client: Impotentia. The small red pill was marketed as "the world's first all-natural male stiffening solution". She had been mortified when she'd found out what she would be working on, and, as an entry-level associate, Tori had the embarrassing job of phoning up customers and asking them about their Impotentia experience. It was far from the glamorous job that Tori had envisioned for herself when she'd first set foot in the city, but it paid the bills. Writing was her first choice of career but when *Fashionist*, her fashion and lifestyle blog, had failed to make its mark, she had had to find something fast. Toronto was an expensive city and her savings would only cover two months' worth of rent. Marketing had sounded okay. Prestigious even.

She would still get to write—crafting promotional material for companies—and she would still get to be creative—pitching marketing ideas for new products.

Oh, how wrong she had turned out to be.

At the age of twenty-three Tori thought that she had landed her first adult job. Immediately after being hired she had gone out and dropped a month's worth of salary on smart suits and separates. At H&M and Joe Fresh, of course—a month's salary wouldn't go very far in Toronto's upscale Bloor Street shops. And with her closet full of corporate clothes and a smart new "adult" haircut, she'd shown up half an hour early on her first day of work, ready to prove her marketing skills to her new employer.

Instead, she'd spent the day fetching coffee for her colleagues and answering the telephone. Her Monday-to-Friday schedule hadn't deviated much since that day. She still spent a large portion of her time quenching her colleagues' coffee thirst and fielding phone calls, but her responsibilities had extended to managing the database of Impotentia consumers and talking to them about the product's effectiveness while addressing concerns, suggestions and questions.

Tori looked at the clock. It was 10:42 a.m. and she had already blown through her coffee run and phone call questionnaires for the morning. She clicked through her office emails, refreshing the page just as she'd done less than a minute ago.

Still nothing.

Heaving a sigh, she switched browsers and opened up a different email tab. TTomlinson@Fashionist.com, she typed, entering "muffin"—the pet name given to her by her high school boyfriend—into the password box. She'd started her blog while still in high school and it had received a lot of hits recently. Unfortunately, the hits were owing to the fast-rising popularity of a recently launched fashion and lifestyle website named *Fashionista*, and not owing to Tori's articles.

Her inbox loaded and twenty-seven email notifications popped up on screen. She'd stopped posting articles to her website over six months ago, demoralized by her less-than-fulfilling day job and inability to garner a single industry invite. But while the posts may have stopped, the spam mail just kept coming. She checked her *Fashionist* account every few weeks now just to keep from drowning in it. Looking at the bottom of her screen she scrolled up the list: Viagra (oh, the irony), Hot Russian Singles, Prince Abaeze Wants to Give You $10 Million (if only, she thought), Munger Carlson's Four Seasons Penthouse Party, Nasty Gal's 40% Off Sale.

Hold on.

Munger Carlson's Four Seasons Penthouse Party?

Odd, she thought. Then she looked at the from line: Black Widow PR. Black Widow PR, as in North America's hottest luxury brand public relations firm? No way. Tori dismissed the thought as she clicked open the email.

Dear Ms. Tinsley Tomlinson,

To celebrate the launch of the new Munger Carlson Vodka collection, which is distilled with the purest water from the Rocky Mountains and crafted with only the highest quality, hand-picked wheat, we would like to invite you to a private party at the Four Seasons penthouse residence to celebrate. You are invited to be among the first in North America to experience the crisp, cool taste of Munger Carlson with the city's most celebrated socialites, celebrities and tastemakers. Join us Thursday, May 4 for an evening of specially curated Munger Carlson cocktails with special guest performances and finger food. RSVP by Monday, May 1 and dress to impress.

Hope to see you there!

Claudia Everett

Black Widow PR

Holy. Fuck. Tori read through the email a second time before her eyes snapped back to the salutation. *Tinsley?* She was confused. *Who the hell is Tinsley?* They must have just gotten her first name wrong, she thought, shrugging it off. Then it hit her: Finally! All of her hard work had paid off! All of those years spent hanging around outside of industry events in order to get a first-hand scoop for her website and she was finally in the big leagues! Black Widow PR managed everyone from Tom Ford and Hugo Boss, to Birks and the Cosmopolitan Hotel. They were *the* PR company of choice when it came to luxury brands. And Toronto-born Munger Carlson was one of the world's biggest playboys. *They must have seen the article that I wrote about their Peter Pilato chocolate launch*, she thought brightly. Sure, the article had only garnered twenty hits and two comments (one of which was from a spammer), but it was well written, Tori told herself. Of course, she hadn't actually been inside of the party. She'd spent the better part of ninety minutes trying to talk her way inside before being firmly escorted to the sidewalk. There, she'd watched minor celebrities and socialites stroll past the velvet rope and into the event. Later, she'd managed to get her hands on a discarded chocolate wrapper that one of the attendees had carelessly tossed aside after leaving the venue. And with that, the celebrities that she had seen, the music that she'd heard every time the door was opened and snippets of conversation that she'd caught from exiting guests, Tori had crafted together a 600-word article that sounded like she had been inside.

Another wave of excitement overtook her as she looked at the date of the email. It had been sent two weeks ago. Today was Monday, May 1. She was lucky that things had been slow at the office today and that her colleagues had been sufficiently caffeinated. She might have missed the invitation otherwise.

Tori clicked the reply button and began to type.

"Dear Ms. Everett," she wrote. "Thank you for the invitation. I would like to inform you that I will be attending the Munger Carlson penthouse party on Thursday." She paused. "And I will be dressed to impress," she added, thinking that it sounded professional. "Regards, T.," she ended the email before hitting Send.

Tori sat back in her chair, an elated smile painted on her face. It didn't matter how many coffee runs or phone calls she'd have to field today, nothing could bring her down from her vodka launch, private-penthouse-party cloud.

"Tori?" came her boss's voice above her. "Tori? Hello, Earth to Tori!" he exclaimed, poking her on the shoulder.

"Hmm!?" Tori sat up straight, exited the browser and turned around. "Keith!" she exclaimed, the ecstatic smile still stuck on her face.

"Why do you have that funny grin on your face?" he questioned, eyebrows furrowing. "Are you on drugs?"

"No!" She immediately wiped the smile off of her face. "Not at all! It's just"—she paused and looked around the room desperately—"such a nice day today!" She gestured to the window, which revealed a veritable monsoon outside.

Keith looked at the window and then back at Tori, both brows raised in question.

"Right," he deadpanned. "Anyway, sheet rain aside, I need you to make sixteen copies of this presentation and then run it to the conference room on the tenth floor. Jensen's presenting our third-quarter results to the shareholders tomorrow morning." He handed her a folder filled with papers. "Think you can handle that?" he asked, eyebrows still raised to his hairline.

"Yes! Definitely! Looking forward to it!" she enthused.

Keith looked at her again, his expression unchanged. "Great," he said, backing away from her slowly before turning on his heel.

Tori's smile returned as she remembered the Black Widow invite. Nothing could burst her bubble, she thought. Not even cranky old Keith. She scooped up the file and headed to the copier. Plopping back down at her desk several hours later, Tori once again opened her *Fashionist* email. Her fifteen-minute task had turned into a nearly three-and-a-half-hour ordeal after being sidetracked by tenth floor coffee requests and a secretary who begged her to cover the phones while she stepped out to pick up her sick son from school.

Tori logged into her account. Sitting there at the top of her inbox was a reply: "Re: re: Munger Carlson's Four Seasons Penthouse Party."

Dear Ms. Tinsley Tomlinson,

RSVP received! So happy that you are able to join us!

Looking forward to seeing you there,

Claudia Everett

Tori's heart rate shot back up again. It was happening! She was going to be on the other side of the velvet rope for a change. She was going to the Munger Carlson launch party on Thursday!

*

The next few days passed pretty uneventfully, minus Tori blowing up the photocopier and spilling coffee all over herself in the Wednesday morning meeting. And finally, after three days that felt more like three years, it was the evening of the party. On Monday night she had torn apart her closet trying to find a dress that would impress and had finally settled on a plain black jersey frock. She'd pulled out her sewing machine, scissors and box of scrap fabric and set to sewing every day after work. The result? Tori looked at herself in the mirror. She'd hacked and sewed and bedazzled to within an inch of her life, taking the dress from simple to . . . if not quite sophisticated, definitely statement making. What that statement was was up for debate, but her outfit would do a drag queen proud. Slipping on black off-the-rack heels Tori grabbed a handful of her business cards (a fashion illustration on one side, T. Tomlinson with her email address and phone number on the other) and stuffed them into her glittery purse.

At the office that day she'd barely been able to contain her excitement. When the workday ended, she'd hurried home as fast as she could to get started on her party prep. And finally, after a three-hour ordeal that included a lavender-scented bubble bath, half a can of hairspray and a liberal application of foundation and black eyeshadow, Tori was ready for her first industry party.

She stood back and surveyed herself in the mirror. Smoky-black eyes, feather-trim dress with a plunging neckline and rhinestone-studded skirt, black heels and slicked-back hair. She looked confident enough. How she felt was an entirely different matter. Tori frowned at her reflection. She didn't feel confident. She felt like an imposter.

Face scrunched up in derision, she put down her purse and headed for her side cabinet. Popping the top off of a bottle of Stoli, she hesitated for a second before putting the bottle to her lips and tipping it upside down.

Fake it till you make it, she thought as she gulped. *Or let vodka fake it for you.* Besides, she justified, she was going to the launch of a premier Rocky Mountain hand-picked wheat vodka tonight. It was necessary for her to imbibe beforehand. How else would she be able to appreciate the crisp, cool taste of Munger Carlson?

She wiped her hand across her mouth and put the bottle back. Picking up her purse, she shrugged on a faux-fur jacket and headed out the door. It took a few minutes for her to flag down a cab and then she was on her way to the Four Seasons.

Traffic wasn't too bad for a Thursday—it was a warm spring evening so there was more foot traffic than car. Tori sat in the back seat trying to keep herself calm but she was unable to contain her excitement. She hadn't told anyone about her invite. She still couldn't believe that she had been invited to this party and she didn't want to embarrass herself if it turned out to be a mistake. She pulled out her cell phone and scrolled through her contact list to the letter *M*.

"Maggie!" she typed. "You're never going to guess where I'm going tonight. So much to tell you!" She hit Send and popped her phone back into her purse. Maggie, her best friend since second grade, lived only a few blocks away from her. But despite the closeness of their living quarters, the pair managed to meet up only once or twice per week, both busy with work and extracurriculars. Well, Maggie was mostly busy with work. While Tori was a journalism graduate with an unrelated nine-to-five and poor advancement prospects, Maggie was a financial analyst for a hedge fund—a job that left her working crazy hours every week with limited time for a social life.

As the vehicle weaved through the city the Stoli came back to haunt her; Tori felt her face flush as the alcohol coursed through her bloodstream. Liquid courage indeed. She was already feeling more calm, cool and collected. The car pulled into the courtyard of the Four Seasons behind a lineup of black town cars and limousines. Leading to a roped-off area, a red carpet lay rolled out in front of the residence. Flashes of light punctuated the scene as photographers clicked away at people exiting the vehicles and making their way down the red-carpeted path. Through the doors Tori could see a large step-and-repeat backdrop. She'd never stood in front of one before, always being relegated to standing outside of the event.

Her taxi finally made it to the front of the queue, and she watched as a handsome tuxedo-sporting man opened the car door and offered her his hand. Tori stood still, momentarily stunned as flashbulbs went off around her.

"Are you okay, miss?" asked the handsome man, gently urging her immobile body towards the carpet.

Tori realized her mouth was gaping and shook herself off.

"Yes! I'm great!" she exclaimed as she willed her legs to start working.

"What's your name, love?" he asked.

"Tori," she replied, stumbling a little as she exited the car. "Tori Tomlinson."

"Well, you'll have a great night tonight, Ms. Tomlinson." He smiled, half dragging her down the carpet. "They flew in Beluga caviar from the Caspian Sea this morning, and Munger Carlson himself designed the drink menu." He deposited her in front of the clipboard-wielding party gatekeeper and bowed to her with a wink. "Enjoy your evening, Ms. Tomlinson," he said before turning away.

"Tomlinson?" asked the clipboard woman.

"Yes." Tori smiled nervously. This was it. This was the moment that they were going to tell her that she wasn't on the list and that there had been some sort of mix-up—that some intern had messed up the invites and that she shouldn't have received one.

"Here you are!" The headset woman smiled warmly. "Tinsley Tomlinson. *Fashionista Magazine*!"

Tinsley. *Fashionista*, not *Fashionist*? Tori was suddenly sober.

"I . . ." she began, and then paused as the headset woman looked at her inquiringly.

"Yes?" the woman asked, one eyebrow raised in question.

Tori was right. She had been mistakenly invited. She would do the right thing and fess up to being Tori Tomlinson from *Fashionist*, a blog with a pitifully small number of readers whose author had never seen the inside of an industry party, and not Tinsley Tomlinson from *Fashionista*, a world-renowned website with millions of monthly readers whose author was probably invited to every exclusive event.

"I . . . I . . . I'm so happy to be here this evening!" Tori gushed.

Okay. She would fess up to it next time. She would pretend to be Tinsley from *Fashionista* just this once. Just for one night. She'd finally experience the glitz and glam parties that she'd longed to be inside of and then she would send Black Widow PR an email telling them that they had her mixed up with the other T. Tomlinson.

The woman smiled and unclipped the red velvet rope.

"We're very happy to have you, Ms. Tomlinson." She motioned for her to walk inside. "Enjoy the evening!"

Tori stood there, her heart beating wildly, not sure if she should make a run for it down the step-and-repeat. Deciding that that was probably the quickest way to get caught and thrown out like the imposter that she was, she shuffled her way down the red carpet, trying to avoid the sea of photographers blinding her with their flashing lights. She quickly found herself at the end of the carpet amongst a small crowd of strikingly attired men and women waiting for an elevator. Helmed by two black-suited bodyguards, she watched the numbers decrease until they hit L and the doors slid open to reveal a spacious compartment with three mirrored walls. The crowd filtered into the elevator, chatting amongst themselves as Tori squished herself into the only available space—right in front of the elevator doors. As the doors slid shut, the man next to her fumbled on the pad, pressing PH, the only button on the lift besides Door Open, Door Close Ground, and Alarm.

Tori struggled not to breathe too deeply as the box began its ascent, her stomach twisting as the lift continued its climb. After what seemed like ages the elevator stopped with a sudden jolt. A faceless voice announced "Penthouse" as the doors opened onto what could only be described as semi-contained chaos.

She had never seen anything like it. Her first timid steps off of the lift bathed her in blue light. Dance music pulsed above the chatter of the bursting-to-capacity crowd and white and clear balloons littered the ceiling between aerial performers conducting sky-high acrobatics. Swan ice sculptures flanked a frosted sign advertising Munger Carlson Vodka and the room danced with bright white and blue lights, casting dark shadows onto the walls and the crowd. She spotted a bar to her right and walked over as a large crowd of people made off with their cocktails. She didn't know anyone at this party, but she wanted to.

Tori stepped up to the empty bar and looked at the drink menu.

"What can I get you?" the bartender, who was sporting a brush mustache and black-rimmed glasses, asked.

"Umm . . ." She hesitated. "What would you recommend?"

"The Mango Munger is pretty good," he said. "A splash of mango, lemon juice and syrup with two ounces of Munger Carlson and a pineapple garnish."

"Okay." Tori nodded. "I'll try one of those, please."

As the bartender poured, shook and stirred, Tori looked around. She should network, she thought. This was her chance to make industry connections. But how? The PR firm thought that she was someone else. She could hardly go around advertising the fact that she wasn't, in fact, Tinsley Tomlinson of *Fashionista*. It would be more embarrassing being escorted out of the party than it ever would have been not being allowed into it in the first place. She picked up the Mango Munger from the bar and took a sip.

Her face scrunched up at the sweet-and-sour combo in the glass before she shrugged her shoulders, threw it back and ordered another.

The bartender laughed.

"One of those nights, hey?"

"You have no idea." She smiled back at him.

Four Mango Mungers later and Tori was lacking neither confidence nor enthusiasm for the sweet-and-sour cocktails. With every downed Mango Munger she felt more self-assured, and after an hour of chatting with the bartender while he mixed up cocktails for the assorted guests, she finally felt confident enough to face the fashionable crowd.

Rick—she'd caught his name after he served her her second Mango Munger—supplied her with a fifth cocktail and bid her good night as she spotted a two-woman, one-man threesome that looked open to out-group conversation.

Tori steeled herself for any potential awkwardness and took a large sip of her drink.

ABOUT THE AUTHOR

Jacqueline Parrish is an Indigenous writer from Treaty 8 territory who lives in Toronto. Her work has appeared in international print magazines, online magazines, and peer-reviewed journals. She enjoys writing chick-lit, rom-coms, and satire, and often borrows inspiration from friends, family and bizarre situations she frequently finds herself entangled in. She is also the author of *A Fashionable Affair*.